MURDER AT THE LOUVRE

By Jim Eldridge

MURDER AT THE LOUVRE

JIM ELDRIDGE

Allison & Busby Limited
11 Wardour Mews
London W1F 8AN
allisonandbusby.com

First published in Great Britain by Allison & Busby in 2023.
This paperback edition published by Allison & Busby in 2024.

10 9 8 7 6 5 4 3 2 1

ISBN 978-0-7490-2908-1

Typeset in 11/16 pt Adobe Garamond Pro by
Allison & Busby Ltd.

By choosing this product, you help take care of the world's forests.
Learn more: www.fsc.org.

FSC
www.fsc.org
MIX
Paper | Supporting
responsible forestry
FSC® C171272

Printed and bound by
CPI Group (UK) Ltd, Croydon, CR0 4YY

For Lynne, my inspiration

CHAPTER ONE

London, July 1899

'You look puzzled,' commented Daniel Wilson to his wife, Abigail.

The pair, known as the Museum Detectives, were sitting in the living room of their house in Primrose Hill, Daniel reading *The Times* and Abigail studying a letter that had arrived for her that morning.

'I am,' said Abigail. She handed the letter to Daniel for him to read.

'This is very flattering,' said Daniel. 'Professor Alphonse Flamand, who one assumes is a prominent figure in the world of archaeology as he's writing from the Louvre in Paris, is inviting you to join him on a dig in Egypt.'

Abigail, as well as working with Daniel investigating serious crimes at museums, was also an internationally known archaeologist who, before she and Daniel had got together, had spent a large part of her life undertaking archaeological excavations, particularly in Egypt, working alongside some of the world's very best archaeologists. This included working with the renowned Flinders Petrie in Hawara in Egypt.

He handed the letter back to her. 'Are you going to accept his offer?'

'You don't understand,' said Abigail. 'Professor Flamand is no fan of mine. On the contrary, he has attacked me in print as a female adventuress. The professor is one of those who doesn't believe that there is any place for women in the world of archaeology, except as some kind of handmaiden to fetch and carry and admire the men. I can't understand why he would be writing to me, of all people, inviting me to work with him on a dig in Egypt.'

'Perhaps he's mellowed in his attitudes as he's got older,' suggested Daniel.

'I hardly think so,' said Abigail. 'It was only about six months ago he wrote an article in a French magazine attacking female archaeologists, as well as female scientists, and made sure to include my name. Although he referred to me by my maiden name of Abigail Fenton.'

'But this letter is definitely addressed to Abigail Wilson,' Daniel pointed out. 'Perhaps he doesn't know that Abigail Wilson and Abigail Fenton are one and the same person.'

'Oh, he knows all right,' said Abigail. 'In this article he accused me of riding on my detective husband's coat-tails in – and I quote – "another ludicrous attempt to prove she is as good as any man".'

'Nice chap,' said Daniel with an ironic smile. 'So, are you going to ignore it?'

'I don't know,' said Abigail uncertainly. 'I'm intrigued to know why he's written with this invitation, in view of his attitude towards me.'

'Where is this dig to be?' asked Daniel.

'He doesn't say. Just Egypt. He says at this moment the details are being kept secret to avoid anyone else finding out and moving in first.' She sighed. 'Sadly, that's not uncommon, so I can understand his caution. He says he will furnish me with all the details if I would care to meet him in his office at the Louvre at 11 a.m. on 10th August.'

'That's just ten days away,' said Daniel.

'Plenty of time to make arrangements,' said Abigail.

'So you're going, then?'

'I am. Hopefully this could lay to rest his ridiculous bias against women.' She looked at her husband. 'Have you ever been to Paris before?'

'No.'

'Then you'll come with me, I hope?'

Daniel looked doubtful. 'Does this professor mention my coming with you?'

'I'm not suggesting you have to meet him,' said Abigail. 'We can enjoy the delights of Paris together. Think of it as a holiday.'

CHAPTER TWO

Paris, 9th August 1899

They arrived in Dunkirk on the boat and made for the railway station and the train to Paris. At the railway station, Abigail did what she always did on arriving somewhere new: she bought a couple of newspapers.

'Just to find out what's happening,' she said. 'It's been a long time since I've been here.'

'You'll have to fill me in,' said Daniel. 'French is a foreign language to me.'

'French is a foreign language to everyone who's not French,' Abigail pointed out.

'You know what I mean. You can read it; I can't.'

Once they'd settled themselves in the railway carriage, Abigail opened the newspapers.

'Good heavens!' she exclaimed, surprised. 'Alfred Dreyfus is back in France.'

'Who?' asked Daniel.

'Alfred Dreyfus. A former captain in the French Army. Do you remember I told you about him last year when there was that article about him in *The Times*?'

'No,' said Daniel.

'It was a major scandal,' said Abigail. 'Still is. He was accused of treason, passing French military secrets to the Germans. He was sentenced to life imprisonment on Devil's Island.'

'Where's that?'

'Some hellhole of a place in French Guiana.'

'I guess he deserved it, betraying his country.'

'No, that's the scandal. He didn't do it. He was set up. It was all in this piece in *The Times*.'

'How come *The Times* did a piece on it? They're not usually that interested in foreign news, unless it's something fairly major. And then only if it's a war involving Britain.'

'This *is* major. Dreyfus was accused of treason on faked evidence. According to the article, the person who actually committed the treason was another officer. I can't remember his name, but he was named, after Dreyfus had been sentenced. But instead of letting Dreyfus go and charging this other man, the army authorities let the guilty man escape to England. It was in England that this reporter spotted him. She did an interview with him in which he admitted he was the one who'd passed the secrets on to the Germans, not Dreyfus. But, according to this piece, the courts and the army refused to have Dreyfus released; they still insisted he was guilty.'

'Why?'

'According to *The Times*, it was because Dreyfus is Jewish and the most senior officers in the French Army are anti-Semitic.'

'That's a bit of an allegation,' said Daniel. 'I'm surprised the French Army didn't sue them.'

'They couldn't because it was published in another country, but when it was republished in France, they took action.'

'People were sued?'

'Not just sued – people were physically attacked. On both sides. Those who supported Dreyfus and demanded his freedom, and those who insisted that Dreyfus was guilty, including some who wanted him executed.' She checked the story in the paper again. 'Anyway, it appears that Dreyfus has been granted a retrial. He's been brought back from Devil's Island for it.'

'So we can expect Paris to be a place of uprisings, with one group attacking the other,' said Daniel wryly.

'No,' said Abigail. 'It seems his retrial is going to be held in Rennes.'

'Where's that?'

'In Brittany.'

'Well, at least he'll get justice this time.'

Abigail looked doubtful. 'I wouldn't count on it. It sems it's going to be held in a military court, so it'll be a court martial, run by the military.'

'Surely they can't convict him again, not with all this publicity?'

'I'm afraid organisations like the military have a habit of protecting themselves at all costs.' She looked at Daniel. 'You should know that from your time in the Metropolitan Police.'

'Yes, that's true,' said Daniel with a sigh. 'It'll be interesting to see how this court martial works out.'

* * *

On their arrival at the Gare du Nord, they caught a cab from the line of hansoms waiting in a queue outside the station, and Abigail gave the driver the name of their hotel in Montmartre, the Olive House. She'd booked it by post once they'd agreed they were both coming to Paris.

'I stayed at it when I was last here in Paris, about eight years ago. It was clean and comfortable and not expensive.'

'The Olive House,' mused Daniel. 'Something to do with olives?'

'No. The owner at that time was a woman called Olive Pascal. She died a couple of years ago. Her daughter runs it now with her husband. She wrote back to confirm our booking, and at the same time told me about her mother dying.'

'What's the area like? Montmartre?'

'It's a hill, very high, but don't worry, the Olive House is at the bottom of the hill so we won't have to haul ourselves up it after a day's sightseeing. I'm due to meet Professor Flamand tomorrow morning, so I suggest we spend this afternoon taking in some of the sights.'

'Sounds good,' said Daniel. 'As you've been here before you'll know which will be the best places for us to visit.'

'It's been eight years since I've been here,' Abigail reminded him. 'Some of the places will have changed.'

'The buildings won't have,' said Daniel.

'Don't count on that,' warned Abigail. 'The Eiffel Tower hadn't been long completed when I was last here, and the Sacré-Coeur church in Montmartre was still under construction. I suggest we do one major attraction, Notre-Dame Cathedral.'

'A church?'

'Not just any church, possibly one of the most famous in Europe. Then we'll stroll around a bit so you can get an idea of the city, so you'll know where to go while I'm seeing Professor Flamand at the Louvre.'

'I expect I'll still get lost.'

She shook her head. 'You've got a good sense of direction. Look at how you find your way around London.'

'That's because I was born and brought up there.'

'What about when we were in Oxford and Cambridge? And Manchester.'

'The difference is the street signs and everything there were in English, and so were the people if I wanted to know where anything was.'

'All right. Then I suggest while I'm at the Louvre you walk around Montmartre, get familiar with the local area.'

That evening, tired after their long journey and their visit to Notre-Dame, they decided to have a meal at their hotel rather than explore Paris for a restaurant that looked to be to their taste.

Next morning, Abigail left Daniel to explore Montmartre while she headed for the 1st arrondissement and the Louvre. It had been a long time since she had last been here, when her main occupation had been as an archaeologist specialising in ancient Egypt. In those days she had spent almost as much time at the Louvre as she had the British Museum, keen to find out about the latest discoveries from the French excavations of the pyramids. In the later days of the eighteenth century and the early part of the nineteenth, the French had dominated

Egyptology with the work of men like Jomard, Coutelle, Lepere, Champollion, Auguste Mariette and Ferdinand de Lesseps. Now, Flamand, Gauthier and Jéquier were seen as the last ones flying the flag for France's role in Egyptian excavations, in the face of the recent dominance of Britain's Flinders Petrie and the German Ludwig Borchardt.

Was this why Flamand had invited her to take part in his forthcoming excavations? Because he would know she'd worked with Petrie at Hawara and would be interested to get as much information from her as possible about Petrie's work and plans.

The 1st *arrondissement* was the least populated of Paris's many arrondissements, as well as being one of the smallest, but in Abigail's eyes it was the most fascinating. Most of the area was taken up by the vast Louvre Museum and the large open space that was the Tuileries Garden. Les Halles was also here, a massive area where vegetables and fruit of all kinds were brought to be distributed to the various greengrocers, the smell from the vegetables, particularly the cabbages, lingering over the whole area.

As she crossed the Place du Louvre and approached the vast and impressive building that housed the Louvre Museum, she puzzled over the invitation from Flamand. It went against everything he'd ever said about her, both in print and – she knew, because she'd been told – in his conversations with other Egyptologists. Why had he invited her?

The museum was contained in the Louvre Palace, which had originally been built in the thirteenth century by Phillip II, and had then been added to over the centuries. It had

15

been in 1682 that Louis XIV had moved the royal household to Versailles, leaving the palace at the Louvre to display the royal collections of art and history. The Louvre as a place of exhibition had outlasted the French royal family, who'd been executed during the French Revolution. It had been during that revolution that that National Assembly had ordered that the Louvre be used as a museum to show the nation's masterpieces. And what masterpieces they were, including Leonardo da Vinci's *Mona Lisa*, Alexandros of Antioch's *Venus de Milo* from 125 BC, and the vast collection of Egyptian artefacts.

Abigail entered the Louvre and asked the uniformed guard on duty inside the entrance for directions to the office of Professor Alphonse Flamand. A few moments later she was walking along the dark-wood walled corridor on the second floor of the museum. She arrived at a door with the name 'Professeur A. Flamand' on it. She knocked at the door. There was no answer so she knocked again. She checked her watch, which showed 11 o'clock, French time. She tried the handle of the door. It moved, so she opened the door and entered.

The office was small, the shelves on the walls – which stretched from floor to ceiling – filled with books of various sizes. The top of the large oak desk that dominated the room was overflowing with papers, some rolled up, resembling old-fashioned scrolls, others piled on top of one another. But the sight that stopped Abigail in her tracks was the body of the professor slumped in the leather chair behind the desk, and the hilt of the knife that protruded from his chest where his heart would be, blood soaking his white shirt. His eyes were open, as was his mouth, his jaw hanging slackly.

Abigail hurried to him, putting her fingers against his neck, desperate to find a pulse, although she knew even before she did it that it was fruitless. The professor was dead.

There was a sound behind her, and she turned to see a young woman enter holding some envelopes. The young woman stopped, bewildered at seeing Abigail, and then she saw the professor's dead and blood-stained body, with the knife sticking in him, and she dropped the envelopes and let out a piercing scream, and a cry of '*Assassin! Assassin!*'

'*Non!*' called Abigail in desperation, and she moved towards the young woman, who shrank back from her, still screaming and wailing, pointing at Abigail. The next second two burly uniformed security guards burst into the office. They took one look at the tableau: the terrified young woman, the dead professor, and Abigail, and then they rushed at Abigail and grabbed her arms, twisting them behind her back and dragging her out of the office, at the same time yelling for the police.

CHAPTER THREE

Daniel arrived back at their hotel after a few hours of exploring Montmartre, expecting to find Abigail waiting for him. Instead, when he enquired at the reception desk in fractured Franglais if Madame Wilson had returned, the man on duty shook his head and took an envelope from the small boxes in the wall beside him where the room numbers were listed, some containing keys, some without. Daniel opened the envelope and was puzzled to find it contained a brief message in French beneath a printed letterhead saying it was from the Paris Police Prefecture. The signature at the bottom was of a Superintendent Jacques Maison.

Daniel passed the letter to the receptionist and asked if he would translate it for him. The receptionist read the letter, then passed it back to Daniel, a worried look on his face.

'It says your wife has been arrested. She is being held at the Prefecture of Police, on the Île de la Cité.'

'Arrested? On what charge?'

'The note does not give details, but it says she is being charged with a very serious crime.'

Daniel stared at the man, then back at the note in a state of bewilderment.

'I do not speak French, nor do I know Paris,' he said. 'Can you arrange for a cab to take me to this Prefecture of Police?'

'Of course, *monsieur*. If you follow me, I shall get the concierge to arrange it.'

Daniel followed the receptionist to the entrance, where a man in a resplendent red uniform adorned with brass buttons stood on the pavement just outside. He talked briefly to the concierge in French, his tone expressing the urgency. Daniel caught the words *Prefecture de Police* and *Île de la Cité*, along with *Il ne parles pas Français*. The concierge nodded and gestured for Daniel to join him at the kerb, then he hailed a one-horse cab at the front of a line a few yards from the hotel entrance. The driver flicked the reins and the cab moved forward and pulled to a halt beside Daniel and the concierge. The concierge rapped out the same words the receptionist had uttered, then pulled open the door of the cab and ushered Daniel inside. The cab set off immediately. Inside, Daniel's mind was in a whirl. It said Abigail had been *charged* with a serious crime, not merely accused of it. What on earth had happened?

He was so lost in thought that he was barely aware of the streets and the buildings they passed. It was only when the cab crossed the bridge over the Seine to the Île de la Cité that he recalled coming this way just the previous day, when Abigail had brought him here to show him the cathedral of Notre-Dame. He could see they were nearing the cathedral now, but the cab turned off the road before they reached it and entered the courtyard of an imposing building at the entrance of which a large board declared that this was the Prefecture de Police. Paris's version of Scotland Yard.

* * *

Abigail sat on a hard wooden chair, filled with a sense of desperation as she looked across the desk at Superintendent Maison.

'I did not kill Professor Flamand,' she said, grateful for the years that she'd spent engaging in conversational French. She pointed at the letter on the superintendent's desk from Flamand inviting her to meet him, which she'd produced from her bag. 'As you can see, he invited me to his office.'

'His secretary says this letter is a forgery,' said Maison. 'She says the professor never wrote to you, and he would never have written to you inviting you to work with him.'

'Then who did write this letter?' demanded Abigail.

'His secretary says you wrote it yourself in order to gain access to him.'

'That's ridiculous,' said Abigail. 'What about the letter I wrote in reply to the professor telling him that I would come to his office at the time and day he suggested?'

'His secretary says she has checked the professor's correspondence and no such letter was ever received. There is no mention of him having an appointment to see you in his diary. Further, his secretary states that Professor Flamand would never have suggested a joint venture with you – she and the other staff who worked with the professor say he couldn't stand you. His secretary has also shown me letters and articles that Flamand wrote showing that he thought you were a fraud whose reputation was built on the work of others. It is his secretary's opinion – and, I have to agree, mine also – that this was your motive for killing Professor Flamand, to stop his attacks on you.'

There was a knock at the door of his office, which opened to admit a uniformed police officer.

'Mr Wilson is here,' he said. 'In response to your note.'

'Tell him to wait,' said the superintendent.

The officer withdrew, pulling the door shut after him.

'I will talk to your husband and inform him of what has happened, and that you are to be further investigated. While that investigation is ongoing you will be taken to La Santé Prison in Montparnasse and held on remand. Before that happens I will allow you to see your husband here, in my office. I will allow you a few minutes alone together.'

'Thank you,' said Abigail, adding, 'My husband doesn't speak French.'

Maison rose and made for the door, summoning the uniformed officer who'd looked in earlier from his station outside in the corridor, to stay in the office and supervise Abigail while he went to see Daniel.

Abigail sat wondering how Daniel was feeling. She didn't have long to wait before finding out, because the door of the office opened and Daniel came in, accompanied by Superintendent Maison. Daniel hurried to Abigail, who got up from the chair, and the two embraced.

'*Non!*' snapped the superintendent.

'I believe he means no hugging,' said Abigail, releasing Daniel.

Maison pulled a chair to his desk for Daniel, before informing them he would give them five minutes alone, then he left. Immediately, Daniel took hold of Abigail's hands in his.

'What's happened?' he asked urgently. 'What are you being charged with? I can't speak French and he doesn't speak English, which is why I guess he's let me see you.'

'I'm accused of murdering Professor Flamand,' said Abigail.

'Murder?!' said Daniel, shocked.

Abigail explained what had happened, her arrival at the Louvre, going to Professor Flamand's office and finding him dead with a knife sticking out of his chest, and the secretary arriving and sounding the alarm.

'But this is ridiculous!' said Daniel. 'Didn't you tell him why you were there? Did you have the letter from the professor inviting you?'

'I did, and I showed it to him, but he says Flamand's secretary insists it's a forgery, and that I forged it in order to gain access to him. She also showed the superintendent various articles the professor had written dismissing me as a fraud, like the one I told you about. And that's apparently the motive for my killing him, to stop him writing any more negative things about me.'

'This is nonsense!' said Daniel. 'We have to get a lawyer to put an end to this farce.'

'That may be the way it's done in England, but I think the judicial system is different here. The fact that you don't speak or understand French is going to be a problem, so I suggest you go to the British Embassy. See if you can talk to a man called Sir Brian Otway. He's someone quite senior there. He might even be the ambassador by now, if he's still at the embassy. These ambassadors move around from country to country.'

22

'Sir Brian Otway.' Daniel nodded. 'Got that. It's been a few years since you were last here, so let's hope he's still there.'

'If not, using his name will get you through to someone senior there. Let them organise the legal side; they're good at that.'

'Where will I find the British Embassy?'

Abigail took a sheet of paper and a pencil from the top of Maison's desk and wrote down the address of the embassy.

'There. 35 rue du Faubourg Saint-Honoré. Show that to a cab driver. They're used to the English doing that.'

Daniel put the piece of paper in his pocket as the door opened and the superintendent reappeared. He spoke in French, and Abigail rose to her feet.

'What's he saying?' asked Daniel.

'Our five minutes are up. I'm being taken to La Santé Prison, which is in Montparnasse, to be held on remand. I'll write that down for you so you can tell the embassy where I'll be.'

She held out her hand and Daniel returned the sheet of paper to her and she added those details before handing it back to him.

The British Embassy at 35 rue du Faubourg Saint-Honoré was a magnificent building in the classical style in a street of equally expensive-looking buildings. Daniel hurried to the imposing entrance and rang the bell. After a while a tall thin man dressed in a dark frock coat and wearing white gloves opened the door to him.

'Is Sir Brian Otway available?' asked Daniel.

'Do you have an appointment?' asked the man.

'No,' replied Daniel. 'But this is a matter of great urgency. My name is Daniel Wilson; I'm a private detective from London. I'm in Paris with my wife, Abigail Wilson, also known as Abigail Fenton, the eminent archaeologist. She has been arrested on a charge of murdering a professor at the Louvre, and been taken to La Santé Prison. She urged me to get in touch with Sir Brian Otway, who knows her, in order to obtain her release from prison. She is absolutely innocent of the charge.'

The man nodded gravely. 'I am afraid Sir Brian is not in Paris at this moment. If you would like to come in, I'll get his assistant, Mr Edgar Belfont, to talk to you.'

Daniel entered and the man showed him to a waiting room just inside the entrance.

'If you'd wait here,' said the man, and he disappeared into the building.

Daniel forced himself to sit down on one of the plush, purple-cushioned chairs, although his agitation was such that he wanted to pace up and down the waiting room. He did not have long to wait before a smartly dressed young man appeared.

'Mr Wilson?'

Daniel jerked to his feet. 'Yes.'

'My name's Edgar Belfont. I'm Sir Brian's assistant. If you'll follow me to my office, we can talk privately.'

Daniel followed the young man out of the waiting room and down a long corridor to a series of doors. Belfont opened a door, ushered Daniel into his office and gestured for him to take a seat in front of his large oak desk. Belfont settled himself into a comfortable chair behind the desk.

'Wilfred said something about your wife having been arrested on a charge of murder?'

'Yes.' Daniel nodded, and he explained the events as Abigail had detailed to him. 'This is some dreadful miscarriage of justice,' he finished. 'That's why she asked me to talk to Sir Brian. He knows her from her time in Paris when she was engaged in archaeological events here at the embassy.'

'Before my time, I'm afraid,' said Belfont apologetically. 'I've only been here for three years, but I'm sure there are older members of the embassy staff who will remember her. However, I'm afraid that at this moment Sir Brian is undertaking some duties in the Loire Valley. He is the British ambassador to France now, by the way. He was promoted when the previous ambassador was relocated to Madrid, but I'm afraid Sir Brian won't be here until the day after tomorrow.'

'The day after tomorrow!' groaned Daniel in despair. 'I was hoping to get her released today. My wife is being held in La Santé Prison, which I understand is in Montparnasse.'

'It is,' confirmed Belfont. 'But arranging her release may not be as simple as it might be in England. Who is the official in charge of the case?'

'A Superintendent Maison at the police prefecture on the Île de la Cité.'

Belfont nodded. 'Yes, I know Superintendent Maison. I've always found him to be a fair person in my dealings with him.'

'Then can't you talk to him? See if you can arrange my wife's release?'

'Unfortunately, it's not that straightforward. I can certainly call on him and let him know of the embassy's interest in the case, but I'm afraid I'm just a junior employee, a rather insignificant cog in this political machine.' He looked at the clock on the wall, then stood up. 'But I'll see what I can do. If we go now to the Île de la Cité, we'll hopefully get hold of Superintendent Maison before he leaves for the day.'

'Thank you,' said Daniel, getting to his feet.

Abigail stood in her cell at La Santé looking out through the barred window at the ominous sight of the guillotine in the corner of the prison yard. They beheaded murderers here in France, she thought with a shudder. She turned away from the dreadful sight of the guillotine and began to pace around the cell. It was narrow, twelve feet long and seven feet wide. The grim walls were composed of solid grey rocks stretching up to the ceiling, ten feet high. There was a metal-framed bed with a thin mattress, a wooden chair, and in one corner a bucket for use as a toilet. A bottle of water had been left beside the bed, presumably for drinking rather than sanitation.

She sat down on the bed, her mind racing with thoughts. How had Daniel got on at the British Embassy? Had he managed to see Sir Brian Otway? Would Sir Brian remember her?

How on earth had she managed to end up in this nightmare? The more she thought of it, someone had planned this. They'd sent the forged letter to her purporting to come from Professor Flamand, arranging for her to arrive at his office at 11 a.m. Just before her arrival, this mysterious person had stabbed the professor, then left. How was it that Flamand's secretary had suddenly appeared at exactly that time? Could she have been part of whatever conspiracy was happening here? Perhaps she, herself, was the murderer.

The superintendent insisted there was no trace of Abigail's reply to Flamand, accepting his invitation. Which meant someone had intercepted her letter. Again, the professor's secretary would have been able to do that. But why? This was obviously a well-planned plot to kill Professor Flamand and plant the guilt on Abigail.

Abigail got up from the bed and walked again to the barred window, the terrifying sight of the guillotine drawing her like a macabre magnet. It was no wonder the French called the Revolution 'The Terror'. That was how the thousands who were dragged to this infernal machine to meet their death must have felt. It was how she felt now.

Oh Daniel, she prayed, *please get me out of here.*

CHAPTER FOUR

Daniel and Edgar Belfont were with Superintendent Maison in his office. Daniel was grateful the young Englishman had accompanied him to the police prefecture; without Belfont's fluent French, Daniel's visit to the superintendent would have been a complete waste of time because there could have been no conversation between them, no exchanges, no questions, no answers. Daniel envied the ease with which the young Englishman and the French policeman conversed and made his own determination to at least begin learning to understand and speak French. The conversation between the two men was hampered in part by the fact that after Maison had spoken, Belfont had to translate his response to Daniel. This, at least, meant Daniel was able to follow the line of questioning the superintendent was pursuing and showed where there were gaps, to Daniel's mind.

'Ask him about the knife that Flamand was killed with,' said Daniel. 'I know Abigail had no knife with her when she went to the Louvre, so whose was it? Where did it come from?'

Belfont translated the question, and Maison replied.

'He says the knife belonged to the professor. It had a

distinctive ornamental hilt of Egyptian design,' said Belfont. 'The professor's secretary, Elaine Foret, recognised it. The professor kept it on his desk and used it as a letter opener.'

'Then tell him that surely proves that Abigail is not guilty. She did not take a knife with her to meet the professor.'

Belfont translated this, and Maison did look uncomfortable. He nodded and responded.

'He says that thought also occurred to him,' said Belfont. 'It suggests that she did not come to his office planning to stab the professor. He says he thinks that some argument happened between them, during which she snatched up the knife and plunged it into the professor's heart.'

'Abigail would never do such a thing,' insisted Daniel.

To this, the superintendent countered with, 'Who knows what people do when they are in a rage. And there is no doubt there has been bad blood between your wife and Professor Flamand for some time.'

'But you've admitted that there was no premeditation, no intent on my wife's part to stab him. She did not have a knife with her when she went to the Louvre. So it cannot be murder.'

'You are suggesting self-defence?' asked Maison. 'The professor attacked her and she picked up the knife to defend herself?'

'No,' said Daniel vehemently. 'She did not stab him. It's obvious to me that someone orchestrated this whole thing with the intention of letting my wife take the blame.'

'Why?' asked Maison.

'At this moment I have no idea,' said Daniel. 'But it's

someone who wanted the professor dead. And that must be someone inside the Louvre.'

'Why do you say that?'

'Because the letter my wife wrote to the professor confirming their meeting has disappeared. Someone intercepted it and destroyed it. That could only have been done by someone inside the Louvre.'

'If she actually sent such a letter,' said Maison.

'She did,' said Daniel. 'I was with her in the post office when she sent it.'

Maison fell silent for a moment, then said, 'There is much to think about. We will take all of this in as we conduct our investigation.'

'But surely you must have heard enough to let her out of prison while you conduct your investigation. She did not go to see Professor Flamand with any murderous intent. She did not go armed, so it cannot be premeditated murder.'

'Whatever it is, it still needs to be investigated,' said Maison stubbornly.

Daniel was feeling angry and bitterly disappointed when he and Belfont left the prefecture. 'I was sure that once the business of the knife came up, Maison would agree to release Abigail,' he told Belfont.

'I'm confident that Sir Brian will be able to sort something out when he returns the day after tomorrow,' said Belfont. 'He has political clout, which – alas – I don't as just a junior member of the embassy staff.'

'You did well there,' said Daniel, still annoyed but wanting to give the young man the compliment he had earned. 'I feel so helpless here, not able to speak or understand French.'

'It would be the same for me if I was sent to somewhere like, say, China, where not even the alphabet nor the vocal sounds are the same as ours. One thing I can do is get us entry to see Mrs Wilson at La Santé Prison and report on our meeting with Superintendent Maison and tell her about Sir Brian returning the day after tomorrow.'

'Can you do that?' asked Daniel.

Belfont tapped his jacket pocket. 'This letter of authority from the embassy will get us in. I've had to use it before when some poor Britisher has found themselves ensconced in a Paris jail cell, usually for some financial misdemeanour over a hotel bill.'

At La Santé there was initially some reluctance to allow Daniel and Belfont to see Abigail.

'There are set visiting hours,' they were informed.

'Yes, but this is a diplomatic matter,' said Belfont, producing his embassy credentials. 'I represent the British ambassador and Her Majesty Queen Victoria. A refusal to allow us to talk to a British national held here on remand will mean I will have to register a strong complaint with the office of the President. And I doubt if President Loubet will be pleased to find himself in a diplomatic confrontation with the British government.'

After much unhappy muttering among the prison officials, eventually Daniel and Belfont were escorted to the visitors' hall, a large room furnished with small wooden tables with three chairs at each. A prison warder stood on guard against the wall nearest to one of the tables, and Daniel and Belfont took their seats. A short while later Abigail appeared, escorted by two prison guards. She joined them at the table. Automatically, Daniel reached out to take her hands, but the guard rapped out '*Non!*', and Daniel reluctantly took his hands away.

'How are they treating you?' he asked.

'Well enough,' said Abigail. She looked at Belfont and said, 'We haven't met before, but I assume I have you to thank for arranging this meeting outside of visiting hours.'

'Indeed,' said Belfont with a friendly smile. 'My name is Edgar Belfont and I'm Sir Brian Otway's assistant. Sir Brian's out of Paris at the moment, but he'll be returning the day after tomorrow and we'll be launching a demand for your release with the full weight of the British Embassy behind it.'

'We saw Superintendent Maison,' said Daniel. 'The knife that killed Professor Flamand was his own knife. His secretary identified it as one he kept on his desk. So Superintendent Maison appears to accept that you did not take it with you to the Louvre, which rules out premeditation on your part. Unfortunately, he insists it still needs to be investigated, but I'm very impressed with Mr Belfont's powers of persuasion, and I feel we shall soon have you out of here.'

'The day after tomorrow,' said Belfont firmly. 'Sir Brian can be very forceful when the situation calls for it.'

'Is there anything I can get you?' asked Daniel. 'Food? Clothes?'

Abigail shook her head. 'If you really think Sir Brian can obtain my release, I shall be fine. The food is adequate and my cell is comfortable enough. However, if you can arrange some reading material for me, I'd appreciate that.'

'Rest assured, Mrs Wilson, that will be done,' said Belfont. 'When we leave I shall buy some books and magazines and bring them here. And I will again use the threat of Queen Victoria being angered if the prison authorities do not give them to you.'

They spent a few more moments talking, with Abigail reassuring them she felt better as a result of the news they had brought her.

'I'm glad you are here, Mr Belfont,' said Abigail. 'I've been worried about how Daniel was faring, with no knowledge of the language.'

'Trust me, Mrs Wilson, I will be Mr Wilson's constant companion until we gain your release.'

'You seem very confident that I'll be let out of here,' said Abigail.

Belfont smiled. 'I've seen Sir Brian in action. I know what he can achieve.'

'Yes, I've seen him in action, too. But that was in his younger days.'

'I can assure you that Sir Brian has lost none of his fire,' said Belfont. 'I will stake my life that he'll have you out of here by the day after tomorrow.'

After they left the prison, Belfont led Daniel to the nearest bookseller's, where he purchased a book on ancient Egyptian art, three magazines and a copy of a newspaper. They returned to La Santé and Belfont gave instructions that these were to be taken immediately to Mrs Wilson on the orders of the British ambassador, Her Majesty Queen Victoria and President Loubet.

As they drove away from La Santé towards Montmartre, Daniel commented, 'You don't think you might be overdoing it with issuing orders from the British queen? As I understand it, this country is not fond of the monarchy. They executed their own and there seems to be no desire to bring it back.'

'It was only a couple of hundred years ago that we British executed our king, Charles I,' pointed out Belfont. 'The thing is, the French respect a strong leader. They despise authority, but anyone who has remained on the throne as long as our queen has, and rules a quarter of the world as Empress of the British Empire, is someone to be looked up to and admired.'

'I have to say, Mr Belfont—' began Daniel, before Belfont interrupted him with, 'Edgar, please. If we are going to be in one another's company, do please call me Edgar.'

'Very well. And please call me Daniel. And, as for being in one another's company, I really do appreciate it, but I don't wish you to ignore your own family for my sake.'

'My family are back in England. That is, my parents. I am not married so have no family to consider. To be honest, Daniel, it is a pleasure to have English company. Can I suggest we dine together this evening? It will save you the awkwardness of having to engage with a menu in French, and French waiters who will make a point of only speaking in French.'

'That is very kind of you,' said Daniel.

'In that case I will drop you off at your hotel and call for you at about seven, if that is agreeable.'

'Very agreeable indeed,' said Daniel.

* * *

That evening, Belfont took Daniel to a small, busy restaurant in Montmartre.

'The food here is excellent and unpretentious, unlike many of the restaurants in the 1st arrondissement, where it is all about being seen in the right company and wearing the right clothes.' He gestured at the framed paintings packed together on the walls. 'Also, here, you will see original works by some of the greatest painters of modern France.' He pointed some particular ones out to Daniel. 'That one there is by Henri de Toulouse-Lautrec. That one, by Claude Monet. Then you have a Degas, a Pissarro, a Renoir, a Paul Cézanne, Berthe Morisot. That one there is by Henri Matisse. These walls hold works by some of the most famous artists of modern times.'

'How could the owner afford to buy them?' asked Daniel. 'I don't know most of the names you mentioned, although Abigail has talked to me about Toulouse-Lautrec and promised to show me some of his works. And I know about Edgar Degas because he was close friends with an English artist we worked with, Walter Sickert.'

'Ah, Sickert.' Belfont beamed. 'He is revered here in France also. The answer is that the owner of the restaurant did not pay for them; they were given to him by the artists in order to pay for meals. Montmartre is like a magnet for young artists when they first come to Paris. Rents are cheap and the artistic ambience encourages them to paint. Before they become well-known, they sell their paintings on the streets. They also use them to barter. Not every shop owner or restaurant is prepared to take a painting in payment, but some have an eye to the future. Like Lucas, the owner of this place. As a result, he now has a small fortune on his walls.'

'Isn't he worried that someone will come in and steal them?'

Belfont shook his head. 'He has an understanding with some of the older local villains.'

'What sort of understanding?'

'He pays them to make sure that the younger unruly element leave his restaurant alone. And that includes his diners.'

'Is there much of an unruly element here in Montmartre?'

'Indeed, as there is in much of Paris. You will see them hanging around in gangs, but they are understandably in awe of the older villains. In the past Lucas has often helped many of these older villains out with food when they were down on their luck, just as he did with all the artists whose work you see displayed. Anyone stealing from Lucas would find themselves hunted down. These paintings are safe here on these walls.'

Their food arrived and they settled down to eat. It was, as Belfont had promised, excellent.

'How did you come to be here?' asked Daniel. 'At the embassy? I would imagine it's quite a sought-after position.'

'My father is Lord Belfont,' said Belfont, 'and it was through a friend of his in the House of Lords that he fixed up this position for me. It's sheer nepotism and I really should be ashamed, but I'm not. I love it here and I doubt if I could have made it on my own.'

'You don't know that,' said Daniel. 'You've shown yourself eminently capable.'

'Yes, but you need more than that if you're to get anywhere in the political service. It's all about family and who you know.

Father knew Sir Brian, and this pal of his in the House of Lords also knew Sir Brian – I believe they were all at the same school – and that's what it takes. Who you know.' He smiled. 'Unlike you, Daniel. I know all about you from a pal of mine. You knew no one. You worked your way up from a lowly place, and here you are, a famous detective. You've done that on your own. No relative pulling in favours from old school pals.'

'I also did it as the result of my partnership with Abigail. Now there *is* someone with contacts. One of the world's most respected archaeologists and Egyptologists.' He gave a wry sigh. 'And currently a prisoner in a Paris jail.'

'Just until Sir Brian gets back,' said Belfont confidently. 'What do you think of the embassy? Impressive, isn't it?'

'It reminds me of a palace,' said Daniel.

'That's exactly what it is. Or used to be. The house used to belong to Princess Borghese, Napoleon's sister, until the fall of the emperor and his exile on Elba. Napoleon was in need of money, so his sister sold the house to the Duke of Wellington in 1814 and went to join him on Elba.'

'The same man who'd defeated Napoleon at Waterloo, which led to his downfall,' said Daniel. 'Why did Wellington buy it? To rub Napoleon's face in his victory over him?'

'No, for practical reasons. Wellington was appointed as Britain's ambassador to the court of Louis XVIII and he needed somewhere grand as his ambassadorial home in Paris. As the princess needed money for her brother desperately, I believe the Duke got the property at a good price.'

'Yes.' Daniel nodded. 'From what I've read and heard about him, Wellington was quite hard-nosed about almost everything. That's why they called him the Iron Duke. But it still must have been a bitter pill for Napoleon to swallow.'

'Not necessarily. His sister passed the money from the sale to her brother. I believe that Napoleon was quite a selfish man. His own needs came first. As it is, the British government own one of the most impressive buildings in Paris.'

'With no resentment from the French?'

'Not as far as we know. But then, our ambassadors have always had a very cordial relationship with the French government, and Sir Brian is no exception. I look forward to introducing you to him when he returns.'

'What time will he be at the embassy the day after tomorrow?' asked Daniel.

'That depends if there's anything he has to deal with after his excursion today. The ambassador's residence is at 39 rue de Faubourg Saint-Honoré, next door to the embassy, which is at number 35.'

'Another palatial building?'

'Even more palatial than the embassy itself,' said Belfont. He smiled. 'Wellington liked the good things in life. Anyway, I expect Sir Brian will arrive at the embassy at about eleven. That's his usual time.'

'In that case I suggest we utilise our time first thing tomorrow by calling on the professor's secretary,' said Daniel.

'Elaine Foret.' Belfont nodded.

'Yes. As Flamand's secretary she will have been in charge of dealing with his correspondence. Yet she claims the professor didn't send that invitation to Abigail. She also says that Abigail's letter to the professor accepting his invitation never arrived. In fact, she claims it was never sent. I know Abigail sent it because I was with her in the post office when she sent it. It must have arrived at the Louvre, but then disappeared. It seems to me that no one is more likely than Elaine Foret to have been able to get rid of it. It also sems to me a great coincidence that the very moment that Abigail entered the professor's office, Elaine Foret walked in.'

'You think she was hovering nearby waiting for your wife to enter the office?'

'It's certainly a possibility. The evidence of the invitation letter asking Abigail to call at a certain time, and the fact that Abigail's reply accepting the appointment has vanished, certainly suggests a conspiracy at work. Usually conspiracies in an organisation depend on someone working within that organisation with internal knowledge being involved.'

'Do you think Elaine Foret killed the professor?'

'I don't know,' admitted Daniel. 'It's a possibility, but killing someone face to face takes a certain ruthlessness. I don't know if she's got that. But if she didn't do the actual killing, I feel she's likely to be a vital part of whatever's going on.'

'Yes, what you say makes sense,' said Belfont thoughtfully. 'So, that will be our first port of call tomorrow. The Louvre, and Mam'selle Foret.'

CHAPTER FIVE

Belfont called for Daniel at the Olive House the following morning and showed him a bundle of newspapers.

'The story's made the morning papers,' he told Daniel. He held one out to Daniel, who shook his head.

'I don't read French,' he reminded Belfont.

'No, but I thought you'd be interested to see the size of type they've used for the headlines. Large. This is a major story.' He read aloud from the paper he was holding: '"English woman kills internationally famous French professor at the Louvre".'

'That's a bit one-sided,' grumbled Daniel. 'Abigail is just as internationally famous as this professor. And are they allowed to say she killed him? There's no proof. Surely that's libel.'

'You have no concept of how the French press work,' said Belfont with a sigh.

'Sadly, I do,' said Daniel. 'The same as some aspects of the English press. I can think of some papers in London that would do exactly the same. The gutter press.'

'Well, at least Sir Brian will be aware of what's happened. If it's in these papers it will also be in those on sale in the Loire.' He groaned. 'Unfortunately I don't know where he's staying or I'd send him a telegram. But hopefully he'll send one to the embassy when he reads about it. He's very proactive.'

They left the Olive House and got into the carriage, which Belfont had told to wait, and headed for the Louvre. During the journey, Belfont did his best to cheer Daniel up with tales of how active and dynamic Sir Brian was when dealing with problems. 'Trust me, if there's anyone who can do anything about this, it's the ambassador.'

They arrived outside the main entrance of the Louvre, and when they descended from the carriage Daniel stood on the pavement and regarded the massive building in awe.

'My God!' he said. 'I hadn't realised it was so enormous. Is this really a museum?'

'Only since the end of the last century, following the Revolution,' said Belfont. 'Before then it was a royal palace, strictly for the use of the elite only. You haven't been here before?'

'No,' said Daniel. 'Abigail said she'd show it to me after she'd found out what Professor Flamand wanted to see her about.'

'It's certainly an experience,' said Belfont as they entered the museum and found themselves in a massively wide corridor whose walls soared up to a curved ceiling high above their heads, decorated with a series of paintings adorned with vibrant blues and golds.

'What an incredible piece of work,' said Daniel. 'It stretches the whole length of the corridor.'

'It was done to praise the King,' said Belfont. 'People think of the Louvre as housing historical artefacts, like the *Venus de Milo*, but initially it was the home of the Royal Academy of Painting and Sculpture. Members of the academy met here at the Louvre to discuss what types of art were officially acceptable.' He gestured at the different exhibition rooms they passed as they walked along the corridor. 'The whole place is laid out in a deliberate structure to show the development of civilisation, starting with ancient Egypt, then the Greeks and Romans, followed by the Italian Renaissance, and then finally French painting, because the French believe that France is the heir to these previous traditions of perfection, and of civilisation. I won't show you the rooms now; I'll leave that to your wife when we get her out of La Santé. We need to see Mam'selle Foret.'

As they neared the end of the long corridor, he made for a flight of stairs in one of the side walls and began to climb them.

'You know your way around this place,' observed Daniel as he followed the young man.

'Sir Brian brought me here soon after I started working for him to introduce me to Georges Deschamps, the curator, and other important people. He said our work as diplomats is about making the right contacts.'

'Have you met Elaine Foret before?'

'No. Nor the professor. Mainly it's been some of the senior administrators, and then only in the company of Sir Brian. But I have a letter of authority from the embassy that should get us access to Mam'selle Foret.'

They reached the top of the flight of stairs and Belfont turned onto another long corridor, though this one was more spartan, lacking in decoration. It was one of a series of similar corridors that branched off, twisting and turning amongst themselves, almost like a maze. Once again, Daniel was grateful he was accompanied by the young man; he'd have been hopelessly lost if he'd attempted to find his way to Foret's office on his own.

'The administrative area,' Belfont told him. 'Elaine Foret's office is just along here, next to the late professor's.'

If Edgar Belfont thought his status as a minor junior diplomat with the British Embassy would make his first meeting with Elaine Foret trouble-free, he was sadly mistaken. It was when he and Daniel entered her office, and Belfont introduced Daniel to her as *Mr Wilson, le mari de Madame Wilson . . .* that their visit began to unravel.

Elaine Foret's immediate rection was to leap to her feet from her chair and shout '*Non!*', and point a finger at the door. Belfont's attempts to show her his letter from the embassy were in vain. Mistaking it for some legal document, she snatched it from him and began to tear it to shreds. When Belfont tried to retrieve the damaged letter from her, she began to shout and scream, her main words being '*Au secours!*'

'She's calling for help,' translated Belfont.

'I rather got that impression,' said Daniel.

Foret's screams resulted in the arrival of four burly uniformed men, who ignored Belfont's protests of innocence and the tattered piece of paper he tried to give them, and Edgar and Daniel found themselves being bundled out of the office, along corridors, then downstairs to the main reception area, where they were unceremoniously pushed out into the street.

'It could have been worse,' observed Daniel. 'They might have thrown us in jail.'

They returned to the embassy, where Belfont was delighted to find a telegram waiting for him.

'It's from Sir Brian,' he told Daniel. 'He's obviously seen the story in the papers. He's coming back today, although he says he won't be back till this evening. He wants us to meet him here. He says, "Train arriving 8.15 p.m.". So I'll pick you up at your hotel at eight so we'll be here when he arrives. Is that all right with you?'

'Excellent,' said Daniel. He looked rueful as he added, 'I suppose it'll be too late to get Abigail out of jail this evening?'

'I'm afraid so. But at least we'll be able to see Superintendent Maison first thing tomorrow at the prefecture with Sir Brian. In the meantime, I suggest we return to La Santé and inform Abigail that Sir Brian's on his way back. Hopefully that will make her feel better.'

Unfortunately for them, their second visit to the prison was not as successful as the first. Different staff were on duty and, without Belfont's letter of authority, which had been torn to shreds by Elaine Foret, they refused to permit them to visit Abigail outside of official visiting hours. This time, Belfont's attempts to use the name of Queen Victoria cut no ice. The only concession they were able to extract from the guards was that a note would be delivered to the prisoner in her cell. The proviso being that it would have to be written in French so that the staff could make sure no inappropriate messages were being sent to the prisoner. Belfont duly wrote the note to Abigail, and they left the prison.

'Will they give it to her?' Daniel worried as they left.

'Yes,' said Belfont. 'I made sure I put in all sorts of references to the British ambassador and the President of the Republic being involved in this situation. They'll make sure she gets it.' He looked at Daniel. 'If Sir Brian's returning this evening, I'll need to make sure I've got everything ready for him. Will you be all right on your own until I pick you up at eight?'

'Absolutely,' Daniel assured him. 'I'll eat at the hotel and wander around Montmartre, making sure I don't stray too far from the hotel and get lost. I thought I'd do my best to learn some French from shop signs. I've already worked out that "*tabac*" is "tobacconist" and "*boulangerie*" is "bakery".'

'An excellent start,' said Belfont. 'I'll drop you back at your hotel now and see you there at eight.'

In her cell, Abigail read Belfont's note again. Sir Brian was on his way back to Paris and would be meeting Daniel and Belfont that evening. Too late to obtain her release today, she thought ruefully, but it boded well for tomorrow. Providing that the Brian Otway she'd known all those years ago was still the same dynamic life-force he'd been then, a man who made things happen, but by using intelligence and not just simply bullying people as some in the British Foreign Service did. She shuddered as she remembered a particular civil servant in Egypt, arrogant, vain and bullying of everyone, except his superiors at the embassy. She thought it no surprise that one morning he'd been found battered to death in a back alley in Cairo. No one had ever been charged with his murder, and although the official report said he'd been killed by some locals, Abigail hadn't been the only one who suspected that the murderer had been a junior member of the embassy staff taking their revenge for the humiliations they'd suffered at the nasty diplomat's hands.

She hoped that Sir Brian was still his same intelligent, caring and able self. She would need that diplomatic skill if she was going to get out of this.

CHAPTER SIX

Daniel and Belfont were already in the reception area at the embassy when the door opened and a tell, elegantly dressed, well-built man in his late fifties strode in.

'Ah, Belfont!' he exclaimed.

Daniel noticed he had an impressive salt-and-pepper beard, which curled at the ends and sides. He held out his hand with a broad smile as he neared them.

'And you must be Daniel Wilson!'

Daniel shook the man's hand.

'Sir Brian Otway,' murmured Belfont.

Yes, thought Daniel, *I'd already reached that conclusion.*

'It's a pleasure to meet you, Sir Brian,' he said.

'Let's hope you still feel like saying that after we've called on Superintendent Maison tomorrow,' said Otway.

'I'm afraid we didn't have any success when we saw the superintendent yesterday,' admitted Belfont ruefully.

'I'm sure you tried your best,' said Otway sympathetically. 'But now it's time for the big guns.' He turned to Daniel. 'I need to make sure I've got all the facts ready, so please accompany to my office and you can tell me everything, right from the very start.' To Belfont, he said, 'See if you can arrange a pot of tea for us. Good tea. The alleged tea they served on the train was undrinkable.'

'Yes, Sir Brian,' said Belfont.

'Along with a bottle of good brandy,' said Otway. 'I feel we're going to need it.'

Once in Otway's office, Daniel filled in the ambassador on the whole story: from the letter allegedly from Professor Flamand inviting Abigail to meet him, to her arrest and imprisonment, and the meetings he and Belfont had held with Superintendent Maison, and their two visits to La Santé Prison. Included in this, Belfont related to Sir Brian the disaster of their visit to the Louvre to talk to Elaine Foret.

'They threw you out?' said Otway, shocked.

'They did,' said Belfont ruefully. 'Fortunately, we remained on our feet.'

'A disgraceful way to treat a member of the British Embassy staff, and a noted British detective,' said Otway. 'I shall have something to say on this matter.'

After he'd listened to Daniel and Belfont, Otway rested his hand on the newspapers he'd brought with him.

'A tale well told, Mr Wilson,' he complimented Daniel. 'And now, if you'll leave me to my thoughts I shall make notes for our meeting tomorrow morning with the superintendent. I am absolutely determined that your wife will be freed from prison tomorrow morning, or else there'll be diplomatic hell to pay. We'll pick you up from your hotel first thing tomorrow.'

Daniel returned to his hotel, leaving Otway and Belfont in conference on the strategy for the next day. As he lay in the bed in his hotel room, his mind was full of thoughts of Abigail in her cell at La Santé.

'Courage, my darling,' he vowed quietly. 'We'll have you out tomorrow, I promise. One way or another.'

Next morning, when Daniel climbed aboard the ambassadorial carriage parked outside the entrance to the Olive House, he found Sir Brian inside grinning broadly and holding a telegram, which he passed to Daniel.

'This morning I received this, which will be the ace in our hand.'

Daniel looked at the name at the bottom of telegram.

'From Sir Anthony Thurrington,' he said.

'The Queen's right-hand man,' said Otway. 'I believe you know him?'

'Yes, Abigail and I were able to give some assistance to Her Majesty recently. Sir Anthony became our liaison during the case.'

'You'll see that he mentions the Queen has taken an interest in this case and exhorts me to obtain Mrs Wilson's release from prison. I assume the story has appeared in the English newspapers. Whatever you did for Her Majesty must have impressed her because I can't recall her taking such an interest in the welfare of a British subject incarcerated here in France before.'

'Her Majesty did say at the time she was grateful to us,' said Daniel.

'I assume you are unable to divulge details of the assistance you gave?' said Otway, with a questioning smile.

'I'm afraid you are right, Sir Brian,' said Daniel. 'Her Majesty was most insistent on secrecy.'

'Yes, that is my experience of Her Majesty.' Otway nodded. He slipped the telegram back into his pocket. 'Well, armed with this missive, I feel it is time for us to launch our onslaught on the French judicial system.'

When they arrived at the police prefecture there was no time spent explaining the purpose of their visit. Sir Brian was obviously a frequent and well-respected visitor to the Île de la Cité because he was shown straight into Superintendent Maison's office, along with Belfont and Daniel. The superintendent welcomed Otway with a handshake and gestured for him to take a seat. Daniel and Belfont were left standing behind Otway.

We must look like a pair of broker's men in a pantomime, ready to do Baron Hardup's bidding, thought Daniel.

Otway showed Superintendent Maison the telegram he'd received.

'This is from Queen Victoria urging me to intervene on behalf of Mrs Wilson and obtain her freedom from prison. As a servant of Her Majesty I have to carry out her bidding, which – in this case – I assume means my making an official presentation to the President. I would rather not do that. You and I have always enjoyed a friendly relationship, and such a request to your president can only harm your career. Mr Wilson has presented his case to you, that this cannot be called murder *if* Mrs Wilson did actually cause the death of Professor Flamand – which Mr Wilson vigorously denies, as does his wife. There was no premeditation; no knife was taken by her into the Louvre. I have known Mrs Wilson for some years; she is a highly esteemed archaeologist, recognised as such internationally. Only Professor Flamand seems to have taken a different point of view. Surely – in view of these facts, and especially in view of this urgent telegram from none other than the Queen of England – she could be released on bail while your investigation continues.'

Maison looked doubtful. 'Bail for someone who could flee the country and return to England?'

'I can assure you that would not happen. You have my word as the British ambassador.' When he saw that Maison's expression was still one of doubt, he added silkily, 'Of course, if you prefer we can always take the course the Queen has ordered: for me to place the matter in the hands of the President.'

Maison shook his head. 'That will not be necessary. I will accept your undertaking for her good conduct, and your promise that she will not attempt to leave France. I must also insist that she does not return to the Louvre while this case is under investigation.'

'Agreed,' said Otway. 'There is another issue here. My assistant, Mr Belfont, accompanied Mr Wilson to the Louvre to conduct an interview with Professor Flamand's secretary, Elaine Foret, but she refused to talk to them. I feel that could be the same situation with other employees of the Louvre. As you know, before I became ambassador I was a barrister. I have taken up Mrs Wilson's legal defence and as such I insist we have access to the staff at the Louvre in order to obtain the answers to the many questions we have. Later, I shall be visiting the senior curator at the Louvre, Georges Deschamps, who is an old friend of mine, in order to arrange such access. It would help enormously if I'm able to tell him that you have no objections to myself and my staff making enquiries, although I accept that Mrs Wilson should remain at a distance for the moment.'

Maison deliberated on this for a moment, then reached out his hand. 'Agreed,' he said.

And the two men shook hands on this agreement.

At La Santé, Otway produced the order signed by Superintendent Maison authorising Abigail's release and presented it to the prison governor. Within a short while, Abigail had joined them in the governor's office. More forms were signed, more handshakes were exchanged, and then Abigail was escorted to the waiting carriage by the three British men.

'It's good to see you again, Mrs Wilson,' said Otway as they settled themselves in the carriage. He beamed at Daniel. 'Although I knew her as Abigail Fenton. I hope you'll forgive me if I occasionally lapse into using her former name.'

'After what you've done in getting her out of that place, I'm sure both of us will be happy with whatever you happen to call her,' said Daniel with a smile.

'Amen to that,' said the relieved Abigail.

'As you know, Mrs Wilson, the superintendent has stopped you from returning to the Louvre for the time being, but I hope to get that amended. No such restrictions were placed on you, Mr Wilson. However, you'll need a translator, and I propose young Belfont assists you until we can get freedom of movement for Mrs Wilson. Will that be acceptable to you?'

'More than acceptable,' said Daniel. 'Mr Belfont has shown himself to be highly efficient in all his dealings on this case.'

'Excellent!' Otway beamed. 'I suggest we begin by my accompanying you to the Louvre.' To Abigail he explained, 'Your husband and young Edgar here attempted to talk to Mam'selle Foret yesterday, but were prevented from doing so.'

'She objected very volubly to us calling on her and we were thrown out of the building,' added Daniel with a rueful smile.

'A situation I intend to overturn,' said Otway. 'I'm afraid you will have to wait in the carriage, my dear, while I introduce your husband and Belfont to the curator, and then to Mam'selle Foret. Hopefully it should not take long.'

'Actually, Sir Brian, I have already met Monsieur Deschamps. He was at a party you gave at the embassy for the French arts community,' said Belfont.

'Ah yes, of course. Excellent! That will make things easier.'

CHAPTER SEVEN

At the Louvre, Otway was greeted by the museum's curator, Georges Deschamps, with a warm smile of welcome.

'*Monsieur l'ambassadeur*,' said Deschamps, shaking Otway's hand vigorously. 'This is indeed an unexpected pleasure.'

'Not entirely unexpected, I would think, Georges.' Otway smiled. 'Not after the recent tragic death of Professor Flamand.' He gestured at his two companions. 'You know Edgar Belfont already; the other gentleman is Daniel Wilson from London.'

'Wilson?' queried Deschamps.

'The husband of Mrs Wilson, who was wrongly accused of Flamand's murder. Superintendent Maison has agreed to release Mrs Wilson from prison, although he has requested that she not be allowed to come to the Louvre until his investigations into the case have been completed. I have accepted that, for the moment, but I hope to overturn that decision. In the meantime, as part of Madame Wilson's defence, which I will be conducting, Superintendent Maison has agreed that Mr Wilson be allowed to question the staff here.'

'Of course,' said Deschamps.

'We wish to talk particularly to the professor's secretary,

Elaine Foret. Unfortunately, when Mr Wilson and Mr Belfont attempted to do that, she protested volubly and they were thrown out of the Louvre. And I do mean literally, by some of your burliest employees. Ejected into the street.'

Deschamps turned to look at Belfont and Daniel, an expression of mortification on his face. He began to apologise profusely. Otway allowed him to get his apology out, then smiled and said, 'I'm sure Mr Belfont and Mr Wilson accept the apology on behalf of the Louvre, and understand that the action of your stewards was obviously a mistake based on erroneous information given to them by Mam'selle Foret. In order to prevent any recurrence, I would be most grateful, Georges, if you would accompany me to Mam'selle Foret's office and tell her that these men are here with the agreement of Superintendent Maison, that they represent not just the British Embassy but Her Majesty Queen Victoria, who has sent a telegram to me today instructing me to conduct enquiries in order to absolutely prove that Mrs Wilson is completely innocent of this charge.' With that, Otway produced the telegram from Thurrington and passed it to Deschamps. The curator gave it the briefest of reads before handing it back to Otway.

'Of course, Sir Brian,' he said. 'If you will all accompany me, I will sort this out at once.'

The curator led them through a series of corridors before arriving at a closed door next to the office that had served as Professor Flamand's base of operations. Deschamps did not knock at the door, merely opened it and strode into the office.

Elaine Foret was sitting at a desk, sorting through papers. She leapt to her feet when she saw Deschamps.

'*Monsieur le conservateur!*' she said. Then her eyes widened as she saw Otway standing just behind Deschamps.

'Sir Brian!' she gasped, shocked, and Daniel noticed that she trembled.

'*Bonjour, Mam'selle Foret*,' said Otway, rather brusquely, thought Daniel. 'These are Mr Belfont from the British Embassy and Daniel Wilson, a detective from London, the husband of Abigail Wilson, who I understand you have met.'

Foret nodded, seemingly stunned into muteness.

Otway gestured to Georges Deschamps, who took over the narrative.

'We have been advised that Madame Wilson is no longer considered as a suspect in this case,' said Deschamps. 'Accordingly, she has been released from prison. The police have given permission for Mr Wilson, Sir Brian Otway and Mr Belfont to conduct enquiries here at the Louvre into the murder of Professor Flamand. I have vowed that everyone in this establishment will answer their questions, and that means everyone. I trust that is clear, Mam'selle Foret.'

Foret almost curtsied as she replied in respectful tones, '*Oui, monsieur le conservateur.*'

Deschamps turned to Otway and announced, 'I shall therefore leave you and your colleagues to talk to Mam'selle Foret, Sir Brian.'

Once Deschamps had departed, Otway turned to Belfont and said, 'I suggest you handle the questions and the translation for Mr Wilson's benefit, Belfont. After all, you've been involved with Mr Wilson right from the start of this and I guess you know what he might be thinking.'

To Daniel, he said, 'So, Mr Wilson, ask your questions and Belfont will translate them into French, along with Mam'selle Foret's answers. I will sit over here and be unobtrusive and just observe.'

With that he settled himself down on a comfortable chair. Daniel noticed that Foret's eyes kept straying towards the ambassador and there was almost a silent plea for help in her face as she looked at him.

'Do you know of any enemies the professor may have had?' asked Daniel.

'No,' said Foret in a firm voice. 'Everyone admired and respected the professor. Everyone except Madame Wilson.'

Daniel caught the words 'Madame Wilson' in between Elaine Foret's French and wasn't surprised when Belfont translated her answer. Instead of reacting with a defence of Abigail, he continued with his questions: Had she seen anyone in the corridor before she went into the professor's office? Again, a firm '*non*' was her response. He asked if anything appeared to be missing from the professor's office after he was killed, and once again came the familiar '*non*'. It soon became obvious that, despite the presence of Sir Brian Otway, Elaine Foret had no intention of giving them any information about the professor, his work or his private life. She was determined to protect his reputation at all costs. To her, Professor Flamand was the epitome of perfection. In the end, Daniel accepted that he would have to look for the answers he wanted from a different source, someone not so passionately devoted to Flamand. He thanked Elaine Foret, then he and Belfont, along with Otway, took their leave of her.

As Daniel, Otway and Belfont made for the carriage where Abigail waited for them, Daniel said to Otway, 'I hadn't realised you knew Elaine Foret.'

'I'd hardly say I know her.' Otway shrugged. 'I'm a frequent visitor to the Louvre to see Georges Deschamps. I've briefly seen her on some of those occasions.'

Abigail was keen to find out how they'd got on when they arrived back at the carriage.

'Not well,' said Daniel. He listed the questions he'd asked Foret, and reported that she had been firm in her defence of Flamand, denying that there was anything wrong with the man or his way of living. 'She insisted he had no enemies. Except you.'

'So you got nowhere,' Abigail said with a rueful sigh.

'I felt her attitude was deliberate stonewalling because she was hiding something,' said Daniel.

'What?' asked Otway.

'If I knew that, it wouldn't be hidden. But it was also there in her manner when you talked to her about the professor.'

'Who knows what she was thinking?' Otway shrugged dismissively. 'I'll drop you at your hotel and then I'll be taking Mr Belfont back to the embassy. If you need me for anything, you'll find me there.'

As the carriage set off, Abigail said, 'I feel Daniel and I need to talk to Professor Flamand's widow – Madame Flamand – in case she knows any enemies her husband might have had.'

'Actually, I would advise against that course of action, Mrs Wilson,' said Otway.

'Why? I have been released from prison. As far as I know I've only been banned from going to the Louvre.'

'But you are still being investigated by the police. I doubt if Madame Flamand will talk to you, as you are the person accused of murdering her husband.'

'But this is ridiculous!' burst out Abigail.

'Actually, I think Sir Brian has a good point,' observed Daniel.

'But who's going to talk to her?' demanded Abigail. 'You? You can't speak French. And I don't believe that Superintendent Maison will ask the questions we want to ask.'

'I speak French,' said Belfont quietly. 'As your embassy representative, I could call on her and ask the questions you want.'

'Yes,' said Daniel thoughtfully. 'That might work. But I'd like to come with you.'

'For what reason?' asked Belfont. 'As Mrs Wilson has pointed out, you won't know what she and I will be saying to one another.'

'No, but reading someone's body language when they're being questioned can be very instructive,' countered Daniel. 'You can often tell when someone's lying. I'll ask you afterwards what you asked her at a particular moment, and what she replied.'

'Agreed,' said Belfont. 'Although I can't guarantee what sort of reception we'll get. Madame Flamand is still the grieving widow and will be within her rights to refuse to talk to us.'

'There's only one way to find out,' said Daniel. 'When are you free to make a call?'

'Tomorrow afternoon?' suggested Belfont. 'I have some important correspondence for Sir Brian that needs to be dealt with before then.'

'My assistant is very conscientious.' Otway smiled. 'Fortunately for me.'

'Tomorrow afternoon will be fine,' said Daniel.

CHAPTER EIGHT

After Daniel and Abigail had been dropped off at their hotel and were in their room, Abigail said, 'You look concerned about something. Ever since you got back in the carriage after talking to Elaine Foret. Did anything happen that you haven't told me about?'

'Yes,' said Daniel. 'I couldn't talk about it before because we were with Sir Brian.'

'Oh?' said Abigail, intrigued.

'It was when we walked into Mam'selle Foret's office. You should have seen her expression when she said "Sir Brian".'

'I'm assuming you mean she looked a bit surprised, but he's a very well-known figure in Paris. Quite famous.'

Daniel shook his head. 'No, there was something else in her face, in her eyes. Passion. Ardour.'

Abigail looked at him, puzzled. 'What are you suggesting?'

'I am suggesting there is more going on between those two than Sir Brian is admitting to.'

Abigail thought about this for a moment, then nodded and said, 'Yes,' in an almost wistful tone.

Daniel looked at her quizzically. 'That's an interesting response,' he said.

'When I knew Sir Brian before when I came to Paris, he had a reputation as a ladies' man. To the extent that he made advances to every woman he met.'

'Including you?' asked Daniel.

She nodded. 'Yes,' she said.

'I can understand that,' said Daniel. 'You were always beautiful. I can imagine that beauty combined with your youth—'

'I wasn't that young,' Abigail cut in.

'Still, I can see why he would chase you.'

'And the question hovering on your lips is: did I let him catch me?' said Abigail.

'I'm not going to ask,' said Daniel. 'It was before you and I were together.'

'Nevertheless, I'm going to tell you. The answer is no. For one thing, I knew of his reputation: enjoy a brief liaison, then move on. Secondly, he was married. I determined many years ago I would not let myself be involved with a married man. I had seen the heartache it caused many of my friends.'

'If he was involved romantically with Elaine Foret, it raises an interesting avenue we might need to look into.'

'Why?'

'Because I'm convinced that, whatever this is about, Foret was involved in the murder of Professor Flamand. Could there be a love triangle?'

Abigail laughed. 'Honestly, Daniel, just because we're in Paris, the city of love, it doesn't mean everyone's involved in passionate affairs. And even if they are, it doesn't mean it automatically leads to murder.'

'Sex and money, two of the most common motives for murder,' observed Daniel.

A knock at their door interrupted them. Daniel strode to the door and opened it, and found a man in his late thirties standing there.

'Monsieur Wilson?' asked the man.

'*Oui*,' said Daniel.

'*Je suis Auguste Perrier*,' said the man.

'Auguste!' came a cry of welcome from Abigail and she joined them at the door. She turned to Daniel. 'Auguste and I worked together on digs some years ago. He came briefly to Hawara when I was there with Flinders Petrie.'

'But the revered Monsieur Petrie and I had very different views of what we were looking for at Hawara, so I left.' Perrier smiled.

'Do come in,' said Abigail.

'Thank you,' said Perrier, entering. 'As what I have to say should be of interest to both of you, I shall use English.'

'I appreciate that,' said Daniel. 'It was getting quite hard to keep up with whoever was translating what people were saying.'

'Would you care for some tea?' asked Abigail. 'If you like, we can always talk downstairs in the restaurant.'

Perrier shook his head. 'It is better if I say what I have to say to you in private where my words can't be overheard.'

'This sounds serious,' said Abigail.

'It is,' said Perrier. 'I read in the newspapers that you

had been arrested on suspicion of the murder of Professor Flamand. I called at La Santé Prison to offer my assistance, but they told me you had been released. So here I am.'

'You know something about the case?' asked Daniel.

'I know about the kind of man Professor Flamand was,' said Perrier. 'I have come to offer my help in solving this case. Finding the murderer. You are, after all, the famous Museum Detectives. I assume that is why you are here.'

'No,' said Abigail. 'We are here in Paris because I was invited by Professor Flamand to discuss working with him.'

'You and Flamand, working together?' said Perrier. 'Never!'

'That is what I thought at first,' said Abigail. 'But then I thought, perhaps he has decided to bury the hatchet. In that case I decided I, too, could let bygones be bygones. So we came here and I went to the Louvre to meet him, as arranged.'

'And found him dead, stabbed.' Perrier nodded. 'Yes, I saw the report in the newspapers. They say no trace of his letter to you was found, nor the reply you sent him.' He shrugged. 'They were destroyed to implicate you; it is obvious. You are the scapegoat.'

'But why me?' asked Abigail.

'Because you are a foreigner, and there was known animosity between you and Flamand.'

'There was no animosity on my part,' said Abigail. 'To be honest, I hardly knew the professor. I met him a couple of times when we were both on separate digs in Egypt. I didn't like his attitude towards me, which was superior and dismissive purely because I was a woman, so I avoided having any contact with him.'

'But you chose to come to see him when he invited you.'

'The tone of his invitation was conciliatory, which made me think that maybe he'd changed as he got older. And he was a brilliant Egyptologist. The problem was he insisted he was the best and everyone else was inferior to him. I hoped that finally we might be able to sit down together and have a proper conversation, equal to equal.'

'Do you have any idea who killed the professor?' asked Perrier.

'It's too early to say at this stage,' said Daniel.

'What you need to do is discover who destroyed Abigail's reply to the professor,' said Perrier. 'It has to be someone within the Louvre, which will be a tall order. The Louvre has two thousand employees, so finding out who might have intercepted Abigail's reply to Flamand is going to be an almost impossible task.'

'We already feel we know who might have done it,' said Daniel. 'Elaine Foret, Flamand's secretary. She was also the one who discovered Abigail with Flamand after he'd been killed.'

'You think she may have been the murderer?'

'Not necessarily,' said Abigail. 'But she may have been part of a conspiracy. We feel there's someone behind her, someone pulling the strings.'

'For which we need to find out what motive there could be behind his death. Who would want to kill him?' said Daniel.

'Many people, I believe,' said Perrier. 'Professor Flamand was not an honest man. I have personal experience of his dishonesty. Last year I was working with Flamand at Saqqara, excavating

Djoser's step pyramid. We found one chamber that contained literally thousands of pieces of pottery. Mostly they were made of alabaster, but there were some – plates and cups – decorated with precious stones. They were supposed to be shipped back to France, and the best pieces to be cleaned and exhibited at the Louvre. But the best pieces never arrived.

'I pointed this out to Professor Flamand, but he dismissed it, saying the pieces were possibly late in being transported. But he didn't seem at all worried at their absence. So I offered to carry out a search for them. After all, I'd been there when they'd been discovered, so I knew what to look for. But that's when his manner towards me changed. He told me firmly that he was in charge of the expedition, not me. He was very firm that he did not want me poking my nose in, as he put it, and upsetting the delicate relationships he had with the Louvre and his sponsors. We had words, and the next thing I know I was removed from the list of those engaged in the expedition.'

'Why?'

'There can only be one explanation: Flamand was instrumental in diverting the best pieces – the precious ones – to somewhere else. To *someone* else.'

'You mean he stole them?'

'I do. But it was impossible for me to prove. He kept control of the paperwork that recorded what we'd found and where, and where it had been sent. The end result was that Flamand blackened my name, saying I was a troublemaker and other such lies. As a result I found it difficult to get backing for my own archaeological digs from within French sources, so lately much of my work has been with German museums.'

'Are you suggesting that Professor Flamand's actions over these precious relics from Saqqara may be a reason why he was killed?' asked Abigail.

Perrier shook his head. 'It's a possibility, but I just told you this to show you the sort of man he was. It's my belief that his murder may actually be related to the Dreyfus affair.'

'Dreyfus?' said Daniel in surprise.

'Captain Dreyfus, a captain in the French artillery, who was convicted of treason and sentenced to life imprisonment,' explained Perrier.

'I was telling Daniel about him earlier,' said Abigail. 'I saw in the newspaper that he's back in France, for a retrial.'

'Which will be a farce!' snorted Perrier. 'It's not even in a proper court of law but in a military court. A court martial run by the army. You know the facts of the case?'

'I know what I read in *The Times*, but that was a year ago. I can't remember all the names of the people involved. I know the real culprit confessed.'

'A French Army major called Ferdinand Esterhazy. A military court held a trial of Esterhazy in secret, at which they found him not guilty. Shortly after this travesty of a trial, where Esterhazy was acquitted, Émile Zola wrote an article exposing the whole nasty charade, which was published on the front page of a Paris daily newspaper. It had the title "*J'Accuse!*" and it accused the highest levels of the French Army of the deliberate obstruction of justice, and also of being anti-Semitic for having sentenced Dreyfus wrongly to life imprisonment for a crime he did not commit.'

'Émile Zola?' mused Daniel thoughtfully. 'He's a writer, isn't he?'

'For the French he is *the* writer, their greatest living writer,' said Abigail.

'Zola's article caused the biggest split there has been in this country since the Revolution,' said Perrier. 'Those who supported Dreyfus – known as the Dreyfusards – were against the pro-army anti-Dreyfusards. Flamand was fiercely on the side of the anti-Dreyfusards. He was a known anti-Semite.'

'And you think that's why he was killed?'

'I do,' said Perrier. 'Passions are running exceedingly high over this matter. People have been attacked, physically as well as verbally. People have died.'

'But why would Dreyfus's supporters want to kill Flamand?' asked Daniel.

'Because Flamand had influence with government ministers. And he had called for Dreyfus to be executed for his so-called crime.'

Perrier looked as if he was about to say more, then he produced his watch from his fob pocket.

'Excuse me, I have an appointment.' He took a card from his pocket and handed it to Abigail. 'Here is my address. Get in touch with me at any time. If there's anything I can do to help clear your name, I will do it gladly.'

He shook their hands, made a brief bow and left.

CHAPTER NINE

'What do you think?' asked Abigail after Perrier had gone.

'Of him, or what he said?' asked Daniel.

'Both,' said Abigail.

Daniel looked thoughtfully at the card Perrier had left with them, then said, 'I'm suspicious of him.'

'Why?'

'He comes in here and the first thing he does is tell us about Flamand's dishonesty over these artefacts. He alleges that the professor had stolen the best pieces and sold them for private gain, cheating the museum. That alone would have piqued our interest. If it's true, there is a motive there for his murder: either revenge, or someone who felt he'd cheated them. But instead of leaving it at that, Perrier then brings in this whole political business about the Dreyfus case.' He shook his head. 'It's too much. It was like he was throwing more than was necessary to confuse the issue.'

'That's not his fault,' said Abigail. 'If he knows something . . .'

'But does he?' pressed Daniel. 'Or is he throwing in this Dreyfus business to throw us off the real story?'

'Which is?' asked Abigail.

Daniel sighed.

'I don't know,' he admitted. 'At the moment we're in the early stages.'

'And we have no official status in the investigation,' pointed out Abigail, 'except with me as a suspect. And, though I've been released from prison, I'm not allowed to leave France or go to the Louvre.'

'Which is why we have to find out who it was who did the murder.'

'I'd like to discuss this allegation of the stolen artefacts with Georges Deschamps, and also this Dreyfus business, but I'm barred,' said Abigail in frustration. 'However, Edgar Belfont will be at the embassy working on Sir Brian's correspondence. I'm sure he'll be able to give us his take on this Dreyfus business. After all, it's all politics.'

Sir Brian Otway had left the embassy, but Edgar Belfont was still there, engaged in writing responses to the various letters that had come for Sir Brian. He greeted them warmly.

'I hadn't expected to see you so soon.'

'We're sorry if we're interrupting your work,' said Abigail. 'We can always go.'

'No, no, do stay. To be honest, dealing with these letters is one of the most tiresome aspects of this job, so I'm grateful to take a break from it. And I'm nearly done. What can I do for you?'

'We had a visit from an old colleague of Abigail's. Auguste Perrier, an archaeologist. He seemed to have the idea that Flamand's murder is to do with the Dreyfus case.'

'The Dreyfus case?' said Belfont, surprised.

Abigail nodded. 'Those who oppose Dreyfus at war with those who support him.'

'With respect, I would caution you about Monsieur Perrier, even though I know you are a friend of his,' said Belfont. 'He has a reputation as an agitator.'

'I wouldn't describe myself as a friend, exactly,' said Abigail. 'We met a few times on archaeological expeditions, and I respect his work and his ambitions, but I wouldn't say I know him that well.'

'Just to warn you, at this moment the furore over Dreyfus because of his retrial is being used by the different sides of political opinion for their own advantage. My advice is to take everything you're told about the case with a pinch of salt.' He looked at them enquiringly. 'To change the subject completely, would you both care to dine with me this evening, at the same restaurant where Daniel and I dined yesterday? To celebrate your release from prison, Mrs Wilson. As I said, I'm very advanced on dealing with this correspondence, and it would be a great pleasure for me.'

'That is a lovely idea,' said Abigail.

'You sure you wouldn't prefer to be alone together?'

'We are always together,' said Abigail. 'And, frankly, having spent the last few days in a grey prison cell within sight of the guillotine, I'd prefer to be out where people are enjoying themselves. And it would be good to see this city through your eyes, Mr Belfont. It's been some years since I was last in Paris and there are bound to have been changes.'

'Excellent.' Belfont beamed. 'I shall call for you at your hotel at seven o'clock, if that is all right. What do you intend to do before then?'

'We thought we'd go and see Superintendent Maison and tell him about Auguste Perrier and his theory about the Dreyfus case.'

Belfont nodded. 'It will be interesting to get his take on that, but bear in mind what I said about people using it for their own ends.'

'We also want to pass on to him something else that Perrier told us. He alleged that Flamand was selling to private buyers some of the most expensive pieces he'd brought back from a dig he was on that was paid for by the Louvre.'

'At Saqqara,' added Abigail.

'Most interesting,' mused Belfont. 'If true, it's grand theft and is surely a motive for some kind of action.' He looked at his watch. 'But we can talk about this more this evening. If you want to catch Superintendent Maison, I would advise making for the Île de la Cité now. He's a conscientious police officer, but he is also a family man and I know he likes to get home to his wife and children for the evening, whenever he can. Sometimes that's not always possible; a policeman's lot is not always a happy one.'

Superintendent Maison was still at the police prefecture when Daniel and Abigail arrived, although he was packing up ready to leave. He already had his overcoat on.

'I do not have much time,' he told them, disapproving of their late entrance.

'We promise we won't keep you,' said Abigail. 'We had a

visit from an archaeologist I once worked with called Auguste Perrier. He has a theory that Professor Flamand's murder is connected to the Dreyfus case.'

'Nonsense!' snapped Maison.

'His reasoning,' continued Abigail, 'is that Professor Flamand was urging the government to execute Dreyfus as a traitor. He thinks that Dreyfus's supporters may have murdered the professor to shut him up.'

Maison shook his head.

'Ludicrous,' he said derisively. 'We know this Perrier. He is a troublemaker. He does his best to stir up trouble for the establishment. He is a left-wing rabble-rouser.' He looked at them dismissively and said, 'Is there anything else?'

'Don't you think it's even worth looking into?' asked Abigail.

'No,' said Maison firmly. 'Now, if you'll excuse me, I have to leave.'

With that he ushered them out of his office and the building and climbed into a one-horse police carriage and drove away.

'Well, that was a wasted journey,' sighed Abigail.

'Not completely,' said Daniel. 'It tells us something about the superintendent and his views on any possible Dreyfus connection.'

'He refuses to consider it,' said Abigail.

'Exactly,' said Daniel. 'Why do you think that is?'

Inside the carriage, Superintendent Maison reflected on the brief encounter with the Wilsons. *So, they want to look into an alleged Dreyfus connection based on the word of a communist agitator like Perrier. Trashing good people's reputations for no other reason than hatred and envy. Well, he wouldn't let that happen.*

Like most French people, he'd followed the case and was now convinced that Dreyfus had been deliberately framed by the military establishment. The man was innocent and should be released. The truth was, he should never have been sentenced. The arrogance of the senior officers who'd chosen to have him tried and then thought they could suppress the forged evidence against him beggared belief. It was they who should have been in the dock and sent to Devil's Island. Not that he would ever declare that publicly. He would not allow his name to be linked to those criminals and traitors who were using Dreyfus as a means of attacking the establishment. Agitators like Perrier.

Was it possible? Of course, anything was possible in France, however unthinkable and corrupt. That was one thing the latest twists and turns in the Dreyfus case had shown. But he would not be investigating these allegations. He would not help these traitors and criminals to bring down the Republic.

Lucas's restaurant was packed when Daniel, Abigail and Belfont arrived, with every table full and five people already waiting. They were invited to stand at the serving counter with drinks until a table became free, but Abigail elected to examine the works of art on display. Belfont explained to her how the restaurant came to have such a large collection by modern French artists ('paintings for food'), to which Abigail responded with, 'Monsieur Lucas has made a very wise investment with that policy. At a cost of a few francs to him for a meal, he will have a fortune if just one of these became famous. And already I recognise one painting by Edgar Degas. And, my God, there's a Lautrec! And a Renoir. And a Monet.'

'If you look at the dates, most were painted in the early 1870s, before they were famous.'

'Yes. As I recall, the first exhibition by the Impressionists, as they came to be known, was in 1874. It was open to any painter who could pay a show fee of sixty francs. It was a painting by Claude Monet, *Impressionism: Sunrise*, which gave the style – the movement, if you wish – its name.'

'You know your art history, Mrs Wilson,' said Belfont.

'I've always been fascinated by artists and their work,' said Abigail. 'And wondered why it is that one particular artist becomes famous, while another of equal talent languishes in poverty. Vincent van Gogh, for example, who I consider one of the truly great painters of the age, whose work will last. Yet he sold only one painting in his lifetime, and that was in exchange for a meal, just as these were.'

Finally, they were told that their table was ready for them, and they settled down and began to study their menus.

'How did you get on with Superintendent Maison?' asked Belfont.

'He refused absolutely to even consider there might be a connection to the Dreyfus case,' said Abigail.

'And the business of Flamand selling artefacts privately?'

'We didn't get a chance to raise that with him. He was eager to leave the office. But we'll raise it with him another time, when he might be more open to hearing it.'

'So we now have a mixture of potential motives,' said Belfont. 'The professor allegedly stealing from the museum. Pro-Dreyfus supporters killing the professor because he called for Dreyfus to be executed. Plus other enemies he may have had, which we don't know about.'

'Hopefully we'll find more from Madame Flamand when we see her tomorrow,' said Daniel. 'You're still all right with that?'

'Absolutely,' said Belfont.

'For me, the key figure is the professor's secretary, Elaine Foret,' said Abigail. 'The fact she just *happened* to enter the office immediately after I went in, the business of my letter to the professor disappearing, it all points to her being involved in some way. I wish *I* could talk to her.'

'Hopefully we'll be able to arrange that,' said Belfont. 'I agree that she needs to be looked into.'

Elaine Foret stood in the shadow of a doorway, her eyes fixed on the main door of the British Embassy, watching out for Sir Brian Otway to appear. At the thought of him she felt her heart start to pound. Why had he changed towards her? So very recently he had held her in his arms. She'd felt the touch of his mouth on her face, then on her lips, gentle, then, as she opened her mouth to him, passionate, urgent, his body pressed against hers. She felt her head swim at the memory.

But then, suddenly he'd withdrawn from seeing her. There had been no contact until today, when he'd called at the Louvre with the two Englishmen. Why? What had she done wrong? She needed to know. She was *desperate* to know.

She saw the door of the embassy open, and then *he* appeared. Sir Brian. He pulled the door closed and then began to stroll leisurely towards his house. Immediately, Foret set off, making for him. She had to get to him before he reached his house.

There was so much she needed to say to him, and hear from him. For her, her desperate need to talk to him, face to face, alone, felt like a matter of life or death. Yes, it was. The agony inside her filled her and drove her forward. She had to see him.

CHAPTER TEN

Daniel and Abigail were just about to go down to breakfast when there was a knock at the door of their suite. Daniel opened the door and found Superintendent Maison there.

'Something has happened,' he said, his tone sombre. 'I need to talk to you both.'

They invited him in and watched him as he walked over to the window and looked out at Montmartre, before turning and announcing, 'Mademoiselle Foret is dead.'

Daniel and Abigail looked at one another, shocked.

'Dead?'

'She was found in her office at the Louvre when the cleaners arrived for work early this morning. The doctor believes she died at about eight o'clock yesterday evening.'

'How did she die?'

'She was murdered. There was a bottle of poison on her desk. I believe it was made to look like suicide, but I do not believe that. We have identified slight bruising on both sides of her nose as those where fingers closed off her nasal airway, forcing her to open her mouth to be able to breathe, and so swallow the poison.'

'What prompted you to look for that bruising?' asked Daniel, curious. 'As you say, it was only slight, and the conclusion most people would have come to would have been suicide.'

'When we talked to Mam'selle Foret before, I discovered that she was a devout Catholic. She went to Mass three times every Sunday. Such a devout Catholic would never have considered suicide: it is the ultimate sin against God. Where were you both yesterday evening?'

'We were having dinner at a restaurant in Montmartre with Edgar Belfont from the British Embassy. Lucas's.'

'All evening?'

'From seven o'clock until ten.'

'Three hours is a long dinner.'

'We had to wait for a table; the restaurant was very busy. We looked at the paintings in the restaurant and talked while we waited,' said Abigail. 'There are plenty of witnesses who can confirm we were there: the waiters, the other diners, Lucas, the owner.'

'And you were with Mr Belfont the whole time?'

'We were.'

'Very well,' said Maison. 'I wish you good day.'

He doffed his hat to them, then left. After the superintendent had departed, Daniel commented, 'I have to admit to being impressed.'

'What by?'

'The superintendent spotting it was murder. I have to admit that nine out of ten detectives in England would have taken the evidence at first sight – the bottle of poison on the desk – and declared it a suicide.'

'It suggests to me that if she was involved in some way in the conspiracy to kill Professor Flamand, one of her co-conspirators has decided to silence her.'

'Unless there's something else going on,' said Daniel. 'This business of Flamand stealing artefacts and selling them, for example. As his secretary, she could have found about it. Another reason to shut her up.'

They headed downstairs to the breakfast room. As they took their seats at a table, the receptionist came from behind the desk and came over to them.

'This has arrived for you,' he said, handing them an envelope.

'You open it,' said Daniel. 'There's no stamp on it so it's been delivered by hand. It's bound to be in French.'

Abigail opened it. 'It's from Georges Deschamps, the curator of the Louvre. He's inviting us to go and meet him at the Louvre.'

'Both of us?' asked Daniel.

Abigail nodded. 'Hopefully this might mean the end of my being barred.'

'Sadly, too late for you to talk to Mam'selle Foret,' said Daniel.

On their arrival at the Louvre, they were shown to the office of the curator by one of the uniformed ushers. There were no questions asked; Deschamps had obviously made sure there would be no obstacles when they arrived.

'Thank you for coming,' he said as they were shown into his office and he gestured at the two chairs waiting for them.

'Does Superintendent Maison know I've been invited to

come here?' asked Abigail. 'He's the one who requested I be kept away from the Louvre.'

'The tragic death of Mam'selle Foret changes everything,' said Deschamps. 'Yes, the superintendent knows. I told him I would be inviting you both here when he was here earlier examining Mam'selle Foret's office. He accepts that. He agrees neither of you could have poisoned Mam'selle Foret. You were both with Monsieur Belfont of the British Embassy and many other witnesses when she was attacked and killed.

'Madame Wilson, I personally feel very bad about the way you have been treated. I understand your desire to prove you are innocent by finding the real culprit. To that end, the board of the Louvre have decided we will pay your fees and costs while you investigate the murders of Professor Flamand and Mam'selle Foret. I know of your reputation as the Museum Detectives and I hope you can achieve at the Louvre what you have achieved at other museums in England. For me, it is vital this case is solved in order to protect the reputation of the Louvre. I advised Superintendent Maison of our intention to hire you in your role as private detectives to investigate these murders.'

'The superintendent didn't object?' asked Abigail. 'I ask because there have sometimes been objections from Scotland Yard when we have been engaged by a particular museum.'

'That will not be the case here. Superintendent Maison is as keen as we are to uncover the culprits. He has given this commission his blessing, but asks that he be kept informed of your progress.'

'Of course,' said Abigail.

'Can we begin by looking at the office where Mam'selle

Foret was murdered?' asked Daniel.

'Of course,' said Deschamps. 'I'll take you there myself.'

They followed him out of his office and along a series of winding corridors that Abigail recalled from her previous visit to Professor Flamand's office, finally coming to Foret's office.

'There is not much to see,' said Deschamps. 'Superintendent Maison has taken various items for examination. The bottle that contained the poison, for example. He has told you about the pinch marks on her nose, which suggest she was forced to swallow the poison?'

'Yes,' said Abigail. 'Along with her being a very devout Catholic.'

'She was,' said Deschamps.

Daniel and Abigail spent some time examining the officer, the chair where Elaine Foret had been found dead, the contents of the desk drawers.

'Can we talk to the cleaners who found the body?' asked Daniel.

'Certainly,' said Deschamps. 'I'll take you to see them.'

'Before we do, there's something we need to discuss with you. We had a visit from Auguste Perrier, who accompanied the professor to the expedition at Saqqara. He told us that he believed the professor diverted some of the best artefacts that were brought back from Egypt to a private collector. In effect, stealing the Louvre's property.'

Deschamps gave a heavy sigh. 'Yes, Perrier came to me with the same accusation.'

'And what did you tell him?'

'I told him it would be looked into.'

'And did you look into it?'

'I gave the task to our head of security, Paul LeMarc.'

'And what did he do?'

'He put the allegations to Professor Flamand. Professor Flamand denied it, of course, and demanded to know where the allegation had come from. He wanted to sue for defamation. LeMarc said he wasn't allowed to divulge that information. He also advised the professor that a legal action on his part would bring the matter into the public domain, which would not be good for the Louvre's image.'

'No smoke without fire?' asked Abigail.

Deschamps nodded. 'LeMarc asked Flamand for the financial records of the expedition. Flamand provided them, but they were quite confused. Scraps of paper with scribbles on them, no real records. The professor's defence was that he was engaged in the dig and that was his priority. He intended to put all these pieces of paper together into a final set of accounts once he had some more accounts that he was expecting.'

'What sort of accounts?'

'Invoices from the transport company who brought the artefacts from Egypt to France. Other expenses that needed to be paid. He explained it would take time because of the distances the artefacts had to travel, and there would be other costs involved to be taken into consideration.'

'And did LeMarc finally manage to get hold of a set of accounts from the professor for the expedition?'

Deschamps hesitated, before saying, 'Unfortunately, Paul LeMarc died a few weeks later, so the investigation was never completed.'

'How did he die?'

'He was attacked in the street while walking home after work. He was beaten over the head with a heavy object.'

'When was this?'

'In January, at the start of this year.'

Abigail translated this for Daniel's benefit.

'Was he robbed?' asked Daniel.

'No. His wallet was still in his coat pocket.'

'Which suggests robbery was not the motive. What did the police say?'

'They said that it must have been someone with personal animosity towards LeMarc.'

'Did they ever find the culprit?'

Deschamps shook his head. 'No.'

'Do you feel it's likely that Professor Flamand sold these artefacts?' asked Abigail.

Deschamps weighed the question up before answering carefully, 'It's possible, of course.'

'What about the rest of the team that were with the professor and Perrier at Saqqara? Did any of them raise any suspicions about pieces going missing?'

'No,' said Deschamps.

'Do you have details of who else was on the Saqqara expedition?' asked Abigail.

'Not to hand, but I can get my secretary to find out the details and let you have them. Shall I have them sent to your hotel?'

'Yes please,' said Abigail.

'And now,' said Deschamps, 'I shall take you to meet the cleaners.'

CHAPTER ELEVEN

General Anatole DeLaGarde of the French Army's General Staff sat in his office at the national barracks and read the report from the spy who'd been assigned to keep watch on the English couple, the Wilsons. According to this, they'd received a visit from that left-wing agitator Auguste Perrier.

He'd put a watch on the Wilsons after it had been brought to his attention that they'd been hired to investigate the murders of Alphonse Flamand and his secretary at the Louvre.

He cursed silently. How had this disaster come about? Everything had seemed so well organised.

Five years previously, a small group of senior officers, including General DeLaGarde, had decided to get rid of the Jews who were in key posts in the army. The French Army should be pure, loyal Frenchmen. The words of the French national anthem, 'La Marseillaise', echoed in his mind:

Grab your weapons, citizens
Form our battalions.
May our enemies' impure blood
Water our fields.

For DeLaGarde, Dreyfus and his kind were those of impure blood and needed to be eradicated from the purity of the French Army.

Their campaign had been provoked when Captain Alfred Dreyfus, then thirty-one years old, had been admitted to the War College and was prophesied to achieve great things in his military career. However, at the college examination in 1892, General Bonnefond, one of the panel deciding on those candidates who would be selected to join the elite General Staff, remarked that he felt that 'Jews were not desired on the General Staff' and gave Dreyfus poor marks. Bonnefond did the same to another Jewish candidate, Lieutenant Picard. Dreyfus and Picard lodged a complaint against Bonnefond with the director of the school, General Lebelin de Dionne.

Dreyfus and Picard were not the only Jews in the French Army; there were about three hundred Jewish officers, ten of whom were generals. However there had begun to be rising prejudice against Jews amongst some of the senior officers, like General Bonnefond. DeLaGarde shared Bonnefond's anti-Semitic views and had been outraged that Dreyfus and Picard had dared to lodge a complaint against the general. From then on, Dreyfus had been a marked man.

In 1894, a torn-up note, known as a *bordereau*, had been discovered by a housekeeper in a wastebasket at the German Embassy in France. The note gave details of a French military secret and had obviously been written by someone in the French military.

This had been exactly what DeLaGarde and his cronies had been waiting for. Despite there being no evidence against him, Dreyfus was arrested for treason. His trial was held in secret. He was found guilty, publicly stripped of his rank with his insignia, buttons and braid cut off his uniform and his sword broken in front of ranks of soldiers in the courtyard of the École Militaire. He was sentenced to life imprisonment on Devil's Island in French Guiana.

Eighteen months later, a new chief of French military intelligence, Lieutenant Colonel Georges Picquart, investigated the case and discovered that the real traitor had been a Major Ferdinand Walsin Esterhazy. The army, determined to protect itself, tried Esterhazy at a secret court martial and found him not guilty. He was told to flee to England, shave off his moustache and settle there incognito. And that would have been that, the end of the matter, with Dreyfus still officially guilty and serving life imprisonment on Devil's Island. But then that idiot Esterhazy had talked to an English journalist, Rachel Beer, the editor of the English newspapers *The Observer* and the *Sunday Times*, who'd recognised him. Even worse, the fool had admitted to her that he had been the real culprit passing secrets to the Germans, telling her, 'I wrote the *bordereau.*'

Rachel Beer published her interviews with him, giving prominence to his confession. She also wrote an article accusing the French military of anti-Semitism and calling for Dreyfus to be retried. When the story appeared in the French newspapers – although it came out only in those that backed Dreyfus; those who supported the army ignored it – it caused a storm, with the army dragged unwillingly into the limelight.

DeLaGarde and his comrades had hoped the furore would die down and go away, but it hadn't.

Then came that dreaded article by the accursed writer Émile Zola, '*J'Accuse*'.

Determined to stop the attacks, the army went on the offensive and, through friends in high places in government, Zola was charge with libel, found guilty and sentenced to a year in prison. However, the campaign by Dreyfus's supporters grew even stronger, forcing a retrial for Zola. The result was the same, the writer being sentenced to a year in prison, but this time he was alerted to the verdict by his solicitor before the trial ended, and encouraged to flee to England.

Meanwhile, the Supreme Court had become involved in investigating the case, and overturned the original judgement against Dreyfus, ordering a retrial, to be held at the military court in Rennes in Brittany.

For DeLaGarde and his fellow conspirator, this was something positive. Having the trial held in a military court meant the army would be in charge, not the judiciary. They could decide which witnesses would be called, and which barred from giving evidence. Esterhazy would be prevented from appearing; he would remain in England.

DeLaGarde's main concern was Fernand Labori, the solicitor acting for Dreyfus at the Rennes court martial who'd also represented Zola. He was young, clever, dynamic and passionate. His speeches to the court, especially if publicised in the newspapers, could prove difficult. He would need to be silenced.

The other problem was the strong lobby on Dreyfus's behalf

that involved so many leading writers, artists, politicians, all writing letters to the government and the press. And now this, these Wilsons, private detectives from England who had achieved great success as investigators in their home country and were now in Paris. Already they'd been contacted by the Dreyfusards. The last thing DeLaGarde needed was for them to become involved. As foreigners, they would be seen as independent, neutrals; anything they discovered about this case would not be easily dismissed as based on prejudice. He needed to take action to silence them.

He picked up the small handbell on his desk and rang it, and immediately his aide and secretary, Captain Martin, entered his office.

'You rang, General?' he asked.

'Yes,' said DeLaGarde. 'Tell Captain Chevignon I wish to see him.'

CHAPTER TWELVE

The cleaners weren't able to tell Daniel and Abigail much more than they already knew: they'd arrived for work at seven in the morning. At half past seven they'd entered Elaine Foret's office, where they found her slumped over her desk, dead. There had been a sweet but acrid smell from her mouth. They had seen the bottle of poison on her desk and one of the cleaners had picked it up to smell it. Then they'd sent for the police.

'I feel it's unlikely that the person who murdered Elaine Foret is a Catholic, or someone who knew her well,' commented Daniel. 'If the murderer had been Catholic, they'd know that suicide would have been dismissed virtually straight away.'

'Possibly,' said Abagail thoughtfully. 'Although there's still so much we don't know about the people involved in this case.'

'I think our next move should be to go to the embassy and inform them about Elaine Foret's death,' said Daniel. 'At the same time we can let Sir Brian and Belfont know we've been hired by the Louvre.'

'Yes,' said Abigail. 'But before we do that . . .'

Daniel looked at her, curious as she hesitated, wondering what was coming.

'As we're here, let's explore the Louvre, at least for a short while. I've been so looking forward to seeing everything here again, what's changed, what's the same, and sharing it with you.' She looked at him in appeal. 'Here we are, inside the Louvre, but with all that's happened we've had no time to even look. An hour or so here can't do any harm, surely.'

'The Egyptian collection?' asked Daniel with a smile.

'I thought we'd leave that for when we have more time to spend. You've never seen the Leonardo da Vinci paintings here, have you?'

'You already know the answer to that,' said Daniel.

'In that case, you are in for an experience.'

Daniel stood and looked at the portrait of the woman with long dark hair and what he thought of as a look of suspicion, set against a hazy countryside background.

'This is possibly the most famous painting in the world,' Abigail told him. 'Leonardo da Vinci's *Mona Lisa*.'

'Who's it of?' asked Daniel.

'We don't know for sure. It's a woman.'

'Yes, but most famous portraits are of someone important.'

'The importance here is that the woman is a mystery. It's said to be of an Italian noblewoman called Lisa del Giocondo, although no one knows for certain. The painting was never given to the Giocondo family, which would have been the protocol if it had been of her. Leonardo left it in his will to his apprentice, Salaì. Eventually it was sold to King Francis I of France.'

Daniel looked closer at the accompanying sign. 'Painted

between 1503 and 1506, and completed in 1517.' He looked at Abigail in surprise. 'Fourteen years?'

'Leonardo often went back to his paintings and reworked them. Look at her mouth. Is she smiling, or frowning?'

'I'd have said she was thinking,' said Daniel. 'And suspicious.'

'About what?'

'About the man who's painting her. Let's face it, after fourteen years you'd start to wonder what he was up to.'

'She didn't sit for him for all the whole fourteen years,' said Abigail. 'As I said, he kept coming back to it and working on it.' She looked at him. 'What do you think of it?'

'It's good,' said Daniel. 'There's no doubt the man had talent.' He studied the painting thoughtfully. 'It's certainly got an air of mystery about it, which is intriguing. It makes you feel . . . uncertain.'

'I agree,' said Abigail. 'Which is why so many art critics disagree about it. Is it just a portrait, or has it some hidden meaning?'

Abigail took him by the arm and led him to another painting. 'There,' she said. 'This is *The Virgin and Child with Saint Anne*.'

'It's by the same artist,' said Daniel.

'Well done,' said Abigail.

'The faces of the two women are similar to the way they've been painted in the other one. The *Mona Lisa*. Look at the cheekbones.'

'We'll make an art expert of you yet.' Abigail smiled.

'I assume the woman holding the baby, who I suppose is

the baby Jesus, is the Virgin Mary, but why is she sitting on the other woman's lap?'

'The other woman is Saint Anne, who is said to be Mary's mother.'

Daniel frowned. 'Her mother?'

'I know, she doesn't look old enough to be Mary's mother, but that's artistic licence,' said Abigail. 'The painters of the Renaissance – Leonardo, Michelangelo – needed to keep their paymasters happy, especially when the paymaster was the pope. A flattering image was required.'

Abigail reached out and took Daniel by the hand. 'There's one more piece I want to show you before we go.' And she led him towards the main staircase.

'More paintings?' asked Daniel.

'No, this one's a statue from ancient Greece, the *Winged Victory of Samothrace*. It's quite remarkable how the sculptor has created the effect of drapery and feathers from a material like marble. It's a must-see for anyone coming to the Louvre.'

He let her lead him up the stairs to the very top, where a monument about fifteen feet high was in place. The top half consisted of a six-foot-tall marble statue of a headless woman with a large wing flying behind her. She was standing on a base made of layers of flat stone, shaped in the form of the tapered bow of a ship.

'This is very impressive,' said Daniel. 'The craftsmanship to recreate in marble the look and the feel of feathers and drapery that way is amazing. Whoever did it was really talented.'

'The sculptor is unknown. It's believed he was Greek, and the sculpture was done some time in the second century BC. It was discovered in 1863 by Charles Champoiseau, the French consul to Greece, who was exploring the ruins of a sanctuary to the gods on the island of Samothrace. Because of the wings he recognised it as a representation of the goddess Nike, also known as Victory. Although the actual statue was mostly intact, apart from the missing head, most of what he found was rubble, fragments of marble and stone. He arranged for the statue and those pieces of marble and stone that were recognisable to be brought to the Louvre, where the curator of antiquities at the museum, Adrien Prévost de Longpérier, took charge of putting the whole thing back together. What you see today is a credit to Longpérier and his team, who did a meticulous job of restoration.'

She turned to him and asked, 'Well? Was it worth that detour?'

He nodded. 'Very much so. And I'm looking forward to returning and you showing me more treasures. But, right now, I think we owe it to the Louvre to get back to investigating these murders.'

CHAPTER THIRTEEN

The arrival of Daniel and Abigail at the British Embassy coincided with Sir Brian Otway walking across the heavily carpeted reception area, possibly on his way to his office.

'Ah, Mr and Mrs Wilson!' he called. 'Good day to you! If you're looking for young Edgar, I've sent him on an errand. But he'll be back in an hour or two.'

'No, it was you we came to see, Sir Brian,' said Abigail. 'Or to see Mr Belfont if you weren't here. We're here to advise you that Monsieur Deschamps at the Louvre has hired us in a private capacity to look into the deaths of Professor Flamand and Elaine Foret.'

Otway stared at them, horrified. 'Elaine Foret? Dead?'

'You didn't know?'

'No. No one has informed us. But then, there's no need; she's a French national, not British.' He suddenly looked very haggard, and he stumbled to a chair and sat down heavily in it. 'I'm sorry, this has come as a dreadful shock. What happened? How did she die?'

'Poisoned,' said Daniel.

Otway gave a groan and buried his head in his hands.

'You knew her well, Sir Brian?' asked Abigail tactfully.

Otway looked up at them, an expression of emotional pain on his face.

'I knew her, but not well,' he said.

'But this news appears to have greatly distressed you,' said Daniel gently.

Otway stood up and gestured towards a corridor. 'Let's go to my office,' he said. 'We can talk privately there.'

Once inside Otway's office, the ambassador sank onto a chair and said awkwardly, 'I saw her yesterday evening.'

Daniel and Abigail exchanged looks of surprise.

'Where?' asked Daniel. 'When?'

'It was about seven o'clock. I'd left the embassy and was walking the few yards to my house, when she appeared. She was in an agitated state.'

'What did she want?'

Otway hesitated before replying, then he admitted, 'A few months ago I dallied with Mam'selle Foret.'

'Dallied?' queried Abigail.

'A light flirtation, nothing more,' he said defensively. 'I felt sorry for her. Unfortunately, she took my interest as something more than it was. She declared herself to be in love with me.'

'You encouraged her?' asked Daniel.

'Because I felt sorry for her,' said Otway. 'She was missing things in life.'

'Someone to love her,' murmured Daniel.

Otway looked at him sharply. 'I was never her lover. I was . . . kind to her. Affectionate. I don't think anyone had treated her that way, with warmth and affection. She

96

mistook it for something more. I felt I had to distance myself from her.'

'Which made her unhappy.'

'Yes. She came to me yesterday evening and pleaded with me not to abandon her.' He gave a mirthless laugh. 'Abandon her? There had never been anything between us for me to abandon. It was all in her imagination.'

'But encouraged by you,' said Abigail.

'I didn't really encourage her,' insisted Otway. 'It was just a friendly flirtation. As I say, she had become obsessed with me. The only thing I could do was keep a distance from her.'

'What did she want yesterday? For you to divorce your wife and marry her?'

'No, she was too devout a Catholic for that. She said she just wanted to continue to see me.'

'And what did you say to her?'

'I said it was impossible with my marriage, my position as the ambassador. I told her we would have to stop seeing one another.'

'How did she react?'

'With tears. And then she fled.'

'You didn't go after her, try to calm her down?'

'No.' He looked at them, agonised. 'And now you tell me she poisoned herself. Because of me!'

'She did not kill herself,' said Daniel. 'She was murdered. Someone forced her to take the poison. They put the bottle to her lips, then pinched her nostrils shut so she had to open her mouth.'

Otway stared at them, stunned. 'Murdered? Why?'

'We believe she may have been part of the conspiracy that was behind the murder of Professor Flamand. It's possible that the person behind it was worried that she might confess, so she was killed to ensure her silence.'

'I told you there was something between them,' said Daniel as they left the embassy.

'He claims it was just a mild flirtation,' said Abigail.

'What do you think?' asked Daniel.

'I don't know,' she admitted.

'Mr and Mrs Wilson!' They looked up at the call and saw Edgar Belfont bearing down on them, clutching an envelope. 'If you were looking for me, I was just doing an errand for Sir Brian.'

'Yes, he told us,' said Daniel. 'No, we came to report that Elaine Foret has been murdered.'

'Murdered?!' Belfont stared at them, stunned.

'In her office at the Louvre. Someone poisoned her at about eight o'clock last night and tried to make it look like suicide, but Superintendent Maison saw through the ruse and false clues.'

'This is terrible!' said Belfont.

'It's another puzzle to solve.'

'And we've been hired by the curator of the Louvre to look into both murders,' added Abigail. 'Which makes me think, as that's now official, perhaps I can come with you both to talk to Madame Flamand.'

Belfont looked doubtful. 'I don't know,' he said. 'This is

the grieving widow, and she will surely have been told at first that you stabbed her husband.'

'But we can discount that now the Louvre have hired us, and with Superintendent Maison's agreement,' insisted Abigail.

Belfont looked at Abigail, then at Daniel. 'Very well, but if she objects . . .'

'If she does I will withdraw immediately and leave it to you and Daniel,' said Abigail.

'That sounds fair,' said Daniel.

Belfont still looked unhappy, but nodded in agreement.

'Very well,' he said. 'And let's hope she's not too grief-stricken to answer questions.'

The Flamands' home was a modest terraced house in the 7th arrondissement, in the shadow of the Eiffel Tower. If Madame Eloise Flamand was grief-stricken, there was little trace of it in her demeanour when she opened the door to her visitors, glaring out at them. Edgar Belfont introduced himself as being from the British Embassy, and then introduced Daniel and Abigail as 'two English detectives the Louvre have hired to investigate the murder of your husband. They are working with the Paris police.'

It was the mention of her husband that brought forth a torrent of abuse. At least, Daniel, who couldn't understand a word, felt it was abuse that was being launched at them, though whether it was because they were English or Madame Flamand was outraged to behold the woman who'd initially been blamed for her husband's death, he wasn't sure. As he watched he got the impression that her very loud and angry diatribe wasn't aimed at them but at someone else. There was certainly a lot of arm-waving, and shaking her fists at the sky, and now and then snarling an angry response to the questions Abigail and Belfont put to her, before she slammed the door shut on them.

'Well, that was interesting,' observed Daniel as the three walked away from the house towards their carriage.

'So, what were your impressions of her body language?' asked Belfont.

'She was angry, but not with you. The fist shake at the sky suggests she's angry with someone who's recently dead, which I guess to be her late husband. She may be a grieving widow, but her grief is for herself.'

'Well done,' complimented Belfont.

'She vented her anger at her late husband for leaving her penniless,' said Abigail.

'Penniless?' said Daniel in surprise. 'I'm guessing he earned a good salary from the Louvre and surely must have put some of it by. We've also been told that he earned money from selling artefacts from Egypt on the side.'

'Despite that, she insists he has left her unprovided for. She also had strong words to say for Elaine Foret, of which the most polite were "harlot" and "whore".'

'Interesting,' said Daniel. 'Was she saying that he spent their money on her?'

'She did, but she didn't give details.'

'She talked of jewellery and fancy clothes,' said Belfont.

'Suggesting that Foret was the professor's mistress?' said Daniel.

'She certainly seems to think so,' said Belfont.

'We need to talk to Georges Deschamps,' said Daniel.

'More importantly, her colleagues at the Louvre,' said Abigail. 'Deschamps, as the curator, will want to protect the good name of the Louvre. Her colleagues are more likely to gossip, especially if they were jealous of her. If she was the professor's mistress, as well as the gifts Madame Flamand talked about, there would have been other favours. I think that's a job for me. I speak French, Daniel; you don't. And the women will be more likely to talk to another woman.'

'That makes sense to me,' said Daniel. 'What do I do while you're engaged in that?'

'I suggest you and Mr Belfont call on Georges Deschamps and ask him about Flamand's financial affairs. Was he in debt? How much was he paid by the Louvre? That sort of thing.'

'So, we travel to the Louvre together and then divide our labours,' said Daniel. 'We have a plan.'

CHAPTER FOURTEEN

As they travelled to the Louvre, Abigail said, 'On reflection, I think it would be better for me to be there when you ask Georges Deschamps about the financial aspect of the professor's expedition to Saqqara. After all, I've been involved in many expeditions, and even led one, so I'll know which questions to ask.'

'Yes.' Belfont nodded. 'That makes sense.'

As they entered Georges Deschamps's office, the curator enquired eagerly, 'Did you get the details of the dig at Saqqara?'

'We'd left our hotel before they'd arrived, but I'm sure they'll be there for us when we return,' said Abigail. 'Our main reason for coming here today is we're still looking into the accusation that Auguste Perrier made about Professor Flamand selling some of the artefacts from Saqqara privately,' said Abigail.

'It is unthinkable,' said Deschamps.

'Unthinkable, perhaps, but we have to look at everything to find the motive for his murder. Was the professor on the museum's regular payroll?'

'He was,' said Deschamps.

'Was his salary paid directly to his bank account, or did it come in the form of cheques?'

'Both,' said Deschamps. 'His regular salary was paid directly into his bank account every month. There were further payments for additional work, which were paid to him by cheque.'

'For his work at the dig at Saqqara, for example?'

'Exactly,' said Deschamps.

'When was the dig at Saqqara?'

'In the last few months of last year. In fact, it coincided with his appointment as a permanent employee of the Louvre. Before that he was paid as an occasional consultant. When he proposed undertaking the expedition to Saqqara we decided to appoint him to the full-time staff.'

'So all the time he was at Saqqara he was being paid a salary?'

'Yes, with additional payments for expenses he and his team incurred during the course of the dig.'

'When did he return from Saqqara?'

'The dig took three months. He and his team went out at the end of August, and he returned at the beginning of December.'

'Eight months ago,' said Abigail.

'Yes,' said Deschamps.

'And since then the only payments the Louvre have paid to him have been in the form of his regular salary, paid into his bank account?'

Deschamps looked thoughtful. 'I think so, but I'll have to check our records in case there may have been some other fees paid that came up as a matter of course. Expenses related to the handling of the artefacts.'

'Thank you,' said Abigail. 'There's one more favour I need to ask of you, Monsieur Deschamps. I'd like to talk to the other secretaries. I remember from my previous visits some years ago that the secretaries were all in one room and able to carry out work on behalf of all of the Louvre executives.'

'That is so,' said Deschamps. 'The exception was Elaine Foret, who had an office of her own. This was at the request of Professor Flamand, who said he needed a full-time secretary with a knowledge of his work.'

'I understand,' said Abigail. 'I'd be grateful if you could take me to the secretaries' room and introduce me to them, so they know I have official permission to talk to them. Otherwise I fear they may be reluctant to do that.'

'Of course,' said Deschamps, getting to his feet. 'I'll take you there now.'

Abigail explained to Daniel and Belfont what she was about to do.

'Fine,' said Daniel.

'It struck me, listening to your conversation with the curator, that it would be good to take a look at Flamand's bank accounts,' said Belfont. 'If we assume that Flamand was selling the most precious artefacts, it can only have happened after he returned from Saqqara. So what we need is access to his bank accounts to see if any large sums were paid in since early December.'

'He might have been paid in cash for these artefacts,' suggested Daniel.

'He might,' agreed Abigail, 'the problem is, I doubt if his bank will grant us access to his bank records.'

'No, but they'll grant it to Superintendent Maison,' said Belfont. 'After all, it's a murder case and he has the power.'

'Then that's a job for Edgar and I, while you talk gossip to Foret's colleagues,' said Daniel to Abigail.

While Daniel and Belfont left to go to talk to Superintendent Maison, Georges Deschamps escorted Abigail to the secretaries' room and introduced her to the six women there.

'This is Madame Wilson,' he explained. 'She has been hired by this museum to investigate the tragic deaths of Professor Flamand and Mam'selle Foret. She would like to talk to you about both persons. It is vitally important for the good name of the Louvre that you give her as much information as you can.' He gestured towards an austere-looking woman in her forties who, like the other women, sat at her own separate desk. 'This is Miss Bertolt, the senior secretary. She is in charge of the secretaries' room. I am sure she will give you all the assistance you require.'

'Certainly, *m'sieur le conservateur*,' said Bertolt.

'Is there a room where I could talk to the ladies separately?' asked Abigail. 'That would mean that work can continue.'

And I can get to hear things the women wouldn't want to say in front of the others, thought Abigail.

'There is Mam'selle Foret's office,' offered Deschamps, but with a doubtful tone. 'I don't know if you will be happy in there?'

'That will be fine,' said Abigail. She looked at Miss

Bertolt. 'Providing Miss Bertolt and the other ladies are in agreement.'

'That arrangement will be satisfactory,' said Miss Bertolt in her clipped tones. She got to her feet. 'If you will follow me, Madame Wilson, I will take you there.'

Abigail resisted telling her that she was well acquainted with that particular office; she needed this woman on her side.

Once inside Elaine Foret's old office, Abigail asked Bertolt for her opinion of both Professor Flamand and his secretary. Her answers were bland: they were people she did not see much of, as the professor had his own secretary. When she did meet them, they were always polite. She knew no gossip about either of them, or, if she did, she wasn't going to repeat it to Abigail.

Abigail thanked her, and then said she'd talk to the other secretaries.

'I would caution you giving too much credence to whatever Miss Perrault tells you,' said Bertolt sternly. 'She is the youngest and inclined to gossip. I have already had to warn her about talking too much in the office; it distracts the others from their work, especially when what she has to say is mere nonsensical chit-chat.'

'I will bear that in mind. Thank you, Miss Bertolt. In fact, it might be a good idea if I saw her first, then I can dispense with her and talk properly to the other ladies.'

'If you wish,' said Bertolt, obviously disapproving of Abigail's suggestion.

'Thank you,' said Abigail. 'Perhaps you'd send Miss Perrault to me.'

Louise Perrault was everything that Abigail had been hoping to find. Young – in her late teens – garrulous and with a love of gossip, especially if there was a salacious aspect to it. It was the girl's mention of Professor Flamand that opened the floodgates.

'Do you know if Professor Flamand was particularly close to anyone here at the Louvre?' asked Abigail.

'Close?' asked Perrault eagerly. 'You mean, having an affair with?'

'Well, yes,' said Abigail. 'Was he?'

Perrault shook her head. 'No,' she said. 'I kept wondering about that especially after the big row.'

'What big row?'

'Between him and his wife. Madame Flamand came in one day, and she was furious. They were in his office and I happened to be passing and I heard her raised voice.'

So you stopped and listened at the door, thought Abigail. *Good.*

'What was she angry about?' asked Abigail.

'She accused him of having an affair with Elaine Foret. He denied it, said he wasn't. That was when she shouted: "Well, you're not having relations with me any more so you must be doing it with someone else." She looked at Abigail, shock and delight on her face. 'Wasn't that a terrible thing to say? And so loudly. Anyone could have heard.'

'Do you believe he was having an affair with someone?'

'If so, it wasn't anyone here.'

'What about with Mam'selle Foret?'

Perrault shook her head. 'No. We could all see that she

107

would have liked to with him, she had that adoring look on her face whenever she was with him, but he didn't want to know. Not in that way.'

'Did you know her well?'

'No one knew her well. She kept herself to herself. She was very aloof. She didn't mix with us. She kept to her office.'

'Was she a bit of a snob?'

'No, I don't think it was that. I think she was just private.'

'And there's no one else that the professor could have been involved with?'

Perrault laughed. 'Who? Miss Bertolt?' She laughed again. 'Wait till you talk to them. You'll see they're all dried up. All they care about is doing their work. And not upsetting Miss Bertolt.'

'Did he ever make advances to you?'

'No. Not that I'd have been interested; I've got a boyfriend who's a better proposition than the old professor. The professor may have been clever at what he did, but he was no young maiden's dream. He didn't wash as much as he ought to have. And he looked odd in the way he dressed: it was all colourful clothes, like he was in a stage show rather than being an archaeologist.'

Yes, thought Abigail, remembering the few times she'd met the professor. He'd had a penchant for brightly coloured waistcoats, and purple jackets and trousers. It was like he wanted to say to the world: *See, I am a famous artist. I dress to show that I am different from the common herd, the run of the mill.*

After Louise Perrault, the other women were very guarded.

They agreed that Elaine Foret seemed aloof and kept herself separate from everyone, but they had nothing negative to say about the professor. Although, as they all pointed out, they did no work for him; he had a secretary of his own. She asked the same question of them that she had of Louise Perrault: had he ever made advances to any of them? They all seemed outraged that she should even ask such an inappropriate question, but their answers were the same: a firm no.

CHAPTER FIFTEEN

Superintendent Maison was in his office when Daniel and Belfont arrived at the police prefecture. Daniel realised that – even more than Chief Superintendent Armstrong at Scotland Yard – a French superintendent's role was management, rather than being directly involved in the nuts and bolts of an investigation. His job was to supervise, send his inspectors where he felt they were needed, then examine what they found and analyse those facts. Daniel wondered if it was this lack of face-to-face involvement that caused the superintendent to look unhappy. Or, possibly, it was some ailment, like ulcers.

'There's been an allegation made that Professor Flamand was privately selling some of the most precious artefacts he brought back to France from his expedition to Saqqara,' said Belfont.

'This scoundrel Perrier telling lies and making false accusations again!' snorted Maison.

'We've heard this from more than one source,' said Belfont. 'We think it worth looking into in case it reveals a motive for the professor's murder.'

'And how am I to look into it?' demanded Maison. 'Madame Wilson is the expert in Egyptian artefacts.'

'We believe if the accusation is true, the evidence will be found in the professor's bank account, which we do not have access to, but we believe you will.'

Maison fell into a thoughtful silence, then said, 'You realise that to start asking questions of his bank manager is tantamount to accusing the late professor of some sort of financial misdemeanour? This is a man with a high reputation, one of France's most esteemed archaeologists.'

'You do not have to say why you are looking into his accounts. Just say it's a formality of some sort. French financial laws are full of various forms of formalities.'

Maison thought it over, then he asked, 'What would you be looking for?'

'Monies paid in over and above his regular salary from the Louvre, and any other payments made by the Louvre. Large sums of money paid in from other sources. If there are any, it would be good to know who paid them. If the allegations are true, such payments could have been made by a private collector, or another museum.'

Maison sat deep in thought, weighing this up, then he said, 'Such payments could have been quite legitimate.'

'They could,' agreed Belfont. 'But it would be good to know who might have paid him, and for what.'

'If they are important people, and the rich usually are important, they could refuse to answer.'

'They could,' said Belfont again. 'But Mr and Mrs Wilson would be happy to be the ones asking the questions. After all, that's what the Louvre has hired them to do: to dig deep and find out who killed the professor, and why. They could ask the questions and report back to you what they find.' Belfont added, 'I understand the delicate situation you feel you would find yourself in. If it involves the rich and powerful, they have influence. It's the same in Britain with our police force. The last thing we want is for you to find yourself in a precarious position. Trust us, your name will not be mentioned if the Wilsons have to talk to some of these people.'

'This may all amount to nothing,' persisted Maison. 'Merely scurrilous rumours and gossip spread by people who were jealous of the professor.'

'That may be true,' said Belfont. 'The key will be finding if any large payments were paid to Professor Flamand's bank account since early December last year.'

Maison once more sank into a thoughtful silence, before nodding in agreement. 'Very well,' he said. 'I'll see what the bank can tell me.'

'It would also be interesting to find out if there have been any large withdrawals of payments made from the professor's bank account,' added Belfont.

'Why?' asked Maison.

'Because when we visited Madame Flamand, she told us that the professor was involved in a relationship with Mam'selle Foret, and he spent large amounts of money on her. Did she say the same when you talked to her?'

Maison looked uncomfortable. 'She did say things to that effect, but I put it down to grief. I had intended to raise the matter with Mam'selle Foret, but sadly she died before I could talk to her about it.'

As Daniel and Belfont walked out of the police building, Daniel commented, 'He's not a happy man.'

'No, he isn't,' agreed Belfont.

'Do you think he'll contact the bank about Flamand's financial affairs?'

'Yes, I do. He's a fair and honest man.'

Belfont and Daniel returned to the Louvre, where they met up with Abigail.

'How did you get on?' Daniel asked her. 'Any good gossip?'

'Yes,' said Abigail. 'I suggest we go to our hotel, where I'll tell you what I picked up and you can see what you make of it. And you can tell me how you got on with Superintendent Maison.'

When they got to the hotel, they found the details of the expedition to Saqqara from Deschamps's secretary waiting for them. They took them to the lounge, where they ordered coffee, then Abigail and Belfont studied the sheets of paper and translated for Daniel's benefit.

'Flamand is listed as leader, then there were three assistants,' said Abigail. 'Auguste Perrier, who it says later resigned.'

'Resigned?' asked Daniel. 'Are you sure?'

'That's what it says in these records.'

'He told us he'd been sacked by Flamand. We need to talk to Perrier again and ask him.'

'The other two assistants were Maurice Larchet and Hugo Sanders,' added Abigail. 'Both are based in Paris.'

'Do you know them?' asked Daniel.

Abigail shook her head. 'No. They're both in their twenties, so I'm guessing they were only recently students.' She turned to Belfont. 'Do you know either of these two men?'

'No,' said Belfont. 'But then I don't move in their kind of circles.'

It was fortunate for Superintendent Maison that the manager of the bank where Professor Flamand had his accounts was an old friend of the superintendent's. This meant that long explanations and invoking different laws involving private financial records were not raised. It was, after all, as Maison pointed out, a murder inquiry.

'And you believe that having copies of the professor's bank records may help you find his killer?' asked the bank manager.

'It would certainly help us greatly,' said Maison.

The bank manager nodded. 'Very well. I shall get one of the clerks to copy them and have the copies sent to you at the Îsle de la Cité.'

'When do you think they might be ready?'

'I shall have the clerk start work on them immediately,' said the manager. 'They should be with you later today.'

'Thank you,' said Maison.

He returned to the police prefecture, where the sergeant on duty at the desk informed him that an army officer was waiting to see him.

'He is a Captain Chevignon,' said the sergeant. 'He says you know him.'

'I do,' said Maison. 'Where is he?'

'In the waiting room.'

'Give me a couple of minutes to get back to my office and settle myself down, then send him along,' said Maison.

The army captain was obviously very eager to see him, because the Superintendent had barely entered his office and removed his coat, when there was a knock on his door, which opened before he could say 'Enter', and the tall, moustached figure of Captain Chevignon walked in.

Maison had known Chevignon for a few years, meeting him at various get-togethers of the anti-Dreyfus caucus in which they had a common interest, although Chevignon had always been much more vocally anti-Dreyfus than the police superintendent. Maison assumed that was because Chevignon was a long-serving army officer and would be only too aware of the recent discussions about the case with the accusations about the army creating false evidence.

'Good morning, Superintendent,' said Chevignon.

'Good morning, Captain Chevignon,' returned Maison. 'How can I help you?'

'You are in charge of the investigation into the death of Professor Flamand at the Louvre, is that not so?'

'It is,' said Maison, curious as to what had brought Chevignon to the prefecture about this matter. As far as Maison knew, Chevignon had no connection with the Louvre, or Professor Flamand. Chevignon was a captain in the French Army, well-connected within the military.

'In that case, why have you allowed these two English people, the Wilsons, to have direct access to the investigation?'

'I was simply acceding to their hiring by the board of trustees of the Louvre.'

'But this is a French matter, for investigation by the French authorities. These Wilsons are not even proper detectives; they are private investigators.'

'They are known as the Museum Detectives because of their success in solving crimes that have taken place in museums in England.'

'Exactly, in *England*. How did it come about that they are being allowed to poke their noses into this case?'

'Madame Wilson had been invited by Professor Flamand to visit him. It was she who discovered his body in his office.'

'And she was arrested for the murder, is that not so?'

'It is, but we discovered that her arrest was an error, based on wrong information.'

'Are you sure it was erroneous?'

'Definitely. And then, when the chief witness against her, the professor's secretary, was also found murdered and it was obvious that the Wilsons could have played no part in her death, Georges Deschamps, the senior curator at the Louvre, took the decision to hire the Wilsons to look into the matter.'

'Thus showing great disrespect to the police, and to you, Superintendent.'

'I do not consider that to be the case. It has been agreed that the Wilsons will work closely with me and my people.'

'But say these Wilsons turn up things that it would be better if they were not made public. Would you be able to intervene and have them silenced?'

'That is not for me, Captain; that is for the Louvre.'

Chevignon thought this over, then said, concerned, 'The people at the Louvre are all artistic types. They have no respect for the army. They have no sympathy for the concept of military honour. They are the sort of people who write letters to the newspapers in support of the anarchists who want to undermine the Republic. People like the fanatic Émile Zola.'

'What does this have to do with the murder of Professor Flamand?'

'Say the Wilsons discover something that might point the finger at the military being involved, what would you do?'

Immediately, Maison remembered the Wilsons raising the issue of the anti-Dreyfusards being involved in the professor's death, something that he had dismissed. But here was a captain in the French Army with known connections to senior army top brass suggesting that the military may have been involved in Flamand's death.

'This makes no sense,' said the superintendent. 'Yes, the Wilsons came to me suggesting there might be a connection to the Dreyfus case . . .'

'Ah-ha!' exclaimed Chevignon.

'But I told them it was ridiculous.'

'What did they say?'

'They said they'd been informed that the professor had been putting pressure on the government to have Dreyfus executed for treason. The same person who told them this suggested that Flamand had been killed to stop him agitating against Dreyfus this way.'

'Who was this person?'

'Auguste Perrier. He's an archaeologist who accompanied

the professor and his team on an expedition to Egypt last year. My own view is that this Perrier made this accusation to discredit Flamand in revenge for the professor sacking him and stopping him getting further work with the Louvre, or any other reputable French archaeological organisations. This Perrier is also a left-wing troublemaker. I do not understand how he can have any connection with the military, or why the military could be involved in Flamand's death. The professor is a known supporter of the military and a strong opponent of Dreyfus.'

Chevignon fell silent, then said carefully, 'That is the opinion of most people. But say it is not so?'

'How could it not be so?' demanded Maison. 'The professor was very public about his opinions on the matter.'

'Which would have been a very convenient cover,' said Chevignon.

'A cover for what?'

'For passing sensitive information about the anti-Dreyfus faction to our enemies, the Dreyfusards. Flamand knew everyone at the top of the anti-Dreyfus campaign; he was intimately associated with many of them, socialised with them, knew their secrets. It is only recently, since the trial of the traitor Zola, that some of my superiors have become aware that the facts they told Flamand about in private conversations have surfaced in the evidence the pro-Dreyfus rabble have been passing to Zola's solicitor.'

'Speculative gossip,' said Maison. 'Lucky guesses.'

'Some of the evidence has been too specific to be just guesswork,' countered Chevignon. 'And when we look at the whole, the details of the personnel in the army who were involved in the prosecution of Dreyfus, my superiors began to suspect that these details came from one high-placed source. That we had a spy in our midst. They now believe that the spy was none other than Flamand.'

'But why?' asked Maison. 'He has always been so vehement against Dreyfus.'

'In public,' Chevignon repeated.

Maison shook his head. 'I cannot believe this.' He looked enquiringly at the captain. 'Are you suggesting that the army had Flamand murdered?'

'No, but there will be those who will spread such gossip if a link is discovered between Flamand and the pro-Dreyfus faction and that he was supplying them with information that was being used to try and free Dreyfus.'

Maison thought this over, then asked, 'Who are you representing?'

'I am here as an officer of the French Army who is concerned about protecting our military's reputation.'

'You mentioned your superiors. Did they send you to tell me to stop the Wilsons investigating?'

Chevignon rose and stood smartly to attention.

'The decision to come here was mine and mine alone,' he said. 'But, if you are able to prevent whatever the Wilsons discover – *if* they find an army connection to Flamand's murder – from being made public, the military will show its gratitude to you.'

With that he saluted, then left.

You are a liar, thought the superintendent. *You did not*

come here of your own volition. You were sent by a cabal of high-
ranking army officers to influence the investigation.

This cabal of senior military officers obviously were worried that the Wilsons would uncover a link between the army and the murder of Flamand. According to Chevignon, Flamand had been leaking secrets from the anti-Dreyfus camp to their opponents, and Flamand had been killed because of that. It was the exact opposite of the motive that Perrier had suggested: that Flamand had been killed by *supporters* of Dreyfus.

When the Wilsons had suggested this last as a motive for the professor's death, Maison had dismissed it out of hand. But this new thought, that opponents of Dreyfus had carried out the killing, opened up a whole new aspect. And the fact that Chevignon had been sent to see him gave validity to the possibility that it might be true.

What to do? Should he pass this latest on to the Wilsons? No. If they discovered it themselves, then he would deal with it. But how? Discredit the idea that the military cabal had killed Flamand? No, in all honesty, he couldn't do that. As a policeman, he'd taken an oath to uphold justice and truth. He knew of many policemen who were prepared to look the other way and ignore evidence for a price. Is that what Chevignon had meant when he said that if Maison suppressed whatever the Wilsons discovered, then 'the military will show its gratitude to you'?

Maison hated corruption. He hated the fact that it went on in government and in many other bodies. When he'd been able to uncover corruption, he'd made sure that charges were made, determined to bring the guilty to justice. Sadly, that did not always work, with some judges working hand in glove with the guilty. So far in his career he'd been able to avoid being part of any conspiracy, but now he was being pressured into joining one in order to protect the military establishment.

I will not do it, he vowed. But even as he made that promise to himself, he was aware that Professor Flamand had possibly died at the hands of this cabal. And, likely, Elaine Foret as well. Did that mean his own life was in danger? Who could he turn to for help? He could not count on assistance from the top brass of the police service; many of the senior officers were sympathetic to the anti-Dreyfus cause. He was going to have to play this one very carefully indeed if he was going to solve the murders, and at the same time remain alive.

CHAPTER SIXTEEN

Over breakfast the next morning, Daniel and Abigail discussed their plans for the day.

'I suppose the next thing is to talk to the professor's other two assistants at the dig, Maurice Larchet and Hugo Sanders,' suggested Daniel.

'Yes,' said Abigail, 'but I have another proposal. I'd really like to go back and see what changes there have been to the Egyptian rooms.'

Daniel smiled at her. 'Absolutely,' he said. 'It will be good to take a break from the case.'

In the carriage that took them to the Louvre, Abigail outlined to Daniel the background of the exhibits they were going to see.

'The Egyptian collection,' she said. 'It was opened in the Louvre Palace in 1827 by King Charles X.'

'Hang on,' said Daniel, puzzled. 'I thought the Revolution of 1790, or whenever it was, ended the line of monarchy in France. The whole royal family were executed.'

'Most of them were,' said Abigail, 'but there's always a relative somewhere. You should know that from the history of the English royal families. There was always someone who popped up with a claim to the throne. After the French Revolution, Napoleon Bonaparte came to power as emperor by military force and established the French Empire.'

'But he was toppled and exiled. Sent to the island of Elba.'

'In 1814. But the next year he escaped from Elba and took back control. He stood down later as ruler that year following his defeat at Waterloo. His son, Napoleon II, took over as ruler. But he was only in power for about three months, and then came the restoration of the royal family, with Louis XVI's younger brother becoming Louis XVIII. Similar to what happened in England after Cromwell, when Charles II was brought to the throne.'

'Louis XVIII?' queried Daniel. 'What happened to number seventeen?'

'Louis XVII was the son of Louis XVI. He escaped the guillotine but was imprisoned by the revolutionary forces. He never actually reigned.'

'So younger brother Louis took the throne?'

'Correct, and he reigned for nine years. When he fell off the perch, his younger brother became Charles X. And when Charles died a cousin of his came to the throne as Louis Phillipe I.'

'I assume they'd run out of younger brothers,' said Daniel.

'In fact, Charles X had a son, also called Louis, but he and his father had a row and Louis renounced the throne.'

Daniel let out a groan. 'It's almost too much to take in. So much so that I'd forgotten where we were in the history of the Louvre.'

'Charles X and the Egyptian collection,' Abigail reminded him. '1827. The new rooms were named the Musée Charles X because it had been Charles who agreed to put this collection together and who appointed Jean-François Champollion as its director. Champollion was a famous archaeologist whose speciality was Egypt. He made his name deciphering ancient Egyptian hieroglyphs. But the roots of the collection go back to the eighteenth century and Napoleon. In the late eighteenth century, there was talk among the revolutionary government about attacking England. France and England had been bitter enemies for many years. Napoleon, however, had another idea to strike a blow at England. He decided to take control of Egypt and kick the English out, and so gain control of the Suez Canal. And it wasn't to be just a military campaign. Over a hundred and fifty non-military people were appointed to the French Commission of Arts and Sciences to work in Egypt. Some were archaeologists, some were surveyors, others were art experts, mining engineers, chemists, botanists, astronomers.'

'That's an impressive assembly,' murmured Daniel.

'It was, and all under the protection of Napoleon's army. In short, the French took Cairo, but then in August 1798 the British destroyed the French fleet in Abukir Bay. With no way to get back to France until new ships arrived, the French spent the next three years exploring Egypt, and especially the pyramids.

'In 1801 the French withdrew most of its miliary force from Egypt, along with a large number of its non-military personnel, who took with them a massive amount of antiquities they'd acquired during their stay in Egypt. Quite a few French archaeologists stayed on and either returned to France with more artefacts, or sent them back where they were documented.

'Champollion had helped create an Egyptian museum in Turin in Italy, and it was he who persuaded Charles X that with all these precious antiquities now in France the country could have one of the greatest collections of Egyptology in the world if they were all assembled in one place. Charles agreed, and the rest, as they say, is history. Literally, in this case.' She looked out of the carriage window. 'And here we are at the Louvre. So, history lesson over, and now for the real thing.'

As Abigail led Daniel through the rooms that housed the Egyptian collection, he could see at once what she meant about this being the greatest display of Egyptology in the world. It did indeed eclipse the displays at the British Museum. For one thing there were the huge, detailed paintings on almost every spare inch of wall space depicting scenes from ancient Egypt. But the one piece that Abigail was guiding him towards was in a glass cabinet. It was a pendant made of gold of three exquisitely carved figures lined up in a row, the outside two each holding up the palms of their hands towards the figure in the middle, who was crouching on a pedestal.

'Look at this! Isn't it wonderful!' enthused Abigail. 'It shows the three main gods from Egyptian religion. The one in the middle on the pillar is Osiris. His wife, Isis, and son, Horus, are the ones on either side. In the original story, Osiris was killed by his brother, Seth. Osiris was revived by his wife, Isis, who gave birth to their son, Horus. Horus avenged his father and succeeded to the throne, thus giving rise to the story of the enduring power of the pharaohs. Horus is also depicted in the wall paintings of ancient Egypt as the falcon-headed god.'

Abigail then took Daniel on a whirlwind tour of the Egyptian rooms, showing him a bewildering number of sarcophagi, many of them highly decorated in bright colours, along with statues and small carvings, and a display of hieroglyph-adorned panels.

'See this?' said Abigail delightedly, stopping by a large granite sarcophagus made of granite, heavily decorated with hieroglyphs and images from ancient Egypt. At one end a large figure of a winged goddess had been carved, while the rest of the box was filled with carvings of smaller figures engaged in rowing large boats or marching soldier-like along the length of the box. 'Familiar?'

Daniel looked at her, then at the large sarcophagus, puzzled.

'No,' he said. 'Should it be?'

'This is the sarcophagus that contained the body of Ramesses III. The lid is in the Fitzwilliam at Cambridge, where we first met. Don't you remember it?'

'No,' said Daniel. 'I was there to investigate a murder, and that's what I concentrated on. And you, of course.'

'The lid was massive,' continued Abigail. 'It's in red granite, weighs about seven tonnes and had a life-size sculpture of Ramesses carved on it. It's magnificent!'

Daniel shook his head. 'No. At that stage, for me, Egyptology was just ancient relics on display in a museum.

It was only after we got together that I began to appreciate it.' He looked again at the ornately decorated sarcophagus. 'When we get back to England, let's take a trip back to Cambridge, and this time I'll take a proper look at things.' He frowned. 'If the base is here and the lid's in Cambridge, what happened to the mummified body that was inside?'

'That went to the Egyptian Museum in Cairo,' said Abigail.

'So everybody got a share,' said Daniel, but he became aware that she wasn't listening to him. Instead, she was making for a huge figure carved in pink granite with the body and head of a lion, but the face of a pharaoh.

'The Great Sphinx of Tanis,' announced Abigail. 'It was supposed to be the living image of a pharaoh, a cross between a man and a lion, always ready to pounce on Egypt's enemies. They were usually found at the entrance to a temple. Isn't it magnificent?'

'It certainly is,' agreed Daniel.

Daniel followed her as she moved from room to room, exhibit to exhibit, and with each piece Abigail launched into an enthusiastic explanation of the purpose or meaning of the particular artefact. For Daniel, it was a delight to see her joy. She was back in her own world, ancient Egypt, and once again it was coming alive to her. She was halfway through translating a panel of hieroglyphs, when she stopped.

'We must move on,' she said suddenly and abruptly. 'Get back to what we're supposed to be doing. Solving the murders.' She looked at Daniel apologetically. 'I'm sorry, I was just losing myself in here.'

'There's no need to apologise,' said Daniel. 'It's great to see you so absorbed in everything here. And later, when this is over, we'll come back and you can show me everything.'

'And not just the Egyptian rooms,' said Abigail. 'There really is so much to see here in the Louvre. But for now,' she added determinedly, 'we need to get on with the case.'

'The two assistants, Maurice Larchet and Hugo Sanders?' asked Daniel.

'I was thinking of Elaine Foret's mother before them,' mused Abigail. 'So far we've been concentrating on the professor, but we've ended up with so many possible motives I wondered whether we might uncover more about both murders if we can find out why his secretary was killed.'

'Yes, that's a good thought,' agreed Daniel.

CHAPTER SEVENTEEN

The address they had for Elaine Foret was in the 11th arrondissement, the Canal Saint-Martin district. The house was in one of the narrow streets of terraced houses not far from the canal that wound its way through Paris.

'This is a far cry from the wealthy districts we've explored so far,' commented Daniel.

'The working class have to live somewhere,' said Abigail. 'Wasn't it the same for us when we set up in your old home in Camden Town?'

They located the house and Abigail knocked at the door. It was opened by a sullen-looking youth in his late teens, who scowled at them.

'*Bonjour,*' said Abigail. '*Parlez-vous anglais?*'

'*Non,*' he said, and started to close the door on them, but Abigail thrust her foot in the gap. In French, she explained that they had been hired by the Louvre to look into the death of Elaine Foret, who they had been led to understand had lived at this house.

'There is nothing to look into,' he snapped surlily in French. 'She killed herself with poison.'

'The police say different,' said Abigail. 'We'd like to talk to you and the rest of your family about her, if we may.'

From inside the house they heard an elderly-sounding woman call out to ask who was calling and what did they want.

'*Les flics, maman!*' the young man called back.

'*Non*, we are not police,' said Abigail. 'We are private detectives.'

'Patrice!' called the elderly woman.

'You'd better go and talk to her,' grunted the young man. He reached out and took a jacket from a peg on the wall, which he put on, and pushed past them and then walked off down the street.

'Friendly character,' commented Daniel.

'But he did say we could go in,' said Abigail.

They walked along a short narrow passage and came to a kitchen, where an elderly woman was sitting by a cast-iron stove.

'Madame Foret?' asked Abigail.

'*Oui*,' she said.

They saw at once there was a white film over both her eyes. The stick propped beside her chair confirmed this first impression.

'She's blind,' muttered Daniel.

'I may be blind but I'm not deaf,' snapped Madame Foret. 'And I understand English because I worked for an English family here in Paris. Come in and sit down. I heard the door slam, so I assume my son has left. I apologise for his behaviour. He has been this way since my husband died.'

130

Daniel and Abigail took the two empty chairs near the stove. In French, Abigail said, 'We have been asked by the Louvre to look into your daughter Elaine's death.'

'We can talk in English,' said Madame Foret. 'That way the man with you can understand. I will be slow at first because it is a long time since I used English, but I like to hear it. The family I worked for were very good people, very kind.' Then she added as a rebuke, 'Your man should learn French if he is to stay in this country.'

'The man is my husband, Daniel Wilson,' said Abigail. 'My name is Abigail Wilson. We are not intending to stay in France. Once our work is done here we shall return to England.'

'Wilson,' mused the old lady thoughtfully. 'They said you had killed Professor Flamand. Stabbed him.'

'That's what they thought at first,' said Abigail. 'But the police discovered it was nothing to do with me.'

'Elaine told me it was you, but later she said she'd been wrong,' said Madame Foret. 'I heard Patrice say that Elaine had killed herself with poison, but the policeman who came to tell me about her death told me she had been murdered.'

'Yes,' said Daniel. 'Was it a Superintendent Maison?'

'Yes,' she said. 'He was a fat man.' She chuckled. 'I do not need eyes to hear a man drop into a chair and make it squeak and know he is fat. But he seemed clever.'

'Yes, he is,' said Abigail. 'Why do you think anyone would want to harm your daughter?'

The woman shrugged. 'Who knows?'

'Did she have any enemies?'

'Not to my knowledge.'

'What was her relationship with Professor Flamand?' asked Abigail.

Madame Foret smiled. 'You think she had a relationship with him?'

'We know she worked for him. We wondered what her attitude was towards him,' Abigail clarified.

'She thought he was a great man. Me, I thought he was a pig.'

'Did you ever meet him?'

'No. Why would I bother to go to the Louvre?'

'He may have called here to see Elaine.'

She shook her head. 'No one from her work came here to see Elaine. She kept people away.'

'Do you know why?'

'Because of Patrice.'

'Why?'

'Because he embarrassed her. She was devout, a strong Catholic. Patrice makes fun of the church. He calls them hypocrites, and that made Elaine upset. Patrice is also an angry young man who derides everyone. Makes fun of them. It is because he envies them. He did not do well at school. He finds it difficult to keep a job because of his tongue; he answers back when he is told off. He runs around with worthless bad companions. They rob. They steal.'

'Why do you say you thought Professor Flamand was a pig?' asked Abigail.

'He stole money from Elaine.'

'Stole?'

'He asked her for money and promised to pay it back, but he never did.'

'How do you know?'

'Because once I asked her for money to pay for something, and she said she hadn't got any. I knew she had been paid the day before so I asked her what she had done with it. At first she wouldn't tell me, but when I pressured her she admitted Flamand had asked to borrow some money from her. She said she had given it to him because he was a great man and she felt she needed to help him. I told her she was a fool; he was using her.'

'Did he pay her back?'

'She said he did, but I don't think so. She thought because I was blind I wouldn't be able to see the expression on her face when she lied, but I could hear it in her voice.'

'Did she talk about the professor and his money troubles?'

'No. She wouldn't talk about him at all except to say what a great man he was.'

After, as Daniel and Abigail walked away from the Forets' house, they mused over what they'd learnt from Madame Foret.

'There's a great deal that doesn't add up,' said Daniel. 'On one hand we have Perrier telling us that Flamand sold priceless artefacts, which – and we assume he sold to private collectors – he must have got good money for. On the other hand we are told by Madame Flamand that he left her destitute. Now we hear that Flamand borrowed money from Elaine Foret, so he must have been in financial difficulties. So, which is it? He made money, or he was broke?'

'The two things could both be true, if the professor had a penchant for spending,' observed Abigail.

CHAPTER EIGHTEEN

Maurice Larchet lived in a house in the 5th arrondissement.

'The Latin Quarter,' explained Abigail as they walked along a narrow, winding, cobblestoned street towards the address they'd been given. 'It dates back to when Paris was a Roman settlement. Now it's where you'll find many of the French universities, like the Sorbonne. As a result it's also home to many of the city's students.'

The house was very old, tall, made of sandstone. Over the years it had sagged and twisted slightly, but it stayed upright, supported by the houses on either side. Maurice Larchet lived on the top floor, and Daniel and Abigail made their way up the twisting wooden staircase.

'It really is a crooked house,' commented Daniel.

'It's remained standing for this long,' said Abigail.

As they approached the door of Larchet's flat, Daniel said: 'I trust you'll be doing the talking?'

'Unless he speaks English.'

She knocked on the door, which was opened by a tall, thin young man in his middle twenties.

'*Bonjour*,' said Abigail, and in French proceeded to

introduce themselves. 'We are Monsieur and Madame Wilson from England. We've been asked by the Louvre to look into the death of Professor Flamand.'

'Why?' asked Larchet suspiciously 'The police will be doing that.'

'They think, because I have experience of the world of archaeology, I might have insights into the professor's world that the police do not.'

Larchet frowned. 'What experience? The name Wilson is not familiar to me.'

'I used to be Abigail Fenton before I married,' said Abigail.

Immediately, Larchet's manner changed. He stepped forward, his hand outstretched, and took Abigail's hand in his.

'Abigail Fenton! Of course! Forgive me, I know of your work, obviously. We studied it, your writings, your experiences. You led the expedition last year to the Sun Temple of Niuserre at Abusir. It was in the *Archaeology World* magazine. There was a photograph of you. I'm so sorry I did not recognise you.'

'I looked very different on that dig to how I look when I'm in the Europe,' said Abigail. 'There's no need for any apology, I assure you.'

'Please, do come in,' said Larchet.

The small flat consisted of two rooms: a living room that also served as a bedroom, and a small kitchen. Larchet was not a man for whom tidiness was important; the room was bestrewn with books, magazines and newspapers and there were two ashtrays overflowing with cigarette ends. Larchet began by picking up some of the books and magazines from where they'd been left on a settee and dumped them on the floor.

'Pleaser, sit,' he said.

'*Parlez-vous anglais?*' asked Abigail as she and Daniel sat.

'*Non*,' said Larchet.

'No matter,' said Abigail. 'My husband doesn't speak French, so we'll stick to French and I'll tell him what we talked about later. You were at Saqqara with the professor.'

'I was.' Larchet nodded.

'How did you get on with him?'

Larchet hesitated before replying, 'He was not an easy person to get on with. At least, as far as I was concerned.'

'In what way?'

'Everything was always about him, rather than the exploratory work we were doing. I got the impression he felt he deserved more notice. Fame. He seemed to feel he did not get the credit he felt he deserved.'

'Did the others on the expedition feel the same way?'

'You'd have to ask them,' said Larchet guardedly.

'We know that Auguste Perrier left, although we've had two different reasons why. The official report says he resigned, but Perrier told us he was sacked by Flamand.'

'I did not see the final confrontation between them, which I believe took place after we returned to France from Saqqara,' said Larchet. 'All I know is that Perrier's name was removed from the list of those taking part in the expedition.'

'How did you find out about this?'

'Professor Flamand told me. To be honest, he used it to threaten me. He and I had not got on during our time at Saqqara. He resented the fact that I questioned some of his decisions. His actual words to me when he told me that

136

Perrier had gone were: "That's what happens to people who oppose me.""

'Which you took to mean by questioning his decisions?'

'Yes, in some way, but I knew that Perrier had his suspicions about what Flamand was doing with the artefacts we'd brought back from the trip. He had an idea the professor was selling them for his own gain.'

'Perrier told you this?'

'He did.'

'And do you think Perrier was right?'

'I don't know, but in my opinion it was feasible. I did not trust Professor Flamand. There was something false about him.'

'False?'

Larchet nodded. 'For all his fame and great reputation, I began to wonder just how much of it was justified. I believe he earned that reputation based on the work of others.'

'What gave you that idea?'

'He made mistakes when talking about some of the digs he claimed to have been on.'

'You think he lied about his past experiences?'

'I do. In fact, I think he lied about many things. There was something . . . not right about him. It was all a front. I think he'd fooled a great many people, including the Louvre.'

Their next call was to a terrace of houses in the 6th arrondissement, the address for Hugo Sanders. If the 5th arrondissement flaunted its ancient history, the 6th arrondissement – the district of Saint-Germain-des-Prés – was prettily quaint, flowerboxes adorning the windowsills of many of the houses.

Abigail knocked at a mid-terrace house and the door was opened by a young man with Middle Eastern features and complexion. He looked at Abigail and Daniel suspiciously.

'*Bonjour*,' said Abigail. '*Est-que c'est Monsieur Hugo Sanders ici?*'

The young man looked startled, then he called out something in a language that was not French before rushing off into the house. Daniel looked questioningly at Abigail.

'Arabic,' she told him.

A man in his mid-twenties appeared. 'Who are you?' he demanded aggressively. 'And what right do you have to come here and harass my guest?'

'We did not harass him,' said Abigail. 'We merely asked him if Hugo Sanders was here. I assume that is you?'

'What if it is?' snapped the man. 'Who are you and what do you want?'

'My name is Abigail Wilson, although you may know me as Abigail Fenton . . .'

At this the man's mouth fell open in astonishment. 'Abigail Fenton the archaeologist? Who was at Hawara with Flinders Petrie?'

'The same.' Abigail nodded.

As Larchet had done, Sanders thrust his hand forward. 'Please allow me to shake your hand. We studied you at college.' Abigail took his hand and shook it, and he continued to stare at her. 'To have you here in person, at my house, is . . .' He faltered as words failed him.

'This is my husband, Daniel Wilson. Latterly, my work is with him as private detectives. We have been hired by Georges Deschamps at the Louvre to investigate the murder of Professor Flamand, who we understand you were with at Saqqara.'

'Yes. I saw about his death in the newspapers.'

'Do you mind if we came in and asked you some questions about the expedition to Saqqara, and the professor?'

'No, please do come in.' As they stepped into the house, he called out 'Abdul!', and as the young Arab appeared he rattled off some words in Arabic. The young Arab looked at him, and then at Abigail and Daniel, in surprise.

'I have asked him . . .'

'To bring us tea.' Abigail nodded. 'Thank you, that will be appreciated.'

'Of course, I forgot that you speak Arabic. Not every European bothers to learn it. Some think that just by shouting louder the Egyptian workers will understand. Such arrogance!'

They followed him to a small living room that was decorated in the style of the Middle East.

'I see you have brought Egypt with you to Paris,' observed Abigail. 'It's wonderful.'

'Thank you,' said Sanders.

'My husband does not speak French, so I'll be the one talking, if that's all right.'

'It will be an honour to converse with you, Mam'selle Fenton.' Then, apologetically, he corrected himself. 'Pardon. *Madame Wilson*.'

'Fenton will be fine. In fact, you may call me Abigail.'

'In that case, I am Hugo.' He frowned as he asked, 'Do you know why the professor was killed?'

'At the moment we are still gathering information.'

'You think it has something to do with Saqqara?'

'We're not sure. We're trying to get a picture of the professor, people he might have upset, what sort of person he was.'

'But you have met him,' said Sanders.

'Yes, but that was many years ago. And he did not care for me, so we're talking to people who knew him recently and worked with him. What did you think of him?'

'He was a genius!' enthused Sanders. 'Possibly one of the greatest archaeologists France has ever known. Up there with Coutelle and Lepere, Gauthier and Jéquier.'

'You admired him.'

'Enormously!'

Just then Abdul reappeared carrying a tray with three glasses of pale-coloured tea, which he put down on the low table.

'Thank you, Abdul,' said Sanders. The young Arab nodded and then retreated. Sanders gestured at the glasses. 'Egyptian style,' he said.

Abigail lifted one and took a sip. 'Delicious,' she complimented. 'Tell me, what was Professor Flamand like to work with?'

Sanders hesitated momentarily, then he said, 'At first, he was wonderful. So insightful. An inspiration. But, towards the end of the expedition, his attitude towards me changed.'

'Why did you think that was?'

Sanders hesitated again, then he said reluctantly, 'Because

of Abdul. We became friends, and the professor didn't like that. He said we shouldn't socialise with the locals, the workers. It was then I realised he was a snob. No, more than a snob, he thought that Egyptians, or any native people, were of a lower order. He ordered me to stop seeing Abdul except at the site. And, at the site, I was to distance myself from Abdul. Distance myself from all the local Egyptians.'

'He was racist?'

'Yes. It showed me a side of him that I found very displeasing.' Then, suddenly agitated, he burst out with, 'It's the same here, in Paris. People look at us suspiciously. They make remarks about Abdul. That's why I was defensive at first; I thought you might be from the government come to check his status, possibly even deport him. I've heard some of the people around here mutter things like "Send him back from where he came. We don't want people like him in this country." Not everyone, of course. I suppose it's just a minority, really, but it's so hurtful. It frightens Abdul.'

'Why did he come here?' asked Abigail.

'I invited him,' said Sanders. 'He had no money, so I paid his fare.'

'He must be important to you,' said Abigail carefully.

'What do you mean?' demanded Sanders defensively.

'Nothing. Just that it is an exceptional and very kind thing for you to do.'

'Yes.' Sanders nodded, mollified.

'How did you get on with the others in the party?' asked Abigail. 'Auguste Perrier? Maurice Larchet?'

'Perrier was a troublemaker,' said Sanders. 'He was constantly challenging the professor. In the end, it was no surprise when the professor told him he was off the official expedition.'

'When did that happen?'

'Not until we were back in France.'

'How long after you were back?'

Sanders thought it over. 'A month. Maybe more. It was when we were cataloguing the artefacts we brought back. There was a row between the two of them.'

'What about?'

'I don't know.' He sighed. 'Sadly, the professor had stopped talking to me by then. He'd discovered that Abdul was coming to France to join me. He was angry.'

'Did Perrier tell you what the row was about?'

'No. Perrier was very difficult. He and I didn't have much to do with one another. Perrier seemed so angry much of the time and I didn't want to get caught up in that. Be thought of as his conspirator.'

'His conspirator?'

'The professor was convinced that Perrier was fomenting some sort of conspiracy against him. I didn't want the professor reporting me to Monsieur Deschamps as part of it. It would affect any future work with the Louvre.'

'Have you had much more work with the Louvre since you came back from Saqqara?'

'Sadly, no,' admitted Sanders. He sighed. 'I believe that was the professor's doing.'

'Because of Abdul?'

Sanders nodded. 'He could be very obstructive if you didn't do things his way.'

CHAPTER NINETEEN

They decided to walk back to the central area of Paris. Daniel had always found that walking helped him think, a habit that Abigail had picked up from him.

'What did you think?' asked Abigail. She'd filled him in on what Sanders had told her about Flamand and Abdul.

'I think it opens a whole new avenue of investigation,' said Daniel. 'Put it with what we know. Flamand no longer had sexual relations with his wife, if he ever did in the first place. By all accounts, he had no relations with anyone. At least, not with women.'

'You're suggesting he had relations with men?'

'It's a possibility. It's not a criminal act between consenting adults in France. The law decriminalising it was brought in over a hundred years ago. But, socially, there's still a stigma attached to it in some circles.'

'You think that Professor Flamand and Hugo Sanders were involved?'

'It's a hunch. The way I see it, Flamand and Sanders became involved at the start of the expedition to Saqqara. Then Sanders becomes involved with Abdul. Flamand is jealous, angry, and even angrier when he discovers that Sanders has invited Abdul to come to France to live with him.'

'It's an interesting theory,' said Abigail, 'but we need evidence to back it up.'

'Let's talk to Auguste Perrier again,' said Daniel.

'Even if he confirms it, how will it help us discover his murderer?'

'It could mean that the person who killed Flamand could be part of that same demi-monde. Who knows who else he had a relationship with?'

Abigail chuckled. 'Demi-monde? My heavens, Daniel, you're talking French!'

When they found Perrier at his lodgings, he was packing a suitcase.

'Off somewhere?' asked Abigail.

'I am leaving Paris,' he said sourly. 'There is no future for me here. I have a meeting arranged with a German university in Bonn who are planning an expedition to Egypt.'

'It's lucky we caught you before you go,' said Abigail. 'We have a couple of questions we'd be grateful if you'd sort out.'

'Ask away,' said Perrier.

'According to the records at the Louvre about the dig at Saqqara, Professor Flamand says you resigned from the expedition.'

'Resigned?' echoed Perrier, outraged. 'Never! Professor Flamand told me he did not want me as part of the team any longer. So I left.' Bitterly, he added, 'It is not in my nature to beg for my place. It is true I could not work with Flamand, but I would never have resigned. The work is too important.'

'You said you were sure Flamand was selling the best pieces to someone for his own profit.'

'Yes,' said Perrier.

'Do you know who the buyer was?'

'No. Flamand played everything close to his chest. I'm sure he got rid of me to prevent me from finding out what was going on, who he was selling the pieces to.'

'Do you know if Flamand and Hugo Sanders had a relationship while you were in Saqqara?'

Perrier studied them carefully. 'Do you mean: were they lovers?'

'Yes.'

Perrier shrugged. 'They may have been. I did not bother to look into that side of them. Certainly, they spent a lot of time together the first few weeks we were there.'

'Alone together?'

Perrier nodded. 'It was nothing to do with me. I had no desire to spend time with Flamand.'

'Was Professor Flamand attracted to men?'

'If he was, he never approached me.'

'What about women? Did he spend any time with women?'

Perrier gave a sarcastic laugh. 'He had no time for women. As you should know, Abigail, from the way he acted towards you, simply because you were a woman.'

'Well, that wasn't really conclusive,' said Daniel as they left Perrier's house.

'Auguste doesn't move in the sort of circles where they talk about such things,' said Abigail. 'He doesn't do social gossip; he's more interested in political agitation.' Then she smiled. 'But we do know someone who moves in all sorts of circles, especially gossipy ones.'

'Sir Brian Otway?' asked Daniel. 'Would he know?'

'If there is anything, Sir Brian will know. These diplomats make sure they know *everything*.'

'So he's our next port of call?'

'No,' said Abigail, 'Next, our hotel for lunch. I don't know about you but I'm getting hungry.'

On their arrival at their hotel they met Superintendent Maison as he was leaving. He was carrying a briefcase.

'This is fortunate,' he said. 'I have left a note at reception asking you to call on me at the prefecture, but as you are here we can talk now.'

'Of course,' said Abigail. 'Shall we go to the restaurant?'

'Today, I need to talk to you privately,' said Maison. 'May we talk in your room?'

'Certainly,' said Abigail. She explained to Daniel what the superintendent had said, then they walked with him up to their room.

Daniel and Abigail sat down as the superintendent opened his briefcase and took out some papers, which he passed to them.

'Professor Flamand's bank accounts,' he said. 'You will see that there are instances of large payments being made into his account.'

'Cash or cheque?' asked Abigail.

'Cheques,' said Maison. 'The payer for two of them was Baron Emile de Barque, three thousand francs both times. The last was by a Lancelot Grimaldi for five thousand francs. There are also frequent withdrawals, some for quite large sums.'

Abigail studied the accounts. 'The two payments by this Baron de Barque were made after he and his team returned from Saqqara. The first three months after, the second two months later. The payment by Lancelot Grimaldi was two months after that.' She looked at the superintendent. 'It sems to give weight to the allegation that he sold artefacts he brought from Saqqara to these two men.'

'It does,' agreed Maison. 'It would also suggest that he decided to sell to Grimaldi rather than Baron de Barque because Grimaldi was willing to pay more.'

'True,' said Abigail, 'but it would depend on the particular artefacts. Like everything that has its price, some things are more expensive than others. Do you know these two men, Baron de Barque and Grimaldi?'

Maison shook his head. 'No, I do not move in those social circles. But I suspect that your friend Sir Brian Otway would know them.' He held out his hand. 'They are for you to look at only, not to keep. I have to return them to the bank.'

'Of course,' said Abigail. 'Would you mind if I copied down some of these details?'

'Not at all,' said Maison. 'Perhaps Monsieur Wilson would do that while I talk to you, Madame Wilson. There is something I need to tell you for which I would like your attention. You can tell your husband later.'

'Of course,' said Abigail. She handed the sheets to Daniel

and told him what the superintendent had asked. 'Just copy them down as they are,' she said. 'We'll decipher them later.'

Daniel nodded and took the bank accounts to a table, where he picked up a pencil and began to copy the details on sheets of paper, while Maison sat with Abigail.

'I have had a visit from an officer in the French Army who told me some disturbing information,' he said. 'The problem for me is knowing who to share it with. I cannot pass it on to my own superiors because I do not know who to trust. The same goes for my inspectors. That is also true of most of the politicians who might be involved. Then it struck me that possibly the only people I can trust here are you and your husband.'

'Us?' said Abigail, surprised. 'But you do not know us.'

'I know enough from our short acquaintance to believe that you are honest. I also believe you are impartial, and that is because as English people you have no connection with either of the two opposing sides who are fighting the Dreyfus case.'

'Dreyfus?' echoed Abigail, intrigued. 'But when we mentioned that to you before you told us it was ridiculous.'

'That was before I had this visit from this particular gentleman. I will not tell you his name, but it is enough that you know he is a very well-connected captain in the army. *Very* well-connected.'

'I assume from your tone that he is on the anti-Dreyfus faction?'

'Indeed.' Maison nodded. He then proceeded to tell her what Chevignon had told him. As Abigail listened, she stared at the superintendent, bewildered.

'You're saying that the *anti*-Dreyfus faction in the army killed Flamand?'

'He did not admit as such, but that was the feeling I got.'

'And he wants you to quash any such ideas coming to the surface.'

Again, the superintendent nodded.

'And if you do, you will be rewarded, and if you don't, you will be killed, just as Flamand was.'

'No, he did not threaten me that way.'

'It sounds to me like a threat. And Flamand was killed, we know that for a fact.'

'We do not know if it was the army who were responsible.'

'If they weren't, why was this captain sent to talk to you?'

Maison shrugged. 'Who knows? There may be someone they wish to protect.'

'Who?'

'If we knew that, we would know much more about this case. The fact is, Madame Wilson, there is no one else I can talk to about this. Everyone gossips. You are not involved in any of these different social and political circles.'

'Sir Brian Otway?' suggested Abigail.

Maison shook his head firmly. 'Definitely not. None of these political people are to be trusted. No, my thought in telling you and your husband this is that we should share every piece of information we gather. That way, if anything should happen, at least one of us will have the whole picture, as you English say.'

'If anything should happen,' said Abigail carefully. 'You mean to you?'

'Who knows,' said Maison. 'I have now told you my new piece of information. What have you learnt since we last met?'

Daniel came over to them from the table carrying the bank statements, which he handed to Maison.

'All copied,' he said. He looked at Abigail. 'What's happening?'

'I'll tell you what the superintendent told me after he's gone,' she said. 'Right now, he's just asked what information we've managed to pick up.'

'I won't be much use for that,' said Daniel. 'Not being able to speak or understand French.'

'Yes, you will,' said Abigail. 'I'll tell him what we've learnt, then I'll tell you what I've told him and you can remind me if I've left anything out.'

'It's all very convoluted,' grumbled Daniel.

'It wouldn't be if you'd bothered to learn French,' said Abigail. She turned to the superintendent and began to bring him up to date on their recent investigations.

'We went to see Madame Foret, Elaine Foret's mother,' she said. 'She has a low opinion of Professor Flamand. She says she believed he borrowed money from her daughter, and she doubts if he paid her back.'

'Why would he do that?' asked Maison.

'The professor might have had money problems.'

The superintendent flourished the bank statements before putting them back in his briefcase. 'With the money he was making from selling these precious artefacts? Hardly.'

'But was he spending it? If so, what on? We also met her brother, Patrice. Have you met him?'

'No. He was not there when I called on Madam Foret to tell her about her daughter being killed.'

'You were lucky. He does not like the police.'

'Why?'

'His mother says he runs around with bad companions.'

'Ah, a delinquent. I shall check our records and see if he's ever been arrested. What was your opinion of him?'

'He was surly, rude and unhelpful.'

'Like so many of the young people today,' sighed Mison wearily. 'They are a blot on the good name of Paris.' He gathered his briefcase and rose to his feet. 'By the way, I received the autopsy report on Mam'selle Foret. As well as confirming she was poisoned, it also revealed that she was still *virgo intacta*.'

'She was a virgin?' asked Abigail.

Maison nodded. 'Yes, so we are not looking for a lover.'

CHAPTER TWENTY

After Maison had gone, Abigail told Daniel what the superintendent had told her about the army captain.

'He said he feels we are the only ones he can trust with this information,' she added.

'That's very flattering,' said Daniel. 'But it's also worrying. It means that we can't trust anyone.'

'Except Superintendent Maison,' said Abigail.

Daniel regarded her thoughtfully. 'Are you sure we can trust him?'

'Yes, I feel we can,' she said.

'I'm not so sure,' said Daniel doubtfully.

'Let's leave that aside for the moment,' said Abigail. 'Let's take stock of what we know so far, and who we feel the main suspects are. This latest information from Maison definitely points towards the army possibly being involved.'

'If what he said is right, that Flamand was passing inside information to the anti-Dreyfus camp, that negates the idea that the anti-Dreyfus lot killed Flamand. They would have known he was actually on their side.'

'Perhaps not all of them,' pointed out Abigail.

'Yes, that's true,' conceded Daniel. 'I heard him say "*virgo intacta*". I assume he was talking about the medical report on Elaine Foret.'

'Yes,' said Abigail. 'So, no affair with Sir Brian, nor with Professor Flamand, despite what Madame Flamand thinks. Which lends credence to your thoughts on his sexual proclivities.'

'The problem is we've got almost too much information,' said Daniel. He pulled a sheet of blank paper towards him and took up his pencil. 'We need to start breaking it down. We have two murders, both happening at the Louvre: Professor Flamand and his secretary, Elaine Foret. One stabbed, one poisoned. The two murders have to be connected.'

'But not necessarily carried out by the same person,' said Abigail.

'True,' said Daniel. He began to make a list of possible suspects. 'According to your friend Auguste Perrier, the supporters of Captain Dreyfus killed Flamand because he was agitating for Dreyfus's execution. But, according to the army captain who came to pressurise Superintendent Maison, it was the other side – the anti-Dreyfus lot – who killed Flamand because he was betraying their side to the pro-Dreyfus campaign.'

'And not just the anti-Dreyfus people, but some high-ranking people in the army,' said Abigail.

'Who were the ones who framed Dreyfus in the first place,' said Daniel.

'What about motives?' asked Abigail. 'It now seems clear that Flamand was stealing artefacts he'd collected in Saqqara and selling them to private buyers.'

'But why would anyone want to kill him over that? If the Louvre discovered it was happening, I can't imagine them sending an assassin to bump him off. They'd do the responsible thing and put the matter in the hands of the police.'

'The two buyers?' asked Abigail. 'This baron and Mr Grimaldi?'

'But why would they kill him? They'd got what they wanted.'

'Perhaps they felt he'd cheated them in some way? As it was an illegal transaction, they could hardly report it to any authorities.'

Daniel shook his head. 'It doesn't make sense. The theft and sale of the artefacts may be connected to his murder, but not by the buyers, I feel. More likely someone who was a conspirator in the whole business of taking the artefacts and selling them, but never got their share of the money.'

'One of the other people on the expedition with him?'

'Or someone at the Louvre.'

Abigail nodded. 'Yes, put that down on our list.'

'The other thing is: why was Flamand so short of money? He made thousands from these sales, and he had a good salary from the Louvre. What did he spend it on?'

'Or *who* did he spend it on?' asked Abigail. 'Did he have a secret he was being blackmailed about?'

'Which brings us to Paul LeMarc, who was killed while looking into Flamand's financial affairs. Was Flamand behind LeMarc's death? If so, did someone find out and kill Flamand in revenge?' Daniel jotted that thought down, then said, 'I'm still not entirely convinced that Sir Brian isn't involved. We know he didn't have a full-blown affair with Elaine Foret, but there's still a question over his relationship with her. And, therefore, with the professor.'

'Yes, put him down,' agreed Abigail.

She moved to stand behind him and looked over his shoulder at the list he'd written.

'I think the next person to talk to is Sir Brian. See if he can throw any light on this business of Flamand's sexuality. But before we do that . . .' She tapped his shoulder. 'Lunch, before anyone else turns up and interferes with it.'

Lunch taken, they made their way to the British Embassy, where they found Sir Brian in between appointments.

'That was the German ambassador,' he groaned, as he showed Daniel and Abigail into his office, having just said goodbye to a very serious-looking middle-aged man with a bushy beard. 'I'm convinced the Germans are only satisfied when they're undertaking a war or planning one.'

'Which is it this time?' asked Daniel.

'Oh, a complete denial that they are considering either,' sighed Otway. 'They accuse the French of stirring up ill feeling against them.' He settled himself behind his desk and motioned for them to sit. 'So, what can I do for you?'

'Did Professor Flamand have sexual relations with men?' asked Abigail.

Otway regarded them, curious.

'Why do you ask?' asked Otway.

'Because it may have some bearing on why he was killed.'

Otway looked at them, bemused. 'Why? Same-sex relations are not a crime here in France, providing they are consensual.' He smiled. 'If poor Oscar Wilde had been living in Paris at the time of his persecution by that oaf Queensberry, he would not have gone to prison. Oscar's living here, now, you know. In Paris.' He gave a sigh. 'Sadly, he's not looking well. Everything has pulled him down.'

'Getting back to Flamand, we're fairly certain he may have had a relationship with one of his colleagues on the dig while he was at Saqqara.'

Otway chuckled. 'Let me guess. You're talking about young Hugo Sanders?'

'You knew about it?' asked Abigail. 'Sanders and Professor Flamand?'

'Rumour and gossip are rife in the social circles,' said Otway. 'Especially among those of a certain persuasion. A professor of the arts who works part-time for the Louvre mentioned it to me.'

'You didn't think to mention this to us before?' asked Daniel.

'Why should I?' asked Otway. 'His sexual persuasion didn't seem relevant. And I knew he preferred to keep it a secret. The fact that his wife didn't know should have told you how carefully he guarded his privacy.'

'But why?' asked Abigail. 'It's not illegal here in France.'

'No, but among some sectors of society it's not the done thing. And that includes the world of archaeology. Leading archaeologists need the support of students, and usually young men. You must have noticed that yourself, Abigail.

Strong young men to do much of the lifting, the heavy work.'

'Yes, that's true.'

'If word spread about the professor's proclivities, there are some families – families with money – who would discreetly prevent their sons from joining the professor on a dig in some remote and rather exotic place. And expeditions need money, as you know only too well. Although organisations like the Louvre fund many such expeditions, additional money is often needed. And much of it is provided by rich families to ensure that their offspring are chosen to accompany – and learn from – the very best.'

'But we didn't get the impression that Hugo Sanders or Maurice Larchet or Auguste Perrier came from wealthy backgrounds.'

'They don't,' said Otway. 'Which suggests the rumours and gossip about the professor had been picked up by that wealthy social circle. Hence, the professor had to make his team up from what one could call less financially viable workers. And just the three of them.'

'Yes, I wondered about that,' said Abigail. 'Most of the digs I've been on have had much larger numbers from Europe.'

'Yes. I mentioned this fact to the professor just before he went to Saqqara and wondered if he would be taking a large enough team with him as theirs seemed very small. He said the heavy work would be done by local labourers in Egypt; his team would be managing the dig.'

'The thing is, Sir Brian, this is an aspect of the professor's character that we've only just discovered. We're looking into all aspects of his life to try and find a motive for his murder.

We've uncovered the business of him stealing artefacts from the dig at Saqqara that should be in the Louvre and selling them privately. There's a possible motive, though what it may be we're not sure, but the situation is a possibility. There's also the business of Paul LeMarc being killed after he started to investigate the professor's accounts with reference to Saqqara. Possibly something there. As we said, we're looking into all aspects of the professor's life to find something that may point to why he was killed. And it's possible that his sex life may point to something. Who were his partners? Did he upset any of them so badly that they wanted to kill him?

'What we wondered was if we could find out the kind of places he went to in pursuit of partners, any particular clubs he frequented. It's legal here, so the clubs would be in the open. If we could find an insider in that world who might be able to tell us which clubs the professor frequented, it would save us an awful lot of time. There must be hundreds.'

'There are,' said Otway. He looked thoughtful, then he said, 'It might be worth having a word with young Belfont.'

'Edgar?' said Daniel in surprise. 'You don't mean . . . ?'

Otway smiled. 'You'd be surprised how many chaps live under a cloud in England. At least here they can be open, if they choose to. I'll have a word with Belfont about your theories. That might save you the embarrassment of raising the issue with him yourselves.'

'I can assure you we won't be embarrassed,' said Abigail.

'No, but he might be, at first,' said Otway. 'And he's a good chap. I don't want him upset.'

'There's one other thing,' said Abigail. 'We've discovered

that Professor Flamand was likely selling some of the best artefacts he brought back from Saqqara to private clients.'

'Yes, I've heard that rumoured,' said Otway.

'You didn't mention it before?' asked Daniel.

'I pick up an awful lot of gossip, but if it doesn't impinge on my role as ambassador, I just store it away and let things go on as they are. I've got enough problems to deal with without looking for more.'

'We think we know who his clients were. Baron de Barque and Lancelot Grimaldi. Do you know them?'

'I do,' said Otway. 'The baron is eminently respectable, Monsieur Grimaldi possibly less so.'

'In what way "less so"?' asked Daniel.

'The baron is a collector, whereas Grimaldi is a dealer. To the baron it's about art and history. To Grimaldi, it's about money.'

'But some collectors have been known to be unscrupulous,' pointed out Abigail. 'Especially if they desire a particular piece and are determined to have it, at any cost.'

'That's true,' admitted Otway. 'But, as far as I know, that's not been said about the baron. But in Grimaldi's case there have been suggestions that he's been able to acquire some artefacts and works of art with the aid of some blackmail.'

'Oh?'

'Yes. He discovers something about someone they don't want people to know, and so manages to persuade them to sell for a lower price.'

'But he paid Professor Flamand more than the baron had paid the professor.'

'That also depends what he paid for,' Otway pointed out.

'True,' said Daniel.

'We were wondering if you could arrange for us to meet either or both of these men?' asked Abigail.

Otway thought it over, then said, 'I can give you a letter of introduction to the baron, tell him you've been hired by the Louvre and so on, and would like to talk to him.'

'That would be excellent. Thank you,' said Abigail. 'And Lancelot Grimaldi?'

'As I said, I don't have the same relationship with Monsieur Grimaldi. I suggest you call on him at his *galerie* and introduce yourselves. I'm sure he'll be aware of you and your reputation, Abigail. It's the Galerie Grimaldi in the Marais, in the 3rd arrondissement. I'll give you the address.'

Louise Perrault made her way from the secretaries' office towards the mail room, carrying the bundle of envelopes to be sent out. She was allotted this job as the youngest secretary. Where the other secretaries would have considered it a menial task beneath their status, Perrault was pleased to do it; it was a chance for her to escape – however briefly – from the suffocating atmosphere in the secretaries' room, with the baleful glares of Mam'selle Bertolt seemingly always directed at her. It just needed the slightest start of a few words from the young secretary for Mam'selle Bertolt to give a sharp cough and rap on her desk with her knuckles.

I need to get out of here, get a different job, she thought. *Otherwise I'm going to end up like those shrivelled-up old women in the secretaries' room. All right, they weren't* all *old – but they acted as if they were. I need a job where I can be* me. *Something with a bit of excitement.*

Maybe she could be a detective, like that English woman, Madame Wilson.

Perrault was still in awe of the English woman – to be a detective! Would that be allowed here in France?

She was just imagining herself carrying out investigations, uncovering mysteries, exposing criminals and murderers, when she became aware of someone lying face-down on the floor ahead of her in the corridor. He was wearing the familiar uniform of the Louvre's stewards and security staff, who kept order inside the museum. Puzzled, she approached him. She knelt down beside him, putting the envelopes down on the floor, and gently prodded him.

'Are you all right?' she asked.

When there was no reply, she prodded him again, harder this time, but again there was no response. Was he breathing? Had the fact that he was face-down stopped him being able to do that? She took hold of his shoulder and rolled him towards her so that his face was clear of the floor. As she did so she saw the blood on the front of his tunic and realised from his staring eyes and slack-jawed mouth that he was dead.

She screamed.

CHAPTER TWENTY-ONE

Daniel and Abigail were in the restaurant of their hotel, drinking coffee and rueing their lack of success on the case so far.

'As we said, there's almost too much,' sighed Daniel. 'One thing, there's been a great deal of talk about Saqqara. I know it's a place in Egypt where archaeological digs have taken place, but I don't know what makes it so special.'

'Djoser's step pyramid,' said Abigail. 'You know what a traditional pyramid looks like.'

'Of course. Like four triangle shapes leaning into one another, with a point at the top.'

Abigail nodded. 'Djoser's step pyramid was different.' She took a sheet of paper and with a pencil began to draw a shape. It looked like a series of five flat boxes laid one on top of another, the largest at the bottom, the size of the boxes decreasing as they went higher up to a small flat box laid at the top.

'As you can see, it looks like a series of steps going up, but with no point at the top. It's a pyramid in the fact that as it goes up, the flat areas get smaller.'

'Why is the design so different from the traditional pyramid?' asked Daniel.

'The speculation is that it was a first step in the creation of the traditional pyramid. The earliest burial places, called mastabas, covered huge areas of ground and were slightly raised, but not like the later pyramids. They rose a few levels up from the ground, but were stretched out, like a very long and wide two-storey building. Inside were the burial chambers. They were stepped, like the lower sections of Djoser's pyramid, but they only rose so high. Imagine a two-storey building like a huge warehouse that stretched for perhaps a mile in any direction. These were the standard burial sites during what are known as the first and second dynasties, from about 3000 BC to 2600 BC.

'What you have to understand is that in the religion of ancient Egypt, each pharaoh was an incarnation of the god Horus. When an incarnation of Horus died, the god passed on to the next reigning king. The dead king was entombed inside the mastaba, the burial chambers, and became identified with Osiris, the father of Horus. So you have the dead king, now merged with Osiris, inside the burial chamber, while the new king, who now has the spirit of Horus, sets to work to build his own burial chamber where he will be entombed when he dies.'

'And from what I've read in your magazines, it's not just the dead king who's entombed, but a large part of his court and family.'

'That's right,' said Abigail. 'Along with riches and treasures from his previous life that he will need again in the afterlife. So these burial chambers were packed with all sorts of precious artefacts, which made them susceptible to tomb raiders.'

'Or archaeologists in search of history,' said Daniel with a smile.

'Sometimes the divide between an investigative archaeologist and a tomb raider can be quite thin,' admitted Abigail. 'Some people have speculated that when Djoser built what was to be his burial chamber – this was between 2667 and 2648 BC – he built it in a pyramid shape, with these different flat areas on top of one another, to make it harder for the burial chambers at the heart of the mastaba to be broken into. Others say that what Djoser was doing with his step pyramid was reaching for the heavens. Whatever the reason, the fact is that, with this step pyramid, Djoser gave us the first form of a pyramid made of stone.

'There is every indication that Djoser's successor, Sekhemkhet, began his burial chamber as a step pyramid, like Djoser's, but then he added more stone to the rising sections, so that they became narrower. Each pharaoh after Sekhemkhet did the same, narrowing the steps until they disappeared, and by Sneferu in the fourth dynasty, 2613 to 2589 BC, we have the traditional pyramid shape.

'I suppose that what makes Djoser's step pyramid so fascinating is because it's a transition from the flat burial chambers of the first dynasty, leading towards the pyramids as we think of them. Those huge, solid, triangular creations rising to a point at the top.'

'Ah, archaeological talk,' said Edgar Belfont with a smile as he appeared by their table. 'Sir Brian said you wanted to talk to me, so I thought I'd come over.'

'Would you join us for some coffee?' asked Abigail.

'That would be very nice,' said Belfont, pulling up a chair and joining them.

Abigail hailed the waitress and ordered another coffee.

'Sir Brian told me what it was about,' said Belfont. 'He said you feel that the professor's private life might throw some light on why he was murdered.'

'The key word here is *might*,' said Abigail. 'It could be just another red herring.'

'He said you were looking at clubs he might have gone to.'

'Yes,' said Daniel.

'He never went to the one I usually go to, but I can ask around. I'm sure someone will know.'

'We're sorry to raise this issue with you,' apologised Daniel. 'We want you to know that it's none of our business who you spend time with or what you do. Frankly, we've been grateful for the time you've spent with us. Particularly the time you spent guiding me around while Abigail was in prison. I'd have been lost without you.'

'I'm glad I could be of help,' said Belfont. 'And thank you both for not being condemning, which usually happens with English people when they find out about me. At least we don't have that kind of prejudice here. Well, sometimes we do, but not from the authorities. I've often thought that's why my parents suggested I move here and take up this post.'

'They know?'

'Oh yes. My father sussed it out long ago. And, luckily for

me, he was sympathetic. Many chaps wouldn't have had the same supportive reaction from their parents. But my father is one of the good ones. "If you stay in England you'll only get into trouble sooner or later," he said. He advised France. "They see things differently there." Which is why he pulled strings and got me this posting. He's a sweet old thing, for all his gruff appearance.'

'And your mother?'

Belfont laughed. 'Funnily enough, she was the one who took longer to come to terms with it. She thought it was just a phase I was passing through. And she wanted grandchildren, so that presented a setback for her. But, in the end, she was very supportive, too. I think the old man sweet-talked her into accepting it.

'Anyway, back to Professor Flamand. I'll have a word with some people and see if anyone knows his preference for a particular club. Someone is bound to know. As I said, I moved in different social circles to the professor, a younger set, but there's always gossip about. Gossip is big currency in the scene. How's the case going? Are you any further to finding out who murdered the professor and his secretary?'

'Sadly, we've got too many possibles,' sighed Abigail.

The sound of heavy running footsteps made them turn round. A uniformed policeman drew to a halt beside their table. 'Monsieur and Madame Wilson,' he panted, out of breath. 'Superintendent Maison needs you to come with me urgently. There's been another murder at the Louvre.'

* * *

Daniel and Abigail hurried from the police carriage towards the entrance to the Louvre, close on the heels of the officer who'd been sent to collect them from their hotel.

'It was lucky we were in the hotel and not out and about,' Daniel said to Abigail. 'And we still don't know who's been killed.'

They ran up the stairs to the first floor, passing a notice that said there was no entry for members of the public, then along a corridor. Superintendent Maison was standing beside the body of a man that lay on the floor, a uniformed police officer beside him.

'Good,' said Maison. 'I am glad my man found you. I wanted you to take a look at the scene before the doctor arrived. He should be here shortly.'

'Who is he?' asked Abigail, looking down at the dead man.

'His name is Armand Ruffalo. He is – or rather, was – a steward here. One of those who move around the museum helping visitors.'

'How did he die?'

'I've just had a quick look, but it looks like he's been stabbed. Right in the heart. We'll get confirmation when the doctor arrives.'

Daniel knelt down and began to examine the man's clothing and his hands.

'No defensive wounds,' he said, with Abigail translating his words for the superintendent's benefit. 'Nothing under his fingernails.'

'Yes, we already checked that,' said Maison.

Daniel got up and looked along the corridor. 'Where does this corridor lead to?' he asked.

'That way goes to the secretaries' room,' said Abigail. 'I recognise it from when I was talking to the secretaries.'

'It was one of the secretaries who found him,' said Maison. 'A Louise Perrault.'

'I remember her,' said Abigail. 'She was very helpful.'

'Perhaps you would like to talk to her again?' asked Maison. 'At the moment she is recovering in Mam'selle Foret's former office. She is in a state of shock.'

'Yes, of course,' said Abigail. 'I'll go there now. I know where it is.' She looked at Daniel. 'Unless you want me here to translate for you?'

'No,' said Daniel. 'It's more important for you to talk to her while it's still fresh in her mind. I'll examine the scene here and you can translate what I find – if anything – to the superintendent later.'

Abigail repeated this in French to Maison, and at his nod of agreement hurried off in search of Louise Perrault.

CHAPTER TWENTY-TWO

'When you found him did you notice anyone else around?'

Abigail was with Louise Perrault in Elaine Foret's former office. The young secretary seemed to have recovered from her shock and was now eager to give Abigail as much information as she could. She almost seemed excited to be such a central character in the tragic event.

'No,' said Perrault, 'but I wasn't really looking. I was so shocked. Who could have done it? And why?'

'Did you know him?'

She shook her head. 'No. The stewards are men in uniforms who make sure that no one is causing any problems in the museum. Some people try to touch the exhibits, rubbing their hands over them, despite the notices telling them it is not allowed.'

'Do you ever have any dealings with the stewards?'

'Only now and then, when I am on my way along a corridor.' She looked wistful. 'That's why I am happy to take the post to the mail room.'

'Because it gives you a chance to meet other people?'

Perrault hesitated, then she said awkwardly. 'Yes, but please do not tell Mam'selle Bertolt. She does not like us fraternising with other employees in the museum. Especially those she considers beneath us.'

'She considers the stewards beneath you?'

'Beneath the secretaries.' Then, angrily, she added, 'She is a snob.'

'Yes, it sounds like she is,' said Abigail sympathetically. 'You say you didn't know Monsieur Ruffalo, but had you seen him before?'

'Yes. Twice. Both times when I was taking the post to the mail room. We didn't speak but he smiled at me, both times. Not in the way that some men do, more like a friendly uncle. He seemed a nice man.'

'And both times you met him it was in the same corridor?'

'Yes.'

'Was he standing there, as if he was on duty, or was he going somewhere?'

'He wouldn't have been on duty. That corridor is for staff only.'

'So when you saw him before, was he moving as if he was going somewhere? Or did he appear to be waiting for someone?'

Louise Perrault thought this over.

'I never thought of that before,' she said. 'He wasn't moving; he was just standing.'

'As if he was waiting for someone?'

'Yes. I suppose so.'

'Did you ever see him with anyone?'

'No. The only times I saw him he was standing in the

corridor, and he smiled in a friendly way as I passed him.'

Abigail thanked Perrault, then told her she needed to talk to Superintendent Maison. She noticed that the girl seemed disappointed that their interview was at an end, so she asked, 'Is there anything else you noticed? Anything at all that will help up solve his murder?'

Louise Perrault's face showed she was thinking hard. *She doesn't want this to end*, realised Abigail. *This is her moment of fame, at being the centre of attention.* Finally, reluctantly, Perrault shook her head.

'Nothing at the moment,' she said unhappily.

'Don't worry, we'll talk again,' said Abigail with a reassuring smile, and the girl smiled back, relieved.

When she got back to where the body of the steward lay, Maison and Daniel had finished their examinations of the scene and were waiting for the ambulance to take Ruffalo's body away.

'How did you get on with Miss Perrault?' asked Daniel.

Abigail told him in English what she'd learnt, then did the same for the superintendent in French. 'When she saw him on two previous occasions in that same corridor it seemed he was waiting for someone. So could he have been waiting for someone again, only this time he was stabbed to death?'

'Who?' asked Maison.

'I have no idea,' said Abigail. 'I suggest we have to talk to the other stewards, see if any of them know why he would have been waiting there in that particular corridor.'

'I will do that,' said Maison. 'I know the chief steward,

Jules Delors. I will ask him who Ruffalo was closest friends with. If Ruffalo was waiting in that corridor for someone, hopefully his friends will be able to tell us who. As soon as I find anything out, I will let you know.'

With that, the superintendent left them in search of Jules Delors.

'It looks like we've been dismissed,' said Daniel. He frowned. 'The puzzle is, how is the person who killed Ruffalo connected to Professor Flamand and Elaine Foret?'

'Who says he has to be?' asked Abigail.

'The murder happened in a part of the Louvre that's closed to the public, the same as with the killings of the professor and his secretary. That suggests an employee.'

'But it doesn't have to be the same employee,' pointed out Abigail. 'There are thousands of people who work at the Louvre.'

'Yes, I suppose so,' said Daniel reluctantly. 'It's just that I don't like coincidences. I'm sure the stabbing of Ruffalo is linked to Flamand and Elaine Foret in some way.'

'Based on what?'

Daniel gave a rueful sigh. 'Just a gut feeling,' he admitted.

'Can I suggest that, for the moment, we leave the superintendent and his men to deal with Armand Ruffalo's murder, while we concentrate on the ones the Louvre have hired us for: Professor Flamand and Elaine Foret. If the superintendent uncovers anything that connects the killing of Ruffalo with our cases, I'm sure he'll tell us.'

'I suppose you're right,' said Daniel. With a last look at the corridor where Ruffalo had been killed, he followed

Abigail towards the stairs that led down to the exhibition rooms, and the corridor that would take them out to the street.

'Ruffalo was quite a private person,' said Jules Delors. 'He wasn't one for socialising very much with the others outside of work.'

Superintendent Maison had found Delors in the exhibition rooms, surveying the other stewards. He'd been notified of Ruffalo's murder and felt it was important to move amongst the rest of his staff in the museum to reassure them of his concern for their well-being, talking to them and trying to find out if any of the other stewards had noticed anything strange about Ruffalo. Delors related all this to Maison.

'And had they noticed anything strange?' asked the superintendent.

'No,' replied Delors.

'Was he married?' asked Maison.

'He was a widower. His wife died two years ago. He has two children, aged seven and five, a boy and a girl. His widowed mother lives with him and she looks after the children while he's at work.'

'Who would you say he was closest to among the other stewards? Or anyone else at the Louvre?'

Delors thought it over, then said, 'He often used to have lunch with Bernard Tavenier, one of the other stewards.'

'Where would I find this Tavenier?' asked Maison.

'I will send him to you,' said Delors. He gestured towards the stairs 'You can use my office upstairs to talk to him; that way you won't be interrupted.'

Maison made his way to the first floor and the administrative area, where he settled himself down in Delors's office. After about five minutes there was a knock at the door, which opened to admit a short, portly man in his forties.

'Superintendent Maison?' he enquired.

'Yes,' said Maison. 'I assume you are Bernard Tavenier?'

'Yes, sir.'

Maison gestured for him to come in and sit down. 'You have heard what happened to Armand Ruffalo?'

'Yes, sir.' He shook his head in disbelief. 'It's unbelievable. Who would do such a thing?'

'Did he have any enemies?'

'No,' said Tavenier firmly. 'He was one of the nicest people you could ever meet.'

'I hear he didn't socialise with the other stewards much.'

'That was because he had his children to look after. He was a widower. He wanted to get home as soon as he could after he'd finished work. Also, he was quite a shy man.'

'Shy?'

'Yes, that's why he didn't talk much to the others.'

'We believe he had taken to waiting for someone in the corridor where he was murdered.'

Tavenier looked uncomfortable. 'Yes,' he said.

'Who was he waiting for?' asked Maison.

Tavenier hesitated, then said reluctantly. 'He had taken a fancy to one of the secretaries. The young one.'

'Louise Perrault?'

'He didn't know her name. He had seen her walking along the corridor taking the post to the mail room. He wanted to

174

get to know her, but – as I said – he was shy. He was especially shy with women. He noticed that she took the post to the mail room, so he began to hang around in that particular section of corridor in the hope of seeing her. He told me he was working up the courage to say 'Hello' to her, and ask her out. But each time he found himself tongue-tied. All he could do was smile at her. He hoped that one day she'd stop and say something to him.'

'She was the one who found his body. I suppose he'd been in that corridor waiting for her to arrive.'

'I suppose so,' sighed Tavenier. He looked enquiringly at the superintendent. 'Do you think that was why he was murdered? Someone found out about him waiting for her, perhaps a jealous lover, and stabbed him?'

'Perhaps,' said Maison.

'Maybe it was someone who, like Armand, was shy and waiting for his chance to speak to Louise, and who became enraged when he discovered Armand was planning on doing the same?'

'It's possible,' agreed the superintendent. 'Has there been any talk among the stewards about anyone else wanting to talk to Mam'selle Perrault?'

Tavenier thought it over, then shook his head. 'But it doesn't have to be one of the stewards,' he said. 'There are many people who work at the Louvre. Painters, decorators, the men who move the exhibits around from place to place, carpenters and other workmen. Any of them could have noticed Louise Perrault walking around the corridors, or going home.'

CHAPTER TWENTY-THREE

The following morning, Abigail and Daniel decided their next step was to pay a call to Lancelot Grimaldi.

'Sir Brian doesn't seem to have a very high opinion of him,' said Abigail as they made their way to the address they'd been given for the gallery.

'But he does have a good opinion of this Baron de Barque,' mused Daniel thoughtfully.

'Which means what?' asked Abigail.

'I just wondered if there wasn't a touch of snobbery involved,' said Daniel. 'Sir Brian and the baron meet socially in the same circle. I get the impression that Sir Brian considers Grimaldi to be a crook but he won't allow himself to believe that the baron could also be dubious in his dealings.'

Galerie Grimaldi was a very upmarket establishment in an obviously wealthy area. The locality reminded Daniel and Abigail of expensive areas of London such as Mayfair. The gallery had a double-fronted showcase frontage and large windows encased in cream-coloured frames, behind which were tastefully displayed works of art, both ancient and modern. A bust of a stately Roman head was alongside a Greek vase, both on low stands. There were also two paintings, which Abigail identified, one a small gilt-framed work by Poussin, the other a larger Tintoretto landscape.

'I imagine they'd be expensive,' said Daniel, 'even though I haven't the faintest idea who either of them is.'

'Was,' Abigail corrected him. 'Both are long dead. Which, of course, only increases their value.'

'So we assume that Lancelot Grimaldi has a wealthy clientele?'

'We do indeed,' said Abigail.

She pushed at the door, which triggered a bell attached to the top of it to ring, and almost immediately a tall, slim man in his sixties and wearing an immaculate suit of lilac linen appeared from the back. There were no other customers in sight in the actual shop area, which had paintings and sculptures from different historical periods on show.

'*Bonjour.*' The man smiled.

'*Bonjour,*' said Abigail. In French, she asked if she was addressing Monsieur Lancelot Grimaldi, and when he confirmed it was indeed he, she introduced themselves. 'I am Abigail Wilson and this is my husband, Daniel Wilson.'

'Ah, the Museum Detectives from England,' said Grimaldi in English, with a welcoming smile.

Abigail and Daniel exchanged looks of surprise.

'As our activities have mainly been in England, we're flattered that you've heard of us,' said Abigail.

'The world of the collectors of antiquities is quite small, and people talk,' said Grimaldi. 'I also saw in the newspapers that you were in Paris, Madame Wilson. I congratulate you on your release from La Santé. It is a hideous place.'

'Thank you,' said Abigail. 'It was an unfortunate event that fortunately proved short-lived. I'm delighted to hear that you speak such good English, because unfortunately, my husband doesn't speak French.'

'That is not a problem. As someone who works with many international clients, English is fine by me.'

'Thank you,' said Daniel. 'That is very much appreciated.'

'How can I help you?' asked Grimaldi.

'The Louvre have hired us to look into the murder of Professor Alphonse Flamand.'

'I thought the police were already investigating it.'

'They are, and we are working closely with Superintendent Maison of the Paris prefecture,' said Abigail. 'We've been advised that you bought some objects from Professor Flamand after he returned from Saqqara.'

Grimaldi shook his head. 'No,' he said.

Abigail and Daniel exchanged puzzled looks at this answer, then Daniel said, 'We have seen the cheque you paid him.'

Grimaldi chuckled. 'And naturally you thought it was to purchase some piece of Egyptian antiquity.'

'That did cross our mind,' said Daniel.

'In fact the payment was for Professor Flamand's professional services. I wanted him to examine some articles I was being offered for sale and I was unsure if they were as genuine as the seller claimed. I also wanted him to value them.'

'Your cheque was for five thousand francs,' said Abigail. 'That seems a lot to pay for a valuation.'

178

'Perhaps, but if the pieces turned out to be fake I would have lost more than that sum.'

'Did you know Professor Flamand well?' asked Abigail.

'Not really,' said Grimaldi. 'It was very much a business acquaintanceship.' He gestured at the items on display in his shop. 'As you will have seen, I handle art from many different periods, specialising in the classical periods. But that is such a long time period and with such a wide range – ancient Egyptian, classical Roman and Greek, Baroque, Rococo, Classicism, the Romantics. Everything from the ancients to the modern era. To be successful and not be duped by unscrupulous people, I need to have the best experts in each particular area to advise me. Professor Flamand was my adviser on artefacts of ancient Egypt.' He gave Abigail what he obviously hoped was a winning smile. 'With the tragic demise of the professor, I wonder if you would care to consider taking over his advisory role, Madame Wilson? Your reputation as an expert on the art and culture of ancient Egypt would be invaluable to me, and to my clientele.'

'That is very kind of you, Monsieur Grimaldi, but I'm afraid my present occupation working with my husband on investigations, such as the one we are currently engaged in at the Louvre, rather precludes that.'

'A great pity,' sighed Grimaldi. 'I would make it worth your while.'

'If we were resident in Paris, I would certainly consider it, but as we are scheduled to return to England once we have finished our work here at the Louvre, I'm afraid my answer must remain the same.'

'Alas,' said Grimaldi. 'And how is your investigation going?

Have you unmasked the person who murdered the professor?'

'Not at the moment,' said Abigail. 'We are still gathering information.'

'Can you think of anyone who would wish harm to the professor?' asked Daniel.

Grimaldi shrugged. 'Everyone makes enemies. Although I cannot think of anyone he might have upset enough to want to kill him.'

'What about his secretary?' asked Daniel.

Grimaldi frowned, puzzled. 'His secretary? Mam'selle Foret?'

'You knew her?'

Grimaldi stiffened at the past tense.

'*Knew*?' he queried.

'Mam'selle Foret was also murdered,' explained Abigail.

Grimaldi looked at them, thunderstruck.

'Murdered?' he echoed, horrified. 'I saw nothing in the newspapers about that.'

'Sadly, I feel that's because she wasn't a celebrity like the professor,' said Abigail.

'What happened? How was she murdered?'

'She was poisoned in her office at the Louvre. Did you know her well?'

Grimaldi shook his head. 'No, I only ever saw her when I went to the Louvre to discuss things with the professor. She was usually in attendance keeping notes of what we said, which I was grateful for because sometimes the professor could be quite forgetful about what we'd agreed.'

'In what way?' asked Daniel.

Grimaldi smiled. 'The price. He often had to be reminded that the price we'd agreed for his advice and valuations was usually lower than what he asked for. Therefore, I was grateful for Mam'selle Foret's efficiency.'

'Well, there's a job opportunity for you there, if you ever fancy it,' said Daniel as they walked away from the gallery.

'I think he was just being flattering,' said Abigail. 'It's one of the tricks that salesmen use.'

'We also got confirmation that the professor was in need of money,' said Daniel. 'I was surprised that Elaine Foret didn't back the professor up when he tried to claim he'd been promised more by Grimaldi.'

'I believe she was honest,' said Abigail. 'She was also protecting the professor from himself, against possible charges of financial chicanery.'

Superintendent Maison knew he was taking advantage of his being at the Louvre. For the first time in a long while he had an opportunity to do some proper detecting work, talking to witnesses at the scene of a crime. It made such a change from being trapped in his office at the prefecture, reading reports and giving orders. He was out in the field carrying out an investigation, talking to real people rather than reading the transcripts of interviews with them.

He sat in the chair behind Elaine Foret's desk and directed his attention to Louise Perrault, who he'd summoned for a second interview. He'd seen how distressed she'd become when he'd told her what he'd heard from Tavenier, about Ruffalo being too shy to talk to her, but waiting in the hope she would say something to him.

'I never knew!' she exclaimed, and her eyes filled with tears. Maison offered her his handkerchief and she took it gratefully to wipe her eyes. 'I thought he was nice.'

Maison nodded sympathetically.

'Do you have a sweetheart?' he asked her.

'I have a sort of boyfriend,' she said. 'But it's off and on.'

'Apart from Armand Ruffalo, have you ever felt that anyone has been watching you when you walked along the corridor, or anywhere else? A man, for example?'

She fell silent and Maison could see that she was exploring her memory. Finally, she said awkwardly, 'I think there used to be a man sometimes in the corridor. A young man, and sometimes I wondered what he was doing and wondered if he was waiting to talk to me. But it wasn't like Monsieur Ruffalo. Monsieur Ruffalo used to smile at me. I don't think this young man ever even looked at me. I was just aware he was there, but at a distance. It was only once or twice.'

'Once or twice?'

She thought about it. 'On two occasions,' she said. 'But I didn't think much of it at the time. There are always people around.'

'Whereabouts did this happen?' asked Maison.

'In the corridor,' said Perrault.

'Where in the corridor?'

'Near to this office.'

'Professor Flamand's secretary's office?'

'Yes.'

'When did this happen?'

'The first time was about a week ago.'

'Before she died?'

'Yes.'

'Have you seen this young man since?'

Perrault thought about it. 'I can't be sure. I thought I saw him a few days ago.'

'When was this?'

Perrault strained hard to remember, then she said, 'I'm pretty sure it was the day after she died. I thought I saw him coming out of her office, but I can't be certain if it was the same young man. I only saw his back. It was early. I'd just arrived for work and I was heading for the secretaries' room when the door of Mam'selle Foret's office opened and this man came out.'

'You didn't see his face?'

'No, just his back. But the way he moved, the way he looked from the back and his clothes made me think he was young.'

'Was he wearing the same clothes as the young man you saw before? The one who was watching you?'

'I don't think so.'

Baron de Barque lived in a mansion in one of the wealthier areas of Paris. The door was opened to Daniel's knock by a butler, who looked at the pair with imperious suspicion. Abigail spoke to him in French, introducing themselves and asking if the baron was available. Abigail then produced the envelope containing the letter of introduction from Sir Brian

Otway and handed it to the butler, asking him to give it to the baron.

The butler took the letter, gestured for them to wait on the doorstep and closed the door.

'Friendly chap,' commented Daniel.

'The servants of the very rich are invariably snooty,' said Abigail.

'Usually echoing their master's attitude,' added Daniel.

The fact that this was not to be the case was revealed to them when the door was opened a few moments later by a tall man elegantly attired in a fashionable and expensive-looking suit who looked at them with an expression of pained remorse on his face. In French he made a profuse apology for his butler.

'I must apologise for Francois. Unfortunately, there have been some callers of late who were frankly undesirable, which has put him on his guard. Please, do come in.'

As they entered the house, the baron added in English, 'And please, we will use English, as Sir Brian adds that you, Mr Wilson, do not speak French.'

'Thank you for that, Your Grace, but I intend to learn,' said Daniel. 'We thank you for seeing us.'

The baron led them through the main corridor, bringing them to a conservatory at the back of the house, which was filled with the most beautiful colourful blooms with classical statuary, Greek and Roman, interspersed with the plants. The butler, Francois, was standing waiting for them, looking suitably chastened.

'Drinks!' said the baron. 'What will you have? I have a crisp white from one of my estates.'

'That would be excellent,' said Abigail.

The baron rapped out an order to Francois, and the butler departed to fetch the drinks. 'Please, make yourselves comfortable,' said the baron, gesturing to the cane chairs with their plush purple and gold cushions. Turning to Abigail, he said with a touch of awe in his voice, 'You were with Flinders Petrie at Hawara, weren't you?'

'I was,' said Abigail.

'I am so envious of you,' enthused the baron. 'I have read about you and your work over the years, and to actually have you as a guest in my house is an honour almost beyond words.'

'You're very kind.' Abigail smiled.

The baron rose to his feet as Francois returned bearing a tray with a bottle of white wine and three glasses.

'We shall take wine in the Egyptian Room!' he declared. 'The Egyptian Room, Francois.'

'Yes, Your Grace,' said the butler, and he stood back to let them pass him, led by the baron, then followed them into the wide corridor.

The baron opened a door and led them into a large room the size of a small exhibition hall. The room was adorned with relics and artefacts from ancient Egypt.

'The Roman and Greek statuary are wonderful, but this is where my heart is – the Egyptian Room.' The baron beamed.

The butler poured the wine into three glasses and handed them round. The baron waited until Abigail had taken a sip, then looked at her enquiringly.

'This is a superb wine, Your Grace,' said Abigail. 'And

served at just the right temperature that brings out its proper bouquet.'

'Excellent!' said the baron. 'I am so gratified. And, please, walk with me as I show my exhibits. The collection has taken me years to assemble, and every piece has stolen my heart a little.'

They strolled along the walkways that criss-crossed the large room as the baron pointed out certain objects. His pride in them shone through in his expressions of delight.

'These came from the pyramid of Senwosret I at Lisht. And those over there from Amenemhet I's pyramid, also at Lisht.' He took them to where other artefacts were neatly and almost ceremoniously displayed. 'These are from the royal tombs at Abydos. Amélineau himself gave them to me because I helped sponsor that particular dig.'

Daniel stood and sipped his wine quietly, listening to the baron and Abigail talking about places and people he'd never heard of with names that were alien to him. Flinders Petrie he knew about, because he'd heard Abigail talk of him, but the archaeologists the baron and Abigail were discussing were predominantly French. As they strolled through the room, admiring the exhibits, Abigail said casually, 'It's a wonderful collection, Your Grace, but I'm surprised to find nothing here from Saqqara.'

'Saqqara?' The Baron frowned.

'Yes. We were told that Professor Flamand had passed on to you some of the artefacts he discovered in his recent expedition there. Last year.'

The baron shook his head. 'No,' he said. 'Is this the purpose of your visit? I read in the newspapers that Flamand had been murdered, which was a great tragedy for French archaeology, and I know of your reputation in England as the Museum Detectives.'

'Yes, we have to admit that,' said Abigail. 'Monsieur Deschamps at the Louvre has asked us to look into the murder of Professor Flamand and during our enquiries your name came up.'

'Mine?' The Baron looked puzzled. 'I can't understand why. I knew of Flamand, but I didn't really know him. Our paths crossed only once at the Louvre, after Flamand returned from Saqqara and we discussed his expedition, but in a very casual way.'

Abigail looked puzzled at this, then said, 'In that case, Your Grace, I can only apologise for raising the matter. You see, we were informed that you paid him a substantial sum of money by cheque on two occasions, which made us wonder if you might have purchased any artefacts from the professor. Some that he brought back from Saqqara?'

'Absolutely not,' said the baron. 'Any artefacts that the professor brought back from Saqqara would belong to the Louvre. To purchase them from anyone other than the Louvre would be receiving stolen property.'

'Perhaps the professor told you he was selling them on behalf of the Louvre?'

The baron shook his head. 'If he had told me so, I would have checked with Georges Deschamps, who is an old friend of mine.'

'So you did not buy any artefacts from the professor?'

'As I have told you, no. Absolutely not.'

'Then the money you paid him . . . ?'

'How do you know I paid him any money?'

'We have seen the professor's bank statements with details of monies he received, including two cheques from you. Unless you did not give him those cheques. Perhaps those cheques were stolen from your cheque books and your signature forged?'

The baron hesitated, unhappy, then said, 'I find it concerning that what was a private transaction should have been made public to you.'

'It was made known to the police.'

'Who then passed that information to you?'

'We are working with the police as a result of the Louvre asking us to investigate the murders there.'

The Baron frowned unhappily. 'This sounds highly irregular, and possibly illegal.'

'When murder is involved the police have a wide range of powers at their disposal. They have already raised this issue with Monsieur Deschamps.'

'And what did he tell them?'

'That it was a matter between you and Professor Flamand.'

'Which it was.'

'Would you care to tell us what the transaction was about?' When she saw he made no attempt to reply, Abigail added, 'If you'd prefer we could leave that to Superintendent Maison to ask you about it.'

The baron shook his head. 'No.' He thought it over, then said, 'The payments were a retainer. I knew the professor was an expert on ancient Egyptian artefacts. I am often offered ancient artefacts. The danger is that some of them are fakes, or not as valuable as the seller claims. I wanted to avail myself of the professor's knowledge. Twice recently I have been offered certain pieces. I was keen to add them to my collection, but I wanted their provenance verified. Both times the professor cautioned me against purchasing them.' He looked at his watch. 'And now, I regret that I have an appointment that I cannot delay. But, if you have any more questions, don't hesitate to contact me.'

'Well, we were thrown out,' observed Daniel as they walked away from the large house.

'But in the nicest possible way,' Abigail pointed out.

'True,' admitted Daniel.

'What did you think of what he told us? Considering it was virtually the same story we heard from Grimaldi, that they both paid Flamand to value pieces they'd been offered.'

'Is that possible?' asked Daniel.

'It's possible,' said Abigail. 'Buying ancient artefacts can be a dubious enterprise; there are so many charlatans and fraudsters operating. However, I would have thought both Grimaldi and the baron would have enough experience to be able to spot anything suspicious.'

'You think they're both lying?'

'I do,' said Abigail.

'So, another avenue for investigation,' said Daniel.

* * *

General DeLaGarde looked up from the papers on his desk as Captain Chevignon arrived in front of him, stood sharply to attention and saluted.

'You have something to report?' asked DeLaGarde.

'The solicitor of Dreyfus, Fernand Labori, has been dealt with.'

'You have confirmation of this?' asked the general.

'I expect confirmation to arrive by post later today or, at the latest, tomorrow,' said Chevignon. 'I despatched a man to Rennes to take care of the situation.'

DeLaGarde nodded. 'I do not need the details at this stage,' he said. 'It is enough to know that Dreyfus's defence will not be able to proceed. Next, we need to neutralise these Wilsons from England.'

'It is in hand,' said Chevignon.

'Good,' said DeLaGarde.

CHAPTER TWENTY-FOUR

While Daniel tucked into a full breakfast the next morning, Abigail browsed through the newspaper inbetween nibbling at her croissant. She was in mid-bite when she saw an item that made her stop.

'My God!' she said, shocked.

'What?' asked Daniel.

'You remember Auguste Perrier telling us about the Dreyfus case?'

Daniel nodded.

'You remember that Auguste said people had been attacked and killed because of it. Well, it seems that Dreyfus's lawyer, Fernand Labori, was shot yesterday while on his way to the court in Rennes.'

'Killed?'

'No, but badly injured. He was shot in the back by an assassin who then got away.' She looked at Daniel, concerned. 'It puts a new perspective on what Superintendent Maison told me about Flamand possibly being killed by the army.'

'In that case, it's lucky for us that we're not involved in the case,' said Daniel.

They were aware of someone arriving at their table, and they looked up to see Edgar Belfont.

'Good morning,' he said. 'I decided to try and catch you before you started on your day.'

'Won't you join us?' asked Abigail, gesturing at an empty chair at a nearby table.

'Thank you,' said Belfont, bringing the chair to the table and sitting down. 'Not for breakfast, though. I've already had mine. But a cup of coffee would be nice.'

Abigail gestured for him to pour himself a cup from the jug.

'I've found out about the club Flamand used to frequent,' he told them. 'It's called Teatro. As the name suggests, it's a favourite haunt of the theatre community: actors, directors, playwrights, set designers, dancers. A pal of mine called Kenneth Walton goes there now and then. He's a ballet dancer, and very good. Unfortunately, he couldn't make a go of it in England because of prejudice. It's all right to be a male ballet dancer there if you're Russian, or from somewhere exotic, but parts of Birmingham are not very friendly in some areas of life. So he came to France and joined a ballet company in Paris, with great success. He's changed his first name to Vladimir, but he's kept Walton because he wants his name known. I think he sees himself returning to Birmingham in triumph, the homecoming hero.'

'As Vladimir Walton?'

Belfont chuckled. 'I believe Birmingham has a substantial Russian expatriate population. Kenneth – or Vladimir – has agreed to accompany you to Teatro. You need someone who's known there if you want to get people to talk to you. I suggest you get together privately before you go to Teatro to tell him what you're looking for. I've told him about the professor being murdered, but only the bare outlines. Would it be all right if I brought him here to meet you? He's quite a flamboyant character, possibly a bit too flamboyant for the embassy.'

'That would be excellent,' said Daniel. 'Thank you, Edgar.'

Captain Chevignon sat in the café outside the national barracks, a cup of coffee on the table beside him as he read the newspaper with ever-increasing despair. The traitor Dreyfus's lawyer, Labori, had only been wounded. His man had failed. Even worse, General DeLaGarde would hold him, Chevignon, responsible for the failure. The man he'd given the job to, Lieutenant Poiret, had been of his choosing. What had happened? How badly had Labori been injured? The newspaper report merely said that he had been shot in the back by an unknown assassin, who'd then made his escape.

There was the sound of a discreet cough and Chevignon looked up to see Lieutenant Poiret himself standing in front of him, his face a picture of abject misery.

'I have failed you, my captain,' Poiret said, and there was no mistaking the emotional agony it caused him to say these words.

The lieutenant was in his mid-twenties. When Poiret had joined the regiment a year before, Chevignon had been impressed by his intelligence, his smart appearance and his ambition to succeed. Chevignon had been pleased to take on the role of mentor to the young man, giving him advice, and also opportunities to develop his talents. The task of disposing of Labori, the Dreyfus solicitor, had been the latest of these assignments, and also the most sensitive.

'Did your gun jam?' asked Chevignon.

'No, sir. I believe the target must have been wearing a bullet-proof protector beneath his clothes.'

In which case, why did you not expect that and shoot him in the head? thought Chevignon, but he did not say this aloud. Poiret was obviously mortified about his failure. Instead, Chevignon said, 'There must be nothing spoken about this.'

'No, sir!' Poiret assured him. 'I would die rather than breathe a word of it.' Then, his face still agonised, he asked, 'Is there anything I can do to make amends, sir? I will do *anything* to recover the situation.'

'No,' said Chevignon. Then, unhappy at the young man's obvious distress, he added, 'You were not to know he may have been wearing protective armour.'

But you should have, he thought angrily. Labori and the whole Dreyfus camp would have been expecting some kind of attack on their persons and taken precautions accordingly. But he did not want Poiret to feel worse than he already did.

'Is there anything else I can do for you, sir? Any other task?'

Chevignon shook his head.

'No,' he said. 'You are dismissed.'

Poiret stood there, hesitating, and Chevignon expected him to say something else, continue with his fulsome apologies. Instead, the young lieutenant saluted, and then marched away.

Chevignon watched him go, then reflected on his perilous position. At the moment the general was in Rennes. He'd gone there to talk to the prosecutor who was conducting the case against Dreyfus, and Chevignon had hoped that while DeLaGarde was there the attack on Labori would have been successful and the general would have returned to Paris full of praise for Chevignon's actions. Instead, the captain did not look forward to his forthcoming meeting with the general when he returned. DeLaGarde was not a man who tolerated failure. It would not be enough to allay the blame on a subordinate like Poiret; it would cut no ice with DeLaGarde. Chevignon could see repercussions looming: a transfer to some hellhole in Africa, possibly even demotion. He needed to do something to rescue his situation. It would be foolish to make another attempt on Labori while he was in hospital and under guard. That left the other persons the general had expressed his concern over, the English couple, the Wilsons.

It would have to be them, Chevignon decided. To dispose of both of them, and immediately, before the general returned from Rennes. And this time he would not leave the mission to an underling. The failure by Poiret, one of his best and trusted men, had shown him that it was likely that none of his people could be trusted to carry out a task successfully. He would have to dispose of the Wilsons himself.

Edgar Belfont had returned to the Olive House with Vladimir Walton in tow to meet with Daniel and Abigail. Abigail looked at the young ballet dancer with affectionate humour. She could see what Belfont had meant when he referred to Walton's flamboyance possibly being too much for the staid atmosphere of the British Embassy. It wasn't just the clothes: the pink jacket adorned with red and gold tassels, nor the long, beautifully decorated silk scarf, which looked as if it had been painted by van Gogh after having taken too much to drink, nor the make-up, lipstick and eyeshadow, possibly left on after a performance; it was his dramatic posturing, arms and legs thrown out in gloriously expansive movements. He'd also decided to keep his hair cut very short in order to wear whichever wigs were needed for a particular role.

'Edgar tells me you're the famous Museum Detectives,' said Walton.

'Known in Britain, perhaps, but not here in France,' said Abigail with a rueful smile.

'I remember you solving a case at the British Museum,' said Walton. 'It was in the papers in England when I was still living there. It made quite a stir, as I recall. A professor stabbed to death. And now here you are investigating another professor stabbed to death, this time at the Louvre.'

'Did you know Professor Flamand well?' asked Abigail.

Walton gave a small chuckle. 'The man was a charlatan. He really wanted to be a stage performer.'

'Yes, I got that impression of him the few times I met him,' said Abigail. 'The clothes. The stances.'

'Exactly. An absolute ham. The problem for him was he had no talent at all. As an actor he'd have been dreadful. Over-acting all over the place. He might have suited opera, where they over-emote all the time, but he couldn't sing. Absolutely awful. He couldn't dance, either. When he tried it looked like a drunken buffalo lurching around. He could have been a variety comedian I suppose, with the dreadful outfits he wore, but he had no sense of humour at all. I think that's why he liked coming to Teatro, because he could rub shoulders with stage people with real talent and believe he was one of them.'

'Do you know who his companions were at the club?'

'*Real* companions?' Walton shrugged. 'Hardly anyone. Most people saw him as an object of ridicule. There were some who cultivated him because they thought he had money, but once they found out he didn't, they usually dropped him. Not that it stopped him turning up and blustering about, doing his best to impress. When would you like to visit the club?'

'As soon as possible,' said Daniel.

'In that case, how about this evening?'

'If that's all right with you, that would be excellent. What time?'

'I leave that up to you,' said Walton. 'I will be there already, chatting and sizing up the people who are there, weighing up who'd be best for you to talk to. How should I introduce you? Are you doing your investigation undercover? If so, who are you posing as?'

'No posing,' said Abigail. 'We think it best to be ourselves: Daniel Wilson and Abigail Wilson, formerly Abigail Fenton, private investigators hired by the Louvre to look into the recent deaths there. That way we can't get caught out as liars and cheats. We are what we are.'

Walton smiled. 'That sounds like a description of the clientele at the Teatro.' He turned to Belfont. 'Are you coming too, Edgar?'

Belfont shook his head. 'I shall deliver Daniel and Abigail

to the club, and then disappear. As I'm a stranger to the Teatro, my presence might divert attention from the purpose of tonight's visit.'

Walton laughed. 'That depends on what your purpose might be.' He looked at his watch and suddenly stood up. 'Apologies, but I have to go. We have a rehearsal this afternoon. We're doing *Romeo and Juliet* and the moron who's dancing Balthasar is desperate for me not to turn up so he can take my place.'

'Which role are you dancing?' asked Abigail.

Walton gave a pout. 'What else but Romeo, of course.' He smiled mischievously. 'The older women in the audience adore me.' He blew them kisses, then swept out, sashaying through the restaurant.

'He does rather put it on,' said Belfont with a rueful grin.

'I've heard it said, "If you've got it, flaunt it."' Abigail smiled. 'I like him.'

Belfont looked enquiringly at Daniel.

'I like him too,' Daniel reassured him. 'He has vivacity and flair.'

'He certainly has that,' said Belfont.

'And, I feel, a good heart,' added Daniel.

'Indeed he has,' said Belfont.

'So, you won't be joining us tonight?' asked Abigail.

'No, but I'll accompany you there. It's in the Pigalle, which isn't the most salubrious area.'

'The Pigalle,' said Abigail. 'That's where the Moulin Rouge is.'

'Yes, but Teatro is in one of the less well-known parts of

the district. I know a bar opposite Teatro, Maxim's. I'll see you safely into the club, then wait for you at Maxim's. They have tables on the pavement so I'll be at one of them.'

'You can join us inside the club, if you like, rather than wait outside,' suggested Abigail. 'Or possibly Vladimir can give us a safe escort afterwards, if you think we need one.'

Belfont shook his head. 'No, I don't want to cramp Vladimir's style in case he meets someone. But I do want to make sure you get back to your hotel unscathed. There are still some thugs who delight in beating up the people who go to places like Teatro.'

CHAPTER TWENTY-FIVE

Emile Chevignon was no longer Captain Chevignon, at least not for this evening. Instead of his usual army uniform, which he wore proudly both on and off duty, he was dressed in plain clothes: a jacket with an overcoat thrown over it. All very nondescript. Nothing showy. Nothing that would be remembered by any potential witnesses. He wore a hat, the brim of which threw shadow over his face. He stood in the shadow of a building opposite the Olive House, the small hotel where he knew the Wilsons were staying. He felt the weight of the revolver in the pocket of his overcoat. He'd checked its mechanisms and the bullets he'd put in the chamber. He didn't want the same error to occur as must have happened during the attempt on Labori. He'd already decided on his course of action: wait for the Wilsons to come out of the Olive House and follow them until they came to an area where there were few people around. Walk up behind them and fire two shots, one into the body of the man, one into the woman. Then empty the rest of the gun into them. That's how his man should have dealt with Labori.

There was a movement in the hotel across the street, then

the two Wilsons appeared. A young man came out of the hotel after them, joined them, then set off along the pavement, the English couple following him. Who was this young man? How long would he be staying with them? Would they hail a cab, or keep walking?

Chevignon set off. The only thing he could do was follow all three until such time as the young man left them. Once the English pair were alone, that's when he'd make his move.

'I thought we'd walk to Teatro, if that's all right with you,' said Belfont. 'I remember reading an article about you, when you talked about preferring to walk the streets of London because that's how you got to really know a city.'

'That's true.' Daniel nodded. 'It helps me get my bearings.'

'The other thing is, Pigalle gets quite congested with cabs in the evening, mainly because of the Moulin Rouge and the other shows that are going on. It's very much the entertainment district.' He smiled. 'Although, not necessarily the kind of entertainments that the church approves of.'

'So you've never been to Teatro yourself?' asked Abigail.

'No,' said Belfont. 'A bit too dramatic for me. I know where it is, of course and I've passed it, but it never tempted me to go in and be part of that theatrical scene.'

Behind them, Emile Chevignon kept a discreet distance as he followed the three. Where were they going? he wondered. They seemed to be heading for the Pigalle district, and at this moment there were still far too many people around for his liking. All he could do was stay with them and see what happened. At the worst, he could just follow them back to their hotel and shoot them when they got to Montmartre. There were so many alleys and side streets in that area that he was sure he could get away and vanish into the warren of cobbled narrow streets without getting caught. But first, he had to make sure they'd parted with the young man, who seemed to be acting as their guide.

He carried on walking, still keeping his discreet distance. Fortunately they seemed to be so engrossed in the conversation they were having with the young man that they never once thought to look behind them, to see if they were being followed.

Finally they stopped outside a length of metal railings that formed a fence. There was a gap in the fence with steps going down to a cellar area. A sign above a window overlooking the cellar area bore the word 'TEATRO'. Chevignon became aware that men of various ages were either coming up steps, or going down them toward a door in the cellar area. It was with a shock that he registered that some of the men were dressed in very feminine fashions, with some even wearing dresses. Others dressed smartly, some even very gentlemanly. With a further shock he realised that some of those dressed elegantly in men's suits were actually women.

It is a place for homosexuals, he realised. But what on earth were the Wilsons doing at a place like this?

As he watched, both Wilsons shook the hand of the young man who'd accompanied them, and then he left them and walked off along the street. The Wilsons, meanwhile, had descended the steps to the cellar area.

Damn them! he cursed silently. He would now have to wait for them to leave the club – because that was obviously what it was – and make their way back to their hotel. He would have to wait to waylay them until then. In the meantime, he decided to explore the area immediately around the club to search for fast ways to escape if he was able to shoot them as they left. That would be preferable to dragging behind them all the way back to Montmartre.

Yes, he decided, that's what he'd do. He'd wait for them to leave, shoot them, then disappear into one of the numerous alleyways that warrened this area.

The first person Daniel and Abigail saw when they entered the club was Vladimir Walton, who hurried towards them.

'I've been keeping an eye open for you,' he said. 'I've already found a couple of men who said they knew Flamand. I'm guessing they meant in the biblical sense, but you'll be able to come to you own conclusion when you talk to them.' He gestured at an empty table nearby over which a coat had been draped. 'I've been keeping this one for you. Sit yourself down while I carry on talking to some people, and when I've found what I think you're looking for I'll introduce you.'

With that he scooped up the coat and draped it around his shoulders, then headed off to join the busy throng.

Daniel and Abigail sat themselves down, and a waiter appeared at their table almost immediately. Daniel suggested wine, and let Abigail choose. She opted for a white. While they waited for it to arrive they studied the crowd in the club. It was a varied mixture: men in women's clothes, women in men's, many of the people dressed conventionally but with their own particular personal adornments. The levels of noise were high in such an enclosed space, all of it excitable chatter in voluble French.

'It reminds me of some of the places we used to get in the East End,' said Daniel. 'The difference was this is legal, whereas those were deemed illegal.'

The wine arrived and Abigail tasted it, declared it fine, and they filled their glasses and clinked them together in a toast.

'What are we drinking to?' asked Daniel.

'To Paris,' said Abigail. 'And our first continental holiday together.'

They sipped at their wine, then Daniel suddenly looked towards the entrance, an expression of surprise on his face.

'My God,' he whispered. 'There's Oscar Wilde.'

Abigail looked at the very tall figure who'd just arrived in the club and stood surveying the assembled crowd.

'He looks ill,' she said.

It was true that Wilde no longer cut the elegant figure he had at the height of his fame. His hair was still long, but straggly and thin. His clothes had the sheen that comes with being worn very often and not being laundered. Suddenly he spotted Daniel and his face broke into a smile.

'I believe he's coming over to us,' said Daniel. Then he looked behind them. 'Unless he's spotted someone else he knows.'

'Mr Wilson.' Wilde smiled, arriving at their table. 'This is a pleasure to meet you again. And in such strange surroundings, I would imagine.'

Daniel got to his feet and shook Wilde's outstretched hand, then gestured to the empty chair at the table. 'Please, won't you join us?'

'Thank you. I will be delighted.'

Wilde sat down, and Daniel said, 'Mr Wilde, this is my wife, Abigail.'

'Mrs Wilson, it is a pleasure to make your acquaintance.'

'May we get you something? Wine? Brandy, perhaps?' asked Abigail.

Wilde shook his head. 'No, thank you. My old friend Robbie Ross has persuaded me to try a teetotal existence for a few months. He thinks it will be beneficial for me.' He paused, then added, 'I have been ill and Robbie is determined to aid me to convalescence.'

'I'm flattered that you should remember me, Mr Wilde,' said Daniel. 'After all, you have met many thousands of people. Hundreds of thousands, I should say, when one considers your trips to America.'

'Many people it is true, but not many who have visited me when I was incarcerated at Wandsworth. You came with Bram Stoker and a police inspector.'

'Inspector Feather,' said Daniel. 'You have a good memory.'

'I have a good memory when it comes to kindnesses because, sadly, they have been so rare for me. I remember you, Mr Wilson, because you were the kindest of the policemen I met.'

'Former policeman,' Daniel corrected him gently. 'I was there in a private capacity.'

'I also remember it because of the generosity of your friend,

Inspector Feather. He promised to make sure I was furnished with reading material, and, even more important, writing materials. I thought it was just an empty promise made to get my co-operation, but I was wrong. Within a week, books and writing material arrived for me.'

'John Feather is an honourable man.'

'When you return to England would you pass on my thanks to him and tell him how much his efforts meant to me?'

'I will indeed.'

'So, what brings you to Paris?' asked Wilde. 'And, in particular, to Teatro?'

'We have been asked to investigate the recent murders at the Louvre.'

Wilde frowned. 'Have there been murders there? How dreadful!'

'They have been reported in the newspapers.'

'I rarely read the newspapers,' said Wilde. 'In the old days I would grab them up, eager to see what the critics thought of my latest creation. But now I no longer write I prefer to spend any reading time with a favourite novel or book of poems.'

'It is a great pity to hear you have forsaken your art,' said Abigail sympathetically. 'It was your great works that set the stage alight just a very short while ago. *The Importance of Being Earnest*, *Lady Windermere's Fan*. So many others.'

'You may see it as a short while ago, but my detractors and creditors deem my work positively prehistoric.'

'But something new from you . . .' said Abigail.

'Would not be put on,' said Wilde sadly. 'Alas, since my

fall, I am considered untouchable.' He sighed ruefully. 'At least, in the literary sense. Not as much in the literal sense, but that is dependent on how attractive they are.' He gave a mischievous smile. 'I do still have standards.'

'It is better to be beautiful than to be good. But it is better to be good than to be ugly,' said Abigail, giving an abbreviated quote from *The Picture of Dorian Gray*.

Wilde's face lit up with pleasure. 'Thank you, Mrs Wilson. You have restored my faith in my work. It does sound clever, does it not?'

'Clever, with a terrible truth to it,' said Abigail.

'Mrs Wilson, I wish you had been writing criticism when I was in my pomp; I would have treasured every word,' said Wilde. Then his manner changed to one of seriousness as he asked, 'These murders you've been asked to investigate at the Louvre – who has been murdered?'

'A Professor Alphonse Flamand and his secretary, a Mam'selle Elaine Foret.'

'Flamand,' mused Wilde. 'I see why you are here at Teatro. I saw him here occasionally. Dreadful man. A vain show-off flaunting himself to try to impress.' He gave a self-deprecating smile as he added, 'Sounds rather like a certain Anglo-Irish playwright of our acquaintance, doesn't it.'

'Oscar.'

They looked up at the tall, rather languid young man who had arrived at their table and was looking at Wilde in a slightly reproving fashion.

'Harold, my dear!' exclaimed Wilde. 'I wondered if you were coming.'

'I have been here for some time,' complained Harold. 'I was expecting you to notice me.'

'And I have,' said Wilde. He turned to Daniel and Abigail with an apologetic smile. 'Forgive me, I have a prior engagement. But it has been a great pleasure to see you again, Mr Wilson, and to meet you, Mrs Wilson. Perhaps we shall meet again while you are in Paris?'

'That would be very nice,' said Abigail. 'Where are you staying?'

'I am intermittently at the Hotel Marsollier, but often I am in transit hither and yon. But a message left here will always find me.' With that he rose, bowed and walked away with Harold. They watched the pair get to the door and leave.

'My God,' said Abigail, shocked. 'He used to be so beautiful, but did you notice he has lost his front teeth?'

'I did,' said Daniel. 'I'm surprised he hasn't had false ones made to replace them.'

They became aware that someone had arrived at their table. They looked up to see Vladimir Walton.

'I saw you talking to Oscar Wilde,' he said, 'so I thought it best to wait rather than interrupt. There's someone here who used to go with Professor Flamand. I thought you might like to meet him. His name's Pierre Verdun, a theatre director. Terribly nice, but very upset over Flamand.'

They got up and began to follow him through the throng.

'Poor Oscar,' said Walton with a heavy sigh. 'He's not well, you know. He comes here to meet handsome young men. You'd be surprised at the number who are flattered to receive his attention, despite the fact that he creates a very poor impression physically. Did you notice his lack of teeth?'

'Yes,' said Abigail. 'We wondered why he doesn't get a plate fitted.'

'Lack of money,' said Walton. 'He depends on friends for handouts and loans.' He shook his head. 'I feel so sorry for him. His downfall has been of tragic proportions. Someone told me that recently he went to Genoa to place some flowers on his late wife's grave. He was deeply upset when he read the inscription on it: "Constance Mary, daughter of Horace Lloyd QC". No mention of Oscar at all, her husband and the father of her two sons. It was as if he'd never even existed. Ah, here's Pierre.'

Pierre Verdun was a short, bald, rotund man sitting alone at a table, lost in thought and nursing what looked like a glass of brandy.

'I'd better warn you, he's liable to suddenly start blubbing when you mention Flamand. He said they were *very* close. In fact, *soulmates* was how he described them. Also, he doesn't speak English.'

'That's all right, I'll do the talking for us,' said Abigail.

'Pierre,' said Walton. The short man looked up, startled out of his reverie. 'These are Mr and Mrs Wilson, the people I told you about who have been commissioned by the Louvre to look into poor Alphonse's murder. Mrs Wilson speaks French.'

Verdun looked up at them, and suddenly began to weep.

'I'm sorry,' he said, taking a large handkerchief from his jacket pocket and wiping his eyes and cheeks, 'but even the mention of his name . . .' And more tears flowed.

'We're so sorry for your loss,' said Abigail, as she and Daniel sat down.

'I'll leave you three together,' whispered Walton, and he departed into the crowd.

'He has been such a good friend,' said Verdun. 'Vladimir. He knows how I suffer.'

'You knew the professor well?'

'Better than anyone else. We were true soulmates.'

'Do you know of anyone who hated him so much to want to kill him?' asked Abigail.

'Yes,' said Verdun. 'His wife, Eloise. She hated him. She made his life a misery with her constant demands for money.'

'Why did Alphonse have money problems?' asked Abigail. 'He received a good salary.'

Verdun hesitated, his lips trembling, then he said in a voice so low that Abigail had to strain to hear, 'He had a weakness.'

'What sort of weakness?'

Again, Verdun hesitated, then mumbled, 'Gambling.'

'Gambling?'

'He was always so sure he would win, but he never did. And the more he lost, the more he gambled to try to win his losses back. It was heartache to watch.'

'You went with him to these gambling places?'

Verdun nodded. 'At first I did because I wanted to see him enjoying himself. But, when it became obvious that it was driving him to despair, I did my best to make him stop. I told him I wouldn't go with him any more in the hope it would make him stop, but it just ended up with him shouting at me. He said I was as bad as his wife, trying to control what he did.'

'Did his wife know about you and him?'

'No. Alphonse was desperate she shouldn't find out.'

'How long had you and Alphonse known each other?'

'For the past six months. As close friends that is. Although I had seen him here before, but it was only about six months ago that we became close.'

'Where did you go to be together?' asked Abigail.

'I have a small flat, not too far from the Louvre.'

'You must miss him terribly,' said Abigail sympathetically.

'I do,' burst out Verdun, and he began crying again. 'Please, find the villain who has done this. I must know who, and why.'

Chevignon stood across the road from Teatro, getting more impatient by the second. How much longer were the English couple going to spend in that infernal place? He looked around. At least there was one blessing: the crowds around the place had virtually disappeared. He supposed most were either inside the club, or had left for the evening.

Suddenly he saw the English couple appear at the gap in the metal railings and step out onto the pavement. There they were! He scanned the area. There was no one else about. This was the moment!

He pulled the revolver from his pocket and walked leisurely across the road towards the pair. No sense in moving quickly – the sound of hurrying footsteps might alarm them. As he neared them, he slowed down. First the man, then the woman. He aimed the pistol, his finger tightening on the trigger.

BANG!

CHAPTER TWENTY-SIX

Daniel and Abigail spun around and looked towards the direction of the shot and saw a man lying on the pavement, while another kneeling on top of him slammed his fist into the fallen man's head. Even from this distance they could hear a crunch of bone on flagstone. Daniel began to run towards the pair. Abigail was on the point of shouting a warning to him to be careful of the gun, when she realised the kneeling man was none other than Edgar Belfont.

'Edgar!' she called as she ran after Daniel.

Daniel and Abigail looked down at the unconscious man as Belfont got to his feet.

'Who is he?' asked Abigail, bewildered.

'No idea,' said Belfont. 'I was just coming out of Maxim's and on my way towards you when I saw this character pointing a gun at you. Luckily, I can be quite quick sometimes. I struck his wrist as he fired and the bullet hit the pavement. Then I kicked him in the knee and he went down. I hit him again.'

'Yes,' said Abigail. 'We heard the thump of his head on the pavement from over there.'

'I couldn't take the chance of him firing again,' said Belfont.

Daniel and Abigail both bent to look at the unconscious man's face.

'Do you recognise him?' asked Belfont.

'No,' said Daniel. He turned to Abigail. 'What about you?'

'No idea,' said Abigail.

'Well, he obviously knows who you are,' said Belfont. 'He was pointing the gun right at you.' He looked down at the unconscious man. 'I suppose this is where we call the police.'

First thing the following morning, Daniel and Abigail made their way to the British Embassy, where they found not just Edgar Belfont, but Sir Brian Otway himself.

'This is appalling,' said Otway, shocked. 'Young Belfont told me what happened, which is why I've come in early. I shall accompany you to the Prefecture of Police. I assume you'll be going there?'

'Yes,' said Abigail. 'We had a note from Superintendent Maison delivered to our hotel inviting us to meet him.'

'And you have no idea who this person is who tried to shoot you?'

'None,' said Daniel. 'And if it hadn't been for Edgar's swift action last night, at least one of us wouldn't be here talking to you today.'

'But why?'

'We can only assume it's to do with the murder of Professor Flamand and his secretary. There's nothing else we're investigating.'

'Who might you have upset with your investigation?'

Daniel and Abigail exchanged a thoughtful look.

'We talked to Leonardo Grimaldi and Baron de Barque about them possibly buying stolen artefacts that the professor brought back from Saqqara. They both denied it, but both were uncomfortable with us raising the issue,' said Daniel.

'Especially the baron, it seemed to me,' said Abigail.

'Do you suspect the baron of being behind this?' asked Otway, obviously very shocked at the suggestion.

'To be honest, we have no idea,' Abigail replied. 'Hopefully the suspect will tell us. It was fortunate that Edgar was there to save us, and to summon the police.'

'It was lucky for us that embassy staff were issued with police whistles in case of a serious incident,' said Belfont.

'Yes.' Otway nodded grimly. 'These can be dangerous times in France with so much political upheaval. You heard about Dreyfus's lawyer being shot in Rennes?'

'Monsieur Labori,' said Abigail. 'Yes.'

'Someone suggested to us that the murder of Flamand might be connected to the Dreyfus case,' said Daniel thoughtfully.

'Oh? Who?'

'An archaeologist called Auguste Perrier.'

Otway looked doubtful. 'I've heard about Perrier. He seems to be a bit of a radical. Possibly communist.'

'But then the possibility was also raised with us by someone else,' said Daniel.

'Oh?' Otway looked at them, surprised. 'Who?'

'Someone who told us something in confidence, and asked us to tell no one else,' said Abigail quickly. 'This person doesn't know who he can trust. He also stressed to us that he did not want us to pass this on to any – as he termed it – people involved in politics.'

'Which I suppose would include me.'

'He specifically mentioned you in that category,' Abigail added awkwardly.

'Well,' said Otway with a sigh, 'I don't know whether to be flattered or offended. But one thing's for sure, we'll have to be careful what we say.'

Superintendent Maison sat behind his desk and glared angrily at Captain Chevignon, who still wore civilian clothes, although they were crumpled and stained from the action of the night before and the captain's night in the cells.

'What were you thinking of?!' demanded Maison angrily.

The superintendent had dismissed the uniformed officers who'd brought Chevignon from the cells to his office in order to have a frank discussion with him, which he thought would be more likely to happen if it was just the two of them. He'd also had the handcuffs removed from Chevignon's wrists. At this moment – at Maison's insistence – Chevignon was just recorded as 'unknown assailant', even though the sergeant on reception who'd been on duty when the captain had called to see Maison before, plus at least some other officers who'd been there also at that time, recognised him.

'I refuse to answer any questions,' said Chevignon flatly. 'This is a military matter. I demand to be returned to the national barracks.'

'Are you insane?' demanded Maison. 'You attempted to murder an English person. A famous English person. We have a witness to this, who overpowered you. A member of the staff of the British Embassy. This is an international incident! Luckily, we have been able to stop it getting into the newspapers, but once they find out about it—'

'Any publicity about this must be stopped,' snapped Chevignon.

'How?' asked Maison. 'The left-wing press will leap upon this with glee. It will be all over their front pages once they get the details.'

'They must be stopped from getting the details.'

'How?' repeated Maison. 'You have committed a serious crime, attempted murder. There will have to be a trial.'

'It must be stopped,' repeated Chevignon doggedly.

'The only person who can intercede on your behalf is your lawyer,' said Maison. He pushed a sheet of paper and a pencil across the desk to Chevignon. 'Give me his name and address and I will contact him.'

'The army lawyer will represent me,' said Chevignon.

Maison pointed to the sheet of paper. 'Write his name down and where he can he contacted.'

Chevignon sat to attention and folded his arms. 'I refuse,' he said.

'In that case you will be appointed a public defender,' said Maison, 'and once that happens this will definitely be made public.'

'No!' barked Chevignon and he leapt to his feet.

'Sit down!' shouted Maison. 'Or I will call in uniformed officers who will manacle you to that chair.'

Reluctantly, Chevignon resumed his seat.

There was a tap at the door, and at the superintendent's call of 'Come in!', it opened and a uniformed sergeant looked in.

'Excuse the interruption, sir, but Monsieur and Madame Wilson are here to see you, along with Sir Brian Otway from the British Embassy and his assistant, Monsieur Belfont.'

'Tell them to wait. I will be with them shortly,' said Maison.

When the sergeant had left and the door closed, the superintendent looked at Chevignon.

'The British ambassador. The Wilsons. It is now an international incident. I cannot conceal your identity from them without putting the good name of the police force in jeopardy. You have one chance: tell me why you tried to kill the Wilsons yesterday. Were you acting under orders? If so, whose?'

Chevignon stood up and held out his hands.

'Handcuff me and return me to my cell,' he said.

'Very well,' said the superintendent. He rose and walked round his desk to where Chevignon stood and put the pair of handcuffs on him. 'Your senior officer is General DeLaGarde, I believe. I will summon him here.'

'There is no need for that,' protested Chevignon. 'You should go and see him at the national barracks if you wish to talk to him.'

'You misunderstand your situation,' said Maison. 'This is a criminal matter, not a military one. The investigation will be done officially, and here at police headquarters, not at the national barracks.' He then called out for the sergeant. Almost immediately the door opened, and Maison ordered, 'Return this man to his cell. When you have done that, bring the Wilsons and the ambassador and his assistant to me.'

CHAPTER TWENTY-SEVEN

Otway had instructed Abigail to leave things to him when they met with the superintendent. 'I am your legal representative and I know how the law works in this country. Please, let me do the talking.'

They now sat in Maison's office, Otway, Daniel and Abigail facing the superintendent across his desk and Edgar Belfont sitting behind them, taking notes.

'I am here as Monsieur and Madame Wilson's legal representative,' announced Otway. 'Have you identified their assailant?'

'Yes,' said Maison. 'He is Captain Emile Chevignon, based at the national army barracks in Paris.'

'Has he said why he carried out this attack?'

'No. He refused to answer any questions, insisting he will only be dealt with by the military.'

'But he must have answered at least one question when he admitted his identity,' pointed out Otway.

Maison hesitated, then said awkwardly, 'He did not voluntarily give his name. In fact, I knew it because I recognised him.'

'From where?' asked Otway.

Before Maison could answer, Abigail said, 'Excuse me for interrupting, Sir Brian, but would it be possible for Daniel and I to talk to the superintendent alone for a moment?'

Otway looked surprised, but then nodded. 'Very well. Although I hope you'll explain the reason later.'

'Thank you,' said Abigail.

Otway and Belfont rose to their feet and left the room. Abigail then told Maison in French what she'd asked the ambassador to do. 'I believe that the man who tried to shoot us yesterday evening, this Captain Chevignon, is the same man you talked about to me, the one who hinted that certain members of the army who were part of the anti-Dreyfus caucus may have been responsible for the murder of Professor Flamand.'

The superintendent hesitated, then reluctantly nodded. 'Yes, it is the same man.'

'The fact that he tried to kill us, who are investigating the murder of Professor Flamand, suggests his mission was to put a stop to our investigation.'

'That is speculation,' said Maison guardedly.

'It is a logical conclusion, *if* the army were responsible for Flamand's death.'

'We don't know that.'

'No, we do not,' agreed Abigail. 'But do you agree this murderous attack on us by Captain Chevignon has just made it more likely?'

'Perhaps,' admitted Maison grudgingly.

'Although we are not stating that in any categorical way,' said Abigail. 'At the moment, it is just a possibility. But we cannot ignore the fact that an attack was made on us, and if it hadn't been for the swift action of Monsieur Belfont we would be dead now. We assume he will be charged with attempted murder?'

Maison stayed silent, studying them, then he said carefully, 'If I had my way, that would be certain. But, with the army involved, there are powerful people that may intervene.'

'The same powerful people who ensured that Captain Dreyfus was sentenced to life imprisonment on Devil's Island and are even now doing their best in Rennes to make sure that sentence continues, in spite of all the evidence showing he was innocent of the charges?' asked Abigail. Before Maison could answer, she added, 'The same powerful people who may have been behind the shooting of Dreyfus's lawyer, Fernand Labori, in Rennes the other day? And, therefore, the attempt to kill us last night?'

Maison fell silent, then he asked, 'What are you suggesting I do?'

'Your job as a policeman. Charge Chevignon with the crime of attempted murder. Ask him about Flamand. Was he involved in that murder? Was he involved in the shooting of Labori? Ask him if he was acting on orders. If so, from whom?'

'It is not that simple, *madame*. Here in France, the army are a powerful force with highly placed political friends. I have no doubt they will attempt to intervene.'

'In that case I suggest you tell Sir Brian Otway all you

know about Captain Chevignon and the Flamand case. He is, after all, our legal representative and will need to have full knowledge of all the facts.'

'And if I don't tell him, you will?' demanded Maison, obviously upset.

'No,' denied Abigail. 'We gave you our word that we would not tell anyone. But I feel the attempt on us changes things. For all we know there could be another attempt, and the next one might be successful. You said before there was no one in the police you could trust, so it would be pointless to ask you to appoint police protection for us. However, Sir Brian Otway could organise protection, using British Embassy security. But, for him to do that, he would need to know why. And that means telling him about Chevignon and Flamand. I do not believe he will pass that information on, unless something happens to us. He has proved himself to be very discreet. But, if we are killed, I would want him to know why. And it's not enough for you to say you would tell him. You, also, may not survive, especially now you've arrested Chevignon.'

Maison studied both of them. Finally, he nodded.

'Very well,' he said. 'You may tell Sir Brian.'

'And his assistant, Mr Belfont,' said Abigail. 'After all, he intervened and saved us from Chevignon. Which makes his life at risk. He deserves to know why.'

Maison sighed. 'Agreed,' he said.

General DeLaGarde read the letter from Superintendent Maison with a sense of increasing rage. Captain Chevignon had been arrested for the attempted murder of two English civilians. Even worse, the superintendent was informing him that Chevignon would be charged with the crime, which would have international implications.

A public trial! How had this come to pass?

He picked up the bell on his desk and rang it. When his aide opened the door, he barked, 'Have my carriage brought round.'

Abigail waited until they were back at the privacy of the embassy before telling Otway why she had requested a private interview with Maison, and what had been its outcome. She told him about the earlier conversation with Maison, when he'd repeated what had occurred between him and Captain Chevignon.

'Let me make sure I've got this clear,' said Otway. 'This Captain Chevignon told Superintendent Maison that the army played a part in the murder of Professor Flamand because he was betraying their secrets to the Dreyfusards.'

'He *hinted* that may have been the case,' Abigail corrected him. 'He did not say that for certain, and he may have been just saying it to interfere with the investigation. The superintendent has since told us that Chevignon asked him to stop us investigating the Flamand murder. Maison told him he had no power to do that as we'd been hired by the Louvre.'

'And yesterday evening this same Chevignon attempted to shoot you.'

'Yes.'

'Which indicates that the Dreyfus case is at the heart of the motive for the killing of Professor Flamand.'

'Possibly,' said Abigail. 'Despite us being shot at, Daniel and I feel there are other motives just as valid.'

She turned to Daniel, who took over. 'There's the business of the artefacts from Saqqara he is alleged to have sold privately. Possibly to Baron de Barque or Leonardo Grimaldi. Both were distinctively uncomfortable when we asked them about that. They both knew that if it was true and was revealed, they would be exposed as having done something illegal. A motive for making sure that Flamand and his secretary were silenced.

'I also feel the deaths may be related to the murder of Paul LeMarc, the Louvre's head of security. He was investigating Flamand's finances. It's possible Flamand was behind his murder. Perhaps Flamand was killed in revenge, and Elaine Foret because she knew who the murderer was.'

'What about the murder of the steward at the Louvre, this Armand Ruffalo?' asked Belfont.

'I have a hunch it's a smokescreen to try and put us off the scent,' said Daniel. 'I feel he just happened to be there; anyone else being killed at the Louvre would have had the same effect.'

'It still looks to me as if this Dreyfus business with the army is the most likely,' said Otway thoughtfully. 'Which raises difficult questions about what happens. The French Army is a virtual law unto itself, as the Dreyfus case has shown. The very fact that his retrial is taking place in Rennes in the form of a court martial rather than in a criminal court shows that.'

He gave an unhappy sigh. 'It will be interesting to see how Superintendent Maison handles the case when the army begin to exert pressure on him.'

'You think this Captain Chevignon will get off when he appears in court charged with our attempted murder?' asked Daniel.

'*If* he appears in court,' said Otway ruefully.

General DeLaGarde strode into Superintendent Maison's office and stood stiffly to attention before his desk, glaring down at Maison with a look of barely concealed contempt, which turned to anger as he realised that Maison was making no attempt to stand up but instead remained sitting.

'I am General DeLaGarde,' he snapped.

'Yes,' said Maison. 'We have met previously.' He gestured to the chair on the other side of his desk. 'Take a seat.'

The fact that the statement was not prefaced with a 'Please' riled the general even more.

'I am a general in the French Army,' he barked. 'I expect to being treated with the respect my rank deserves.'

'I am a superintendent in the French police force and also expect to be treated with the respect my rank deserves,' retorted Maison, and again he gestured at the chair on the other side of his desk.

General DeLaGarde hesitated momentarily, then reluctantly took the seat.

'You say we met previously,' he said. 'Where and in what circumstances?'

'At a meeting of senior officials of standing to discuss the way to proceed in the light of the Dreyfus affair.'

'Ah yes,' said DeLaGarde. 'Captain Chevignon was also at that meeting.'

'He was,' confirmed Maison.

'Then you are one of us.'

'At that time I was sympathetic to your opinions. Lately, I have begun to question them, particularly in view of the attempted murder by Chevignon of the English couple, Monsieur and Madame Wilson, yesterday.'

'Mistaken identity,' said DeLaGarde.

'No,' said Maison. 'He was identified as the assassin by one of the ambassadorial staff at the British Embassy who overpowered and disarmed him during the attack. He was then brought here to the prefecture. I, myself, identified him as Captain Emile Chevignon. He does not deny he made the attempt on their lives. Therefore, he must stand trial.'

DeLaGarde glared at the superintendent.

'You have joined the ranks of the radicals. The communists and those who oppose us,' he snarled accusingly.

'I am a policeman sworn to uphold justice,' responded Maison. 'This is not politics; it is a straightforward criminal charge of attempted murder. In order to help me decide what course to take, I wish to know the motivation behind the attack. I have asked Captain Chevignon, but he refuses to answer. I am therefore asking you, as his senior officer, that same question.'

The general sat in stony silence for a moment, then he said, 'This is a military matter. I insist you hand Captain Chevignon to me at once.'

'No,' said Maison. 'This has become a criminal matter. Because of the high profiles of the persons involved, the Wilsons, who are well-known in their own country, and Sir Brian Otway, the British ambassador to France and his assistant, Monsieur Edgar Belfont – who was the one who prevented the killing and overpowered Chevignon – this cannot be buried. Unless I am given a good reason why it should not take place, Captain Chevignon will stand trial for attempted murder.'

DeLaGarde rose abruptly to is feet. 'You have not heard the last of this,' he said warningly.

With that, he left.

CHAPTER TWENTY-EIGHT

The next morning, after breakfast, Daniel accompanied Abigail in going out to buy a newspaper.

'It's part of my learning to speak French,' he said. 'I've got a few basic phrases I can try out, such as remarking on the weather, and also I'm learning about the French money: francs and centimes.'

'That's very commendable,' said Abigail.

They stopped at a newsvendor's stall and Daniel examined the front pages of the papers on display before he reached for a copy of *Le Temps*. Abigail took a copy of a paper called *Les Voix*, which she handed to him.

'Here,' she said. 'Get this one as well.'

'I thought you preferred *Le Temps*,' said Daniel.

'I do,' said Abigail, 'but this one has got an interesting story that may not be in *Le Temps*.'

They took the newspapers back to their hotel, where Daniel did his best to decipher what he could of the front page of *Le Temps*, while Abigail read *Les Voix*.

'There doesn't seem to be anything in here about us being shot at,' said Daniel.

'You can read it?' said Abigail, surprised. 'I'm impressed.'

'Not really, I was just looking for certain key names: ours, and Captain Chevignon's. None of them seem to be here.'

'I expect they've kept a lid on it at the moment,' said Abigail. 'It's politically sensitive.'

'What's the story about that you said looked interesting?' asked Daniel.

'*Les Voix* has the story about the latest murder at the Louvre,' Abigail told him. 'The steward who was stabbed. According to them there's a murderous lunatic at large at the Louvre. In fact that's the banner headline.' She read the article aloud. '"Our reporter has spoken to someone with inside knowledge of the Louvre who told him that it was well-known that there was someone with homicidal tendencies at work at the museum. Previous to the murder of Armand Ruffalo, three people employed at the Louvre have been murdered: Professor Alphonse Flamand, Elaine Foret, who was the professor's secretary, and the museum's head of security, Paul LeMarc. Professor Flamand was stabbed to death, Mam'selle Foret was poisoned, Monsieur LeMarc was brutally beaten. Now Armand Ruffalo has been stabbed to death. Is the cycle starting all over again? Are we to expect a poisoning and a brutal, murderous attack to follow?"'

'The timing of this is interesting,' said Daniel. 'Just after Captain Chevignon has been arrested, and so implicating the army.'

'You think the army arranged for this to appear?' asked Abigail.

'It would make sense,' said Daniel.

'In that case, I'm surprised they used *Les Voix* to put the story out. *Les Voix* is a left-wing paper, not one that favours the army or the establishment. I would have expected it to appear in one of the right-wing papers.'

'No, this is cleverer,' said Daniel. 'No one would think this has been reported to clear the name of the army. Also, at this moment, as far as I'm aware, none of the papers have got the story about the shooting and the arrest of Chevignon.'

'You're right,' said Abigail thoughtfully. 'But the left-wing press would be suspicious of any story being given to them by the army, or anyone associated with it.'

'In which case I expect this was fed to this paper through an intermediary. Someone posing as a radical. But whoever did it, it's someone with an inside connection to the Louvre. The deaths of the professor and his secretary were both featured in the newspapers, so they were common knowledge. But the murder of Paul LeMarc would only have been known to a few people at the Louvre and the police.'

'Could someone inside the police have passed the story to the newspaper?'

'They could have, but LeMarc was killed some time ago. I think we need to go and see Superintendent Maison.'

When Daniel and Abigail were ushered into Superintendent Maison's office at the police prefecture, both of them thought the superintendent looked more downcast than usual. Abigail showed him the story in *Les Voix* about the lunatic on the loose in the Louvre.

'Yes, I've seen it,' grunted Maison.

'We think it comes at a very timely moment for the army and Captain Chevignon,' said Abigail.

'Yes, I would have had the same thought,' said Maison, 'if I hadn't been for this, which was delivered to me by special messenger earlier.'

He passed an official-looking letter across the desk to them. Abigail picked it up.

'It's from the Minister for Defence,' she told Daniel.

'From the government?' asked Daniel.

'Just as in our country, there's only one Minister for Defence. Here in France, it's a very important post in the government. Possibly the most important after that of the President.'

'What's the minister say?'

'"To Superintendent Maison. Upon receipt of this letter you will hand Captain Chevignon into the custody of the army, in the person of General DeLaGarde at the national barracks. From now on this case will be the responsibility of the army. There is to be no mention of it in any way to any other persons, especially to any journalists or persons of the press. Failure to comply will lead to you being charged with treason."'

Abigail passed the letter back to Maison, who took it and put it in his desk drawer.

'I'm sorry,' she said.

'As am I,' the superintendent said with deep bitterness. 'A crime has been committed – a grave crime, which would have been murder if Chevignon had succeeded – and I am ordered to let the culprit go free.'

'What will happen to Chevignon?' asked Abigail.

'I believe he will be admitted to a military hospital, where he will receive treatment for a supposed nervous breakdown.' He sighed. 'You see now why I do not believe the army were behind this story in the newspaper of the lunatic at large. They had no need to do that, when they have a government minister ready to do their bidding.'

'Can the army have this much power?' asked Abigail. 'To get a government minister to intervene in this way?'

'DeLaGarde is a general, the second highest rank in the military,' said Maison. 'Only a field marshal comes higher. People at that level have powerful political friends.'

'So what do we do?' asked Abigail. 'What do we tell the Louvre about the case?'

Daniel weighed up Abigail's translation of her conversation with Maison. 'We could be honest with them. Tell them we believe the army was behind Flamand's murder, but the government have stepped in to hush it up.'

'No, we can't do that,' said Abigail. 'If we tell anyone about it, the superintendent will be charged with treason.'

She translated this for Maison's benefit, and he nodded sadly. 'That is true.'

'Then we do have a problem,' said Daniel. 'If the army were behind Flamand's murder then the attack on us yesterday was intended to stop our investigation. We know they are ruthless in their operations. I suspect that Dreyfus's lawyer, Labori, was also shot by them. And they have been ruthless in framing Dreyfus and stopping all efforts to prove he's innocent. The fact that Chevignon has been released and won't be charged shows how well protected they are. In short, summing up, the fact that the attack on us yesterday failed won't stop them trying it again. So, are we prepared to die for this investigation, knowing that if we do the people who kill us will get away with it?'

'When you put it like that, the answer has to be no. But if we pull out, what do we tell Georges Deschamps at the Louvre?'

'We tell him about Captain Chevignon and the army, but without mentioning the superintendent. We also tell him the government have stepped in to stop our investigation. I'm pretty sure he won't cause a fuss over it; the Louvre depends on the government for its finance.'

'So it's a failure,' sighed Abigail.

She translated what Daniel had said to Maison, who looked at them both thoughtfully. Then he said, 'There is always the possibility that the army were not behind the killing of Flamand. That the real murderer is someone else.' He tapped the newspaper. 'Perhaps it is this lunatic!'

'You surely don't believe that!' said Abigail.

'Actually,' said Daniel thoughtfully after Abigail had translated what the superintendent had said for his benefit, 'there may be something there.'

'A lunatic?' said Abigail in disbelief.

'No, but this piece mentions the murder of Paul LeMarc. As I said to you earlier, the murder of Paul LeMarc would really only have been known to a few people at the Louvre.'

Abigail translated this for the superintendent, who nodded. 'That is a good thought. I shall send for the person who wrote the story, this Julien Amity, to ask him who gave him his information.'

'He might refuse to tell you,' said Abigail. 'In England, journalists insist on protecting their sources.'

'They use the same excuse here,' grumbled the superintendent. 'It is a ruse to cover the fact mostly they make things up and tell lies to sell their story.'

'Can you ask the superintendent about the murder of Paul LeMarc?' Daniel asked Abigail. 'Did anything ever happen about it? Was there a suspicion about who'd done it? Tell him I'm asking because it's mentioned in the paper, which makes me suspicious about why, and who.'

Abigail repeated Daniel's request to the superintendent, who shook his head.

'Sadly, it remains unsolved. I remember the case because Georges Deschamps at the Louvre was greatly upset over it and, during the first few weeks after it happened, kept calling in to see if there was any news on the killer.'

'And there was none?'

'No. That happens occasionally. Someone dies and there is no obvious reason. Possibly a mugging that went wrong, the attacker running off before he could rob the body because he was disturbed.'

'Ask him if he talked to people who knew LeMarc in case there was someone LeMarc had disagreements with,' said Daniel.

Abigail did, and Maison answered, 'Of course. My inspectors talked to his wife, Mirielle. She said LeMarc had no enemies. Everyone liked him. She could think of no one who would want to harm him.'

At Daniel's prompting, Abigail asked the Superintendent

if he had an address for Madame LeMarc. 'We could always ask at the Louvre, but if you've got one that will be quicker.'

'What do you hope to learn?' asked Maison.

'We don't know,' said Abigail. 'The thing is, as time has elapsed since he was killed, after thinking about it she may have had further thoughts.'

'If she had, she would have come to us with them,' countered Maison.

'True,' said Abigail. 'But, please, humour us.'

Maison grumbled under his breath, but sorted through an old file, from which he copied down an address and gave it to them.

'Thank you. We may not do anything with it because we still have the threat of the army hanging over us. We've realised that as long as we are in Paris we are at risk. The only way we can be sure of being safe is to return to England.'

'I understand.' The superintendent nodded. 'But, for me, that would be a great pity. It has been a great pleasure working with you. And there is still the possibility that the murderer may *not* be from the army, but for some altogether different reason. And, as a policeman, I hate the idea that someone may deliberately murder someone and get away with it.'

'So do we, but that would have been the case if Chevignon had shot us.'

'True,' admitted Maison sadly. But then he brightened up. 'There is another possibility, if the murder of Flamand is not connected to the army.'

'*If*,' said Abigail pointedly.

'Hear me out,' pleaded Maison. 'I have a suggestion. I can

234

go to General DeLaGarde and tell him I have ordered you to cease investigating the murder of Professor Flamand. I will also tell him that the attempted shooting of you by Captain Chevignon has influenced you to agree to this. I will tell him there must be no further attempts on you by the army, that if there are the British ambassador will be involved, which means the British government. I'm sure that means they will leave you alone, and you could continue with the investigation surreptitiously.'

'No,' said Abigail. 'That is ridiculous. You may tell the army that we are no longer investigating the murders at the Louvre, but as soon as we return to the Louvre and start asking questions they'll know it's a lie. And we can't investigate the murders at the Louvre without asking questions there.'

The superintendent gave a sly smile. 'But you can if Monsieur Deschamps agrees with my suggestion.'

'What suggestion is that?'

'You, Madame Wilson, are a noted and internationally celebrated Egyptologist. I am sure, as part of this ruse, I can get him to arrange a lecture by you at the Louvre on – say – the treasures of ancient Egypt in their collection. Or perhaps on the expedition that I believe you led last year, a rare honour for a woman.'

'The Sun Temple of Niuserre at Abusir,' said Abigail.

'Yes. This will mean you making frequent visits to the Louvre to examine their collection and make notes for your lecture.' His smile broadened. 'What do you say? We can arrange for this lecture to take place, say, a week hence, to allow for it to be publicised. If you haven't uncovered the identity of the murderer in that time, then we shall say between us that sadly the case is unsolved. You will return to England, and I will continue to keep the file in a drawer, which every now and then I will look at.'

Abigail weighed this suggestion up, then told Daniel what the superintendent was suggesting. Daniel frowned thoughtfully.

'Does he think he can persuade the army to back off, and get Monsieur Deschamps's agreement for this lecture?' Daniel asked.

'He seems confident enough,' said Abigail.

'What do *you* say?' asked Daniel. 'It all depends on you agreeing to do this lecture. And your life is just as much at risk if the army don't believe in the cover story.'

'I'm prepared to give it a try,' said Abigail. 'If it isn't the army who were responsible, I hate the idea of the murderer going free. And if it *is* the army, we know that's a dead end.'

Daniel nodded, then reached his hand across the desk towards the superintendent. 'Tell him we agree, and this is me shaking hands on it,' he said.

Abigail translated his words, and the superintendent shook his hand, then did the same with Abigail. '*Bon!*' he said.

'He said . . .' began Abigail.

'Yes, he said "good",' said Daniel. 'Bit by bit, I'm picking up the language. Slowly, but surely.'

'I will let you know how I get on with General DeLaGarde and Georges Deschamps,' said Maison.

'*Merci beaucoup.*' Daniel smiled as they rose to their feet '*Au revoir pour le temps.*'

They were about to make for the door when Abigail stopped.

'By the way, we think we've found out why the professor was in need of money, and the reasons for all those withdrawals of cash from his bank account,' she said. 'He gambled heavily, and he lost.'

Maison thought this over, then asked, 'Where did you get this information?'

'From a lover of his.'

'A woman?'

'A man.'

Maison looked at them in surprise, then he said, 'A man?'

'Yes,' said Abigail. 'Didn't you know?'

'We did not look into that side of his life.'

Abigail was tempted to say, *Perhaps you should have*. Instead, she said, 'We haven't mentioned this to Madame Flamand. We don't feel it will help the situation.'

'Who have you mentioned it to?' asked Maison.

'Sir Brian Otway. Once we'd got our suspicion about the professor's sexual proclivities, we needed Sir Brian's help in tracking down the kind of places where he might have met his like minded companions.'

'And you found it?'

'A club called Teatro. That was we were last night. It was as we left it that Chevignon took a shot at us.'

'Could Flamand's death have had anything to do with his sexual activities?'

'We don't think so,' said Abigail. 'But it could be connected to his gambling, especially if he was in debt. People who run

237

gambling clubs can be very dangerous when they are owed money.'

'Do you know which gambling clubs he frequented?' asked Maison.

'No,' said Abigail. 'We thought you and your people might have more knowledge about that sort of thing than we could discover.'

Maison made a note on a pad. 'I shall talk to the inspectors who keep a watch on the gambling clubs, ask them to find out which ones Professor Flamand used. Once I know that, I shall pass it on to you. And once I've spoken to this Julien Amity about this article of his, I will likewise be in touch with you.' He smiled and said in English, 'Thank you.'

CHAPTER TWENTY-NINE

Afterwards, as they left the prefecture, Abigail asked, 'What do you think of the superintendent's suggestion?'

'It could work, if he can get the army to agree to leave us alone.'

'You believe the army may not necessarily be connected to the murders at the Louvre, don't you?' asked Abigail. 'And it's not some lunatic on the loose?'

'The deaths of Professor Flamand and Elaine Foret are connected with one another. And, I suspect, the murder of Paul LeMarc because he was investigating the professor's finances,' said Daniel. 'The murder of Armand Ruffalo *is* also connected because he worked at the Louvre and *someone* who is said to have inside information at the Louvre claims a lunatic is at large. Thinking about it, this lunatic story sounds to me like a deliberate diversion tactic, by someone who does have inside knowledge of the murders, confirmed by the fact that they mentioned Paul LeMarc.'

'You think that the person who gave that story to the newspaper reporter, this Julien Amity, could be the murderer?'

'I do,' said Daniel. 'Or they're in conspiracy with the murderer.'

'Just because of the mention of Paul LeMarc's murder?'

'It's the only one that isn't in the public domain.'

Abigail nodded thoughtfully. 'I suppose all we can do is wait and see if Superintendent Maison gets the name of the so-called inside informant from this Julien Amity.'

'And if he doesn't?'

'Then we talk to Amity ourselves.'

'But if he's not going to disclose the name to the police, why would he give it to us?'

'We might be able to offer him an attractive proposition,' said Abigail.

'A bribe?'

'Possibly. Along with an exclusive about the arrest of the murderer.'

'It's certainly worth trying,' said Daniel.

'How sure are you this informant is linked to the murders?'

'It's a gut feeling,' said Daniel. 'It makes more sense than some lunatic roaming around the Louvre bumping people off.'

'So what do we do in the meantime?'

'Carry on looking into the murders of Professor Flamand, Elaine Foret and Paul LeMarc. And I suggest we talk to Madame LeMarc next, as that's the one we've had nothing to do with so far.'

General DeLaGarde looked up from his desk at Superintendent Maison as the policeman entered his office. There was no doubt about it, the general wore a smug smirk on his face.

'I assume you received the minister's instructions as Captain Chevignon is now here, in our care,' he said, his voice full of contempt. 'Are you here to apologise for your foolishness in thinking you could defeat the military?' He gestured at the chair opposite him. 'You may sit.'

'I have no intention of sitting,' snapped Maison. 'I have a message to impart and then I shall leave. Your actions have shown me that you harbour the desire to eliminate the Wilsons. You failed with Captain Chevignon. I expect you to try again.' He stepped forward and fixed the general with a steely and angry gaze. 'You will not make any further attempts on them. As the minister has instructed, the Wilsons will not be investigating the Flamand murder further.'

'Good,' said DeLaGarde, his lips curling in a sneer of derision.

Maison held up his hand to call the general to silence.

'However, as I say, I believe you or one of your minions will make further attempts on their lives. This is to inform you that I have seen the telegram that came to the British ambassador from none other than the British queen herself, Victoria, in which she expresses her concern for the safety of Madame Wilson. I am told they have a personal friendship. Her Majesty asked the ambassador to raise the matter with the President of France. So far he has held off from doing that. But if the Wilsons are attacked again, Queen Victoria and her government will take decisive action with the President, which could bring the French government down. One thing for sure, it will end the career of the minister of defence and the army will be left defenceless. And certainly, if it is found the army are involved in any further attempts on the Wilsons, not only will the officers involved be tried and executed, but so will their superior officers who did not prevent it. Your head will roll, General. If there are any further attacks on the Wilsons, you will be arrested on a charge of conspiracy to murder, and with the greatest publicity as you are taken to the prefecture in handcuffs.' He looked sternly at the general. 'You and the army have been warned. My men stand ready to move in at a moment's notice. And if you try to leave the country, you will be stopped.' He made a slight bow. 'I wish you good day, but I strongly advise you to heed my words.'

With that, he turned on his heel and left, leaving General DeLaGarde staring dumb-struck after him.

Abigail and Daniel knocked on the door of the terraced house they'd been given as Madame LeMarc's address. They waited a while. When there was no answer they knocked again, louder this time. Their knocking resulted in the neighbouring door opening and a middle-aged man looking out at them. In French, he told them, 'She's not there. Nor is that gigolo of hers, if you're looking for him. They've gone away.' He laughed derisively. 'Spending the money that bitch made from poor Paul's death insurance.'

'Her gigolo?' asked Abigail.

'Luigi, his name is,' said the man sourly. 'Got the build of a boxer. In his twenties. Disgusting, it is. There she is, in her forties, taking up with the likes of him. I'm surprised the police didn't look into it after Paul died.'

Abigail put on a look of shock.

'Died?' she repeated. 'Did you say Paul is dead?'

'Yes, didn't you know? He was battered to death in the street.'

'No.' She looked at him enquiringly. 'Do you think there was something suspicious about his death, involving this Luigi?'

He gave another derisive laugh. 'Suspicious? A married woman in her forties carrying on with a man like that, and then Paul dies, battered to death.'

'Were Madame LeMarc and this Luigi an item before Paul was killed?'

The man nodded. 'Three months before he died. He used to come round to the house when Paul was at work. It was so blatant. I told Paul, you'd better watch out, they mean you harm. But he just laughed. "Mirielle wants some younger company now and then," he said. "There's nothing in it."' He shook his head. 'There's no fool like an old fool.'

'Did you tell the police about this?'

'No. I'm not getting involved with anything to do with the police. Especially with that Luigi. A right brute he is. If he'd thought I'd said anything to the police, it would have been me next. I'm only talking to you now because they're away and they might not be coming back. Good riddance if they don't come back, say I.'

'Do you know where they've gone?'

'No idea. I didn't ask. I just saw them leave carrying suitcases and bags.'

'But their furniture's still at the house.'

'It's not their furniture,' said the man. 'They rented the house furnished. Paul was planning to bring in their own furniture when he could afford it.'

'Do you know the name of the person who owns the house?' asked Abigail. 'The landlord?'

The man looked at her suspiciously. 'What are you asking all these questions for?'

'I'm an old friend of Paul's,' lied Abigail. 'Actually, a second cousin. I haven't seen Paul for some years and as we were in Paris, I thought I'd see how he was doing.' She shook her head sadly. 'I can't get over the fact he's dead. No one let us know.'

'Well, she wouldn't,' said the man. 'As to the landlord, it's the same people who own all the houses on this side of the street. Clutonnard. Their office is round the corner in rue Saint-Antoine. You can't miss it. It's got a green shop front with their name over the window.' Then he paused before he went back indoors, and told them, 'Don't tell anyone what I told you, or I'll deny it. I don't want any trouble. It's just that it got to me when Paul died and I've been thinking about it ever since. That bitch and him.'

'You think they did it? Killed him?'

'Who else?' said the man, and he went indoors.

As they walked away from the house, Abigail filled Daniel in on what the man had told her.

'A pity the police didn't talk to the neighbour at the time,' commented Daniel.

'From what he said, I doubt if he would have mentioned anything about Madame LeMarc and this Luigi,' said Abigail. 'He was quite clear he didn't want to get involved with the police. What do you think?'

'I think it puts a whole different perspective on his death.

244

I've been thinking that the death of Paul LeMarc was connected to the murders of Flamand and Elaine Foret. Now it could be totally different, a wife and a lover who want to dispose of a husband.' Then he frowned. 'However, that could be a coincidence. For all we know they had nothing to do with it, it still could be connected to Flamand's murder. I think we have to keep both possibilities in the frame and dig into both.'

'It will be easier for the police to dig into Madame LeMarc and Luigi,' pointed out Abigail. 'For one thing, we don't know where they are. They could be out of the country.'

'Yes, that's a good point,' said Daniel. 'We'll tell the superintendent about it and let him chase them up. We'll carry on with the possibility that Paul LeMarc was murdered because he was looking into Flamand's finances.'

Superintendent Maison arrived back at the prefecture, where the duty sergeant at reception told him, 'The men have returned, sir. They have the man in custody.'

Maison looked at him, uncomprehending. 'They have who in custody?'

'The man you sent them to bring in. The reporter, Julien Amity.'

I'd forgotten about him in my anger at General DeLaGarde, thought Maison. Aloud, he said, 'Good. Give me a few moments then have him brought to my office.'

With that he strode to his office.

Will my visit to the national barracks work? he wondered. *Will DeLaGarde keep his hounds in check?*

If not, and there was another attack on the Wilsons, he'd

ensure the general would learn this was no bluff on Maison's part. He'd have him in a prison cell faster than anything that had ever happened to the general before.

He hung up his overcoat and settled himself behind his desk, and almost immediately the door of his office opened and two policemen ushered in a man in his early thirties. He was dressed casually in a jacket and trousers of a coarse material, and wearing a red kerchief tied round his neck, which was seen as the uniform of a left-wing agitator.

'Julien Amity,' announced one of the officers.

Maison nodded and gestured for them to stay by the door, ready to move in if Amity decided to act rough. He gestured for Amity to sit opposite him.

'I am Superintendent Maison,' he said. 'I have asked you to come in because of the article you wrote in *Les Voix* claiming there is a murderous lunatic at large in the Louvre.'

'You did not ask me to come in,' snapped Amity. 'Your men hauled me out of the newspaper offices and bundled me roughly into a police carriage. It was police brutality.'

Maison looked inquisitively at the uniformed officers.

'He refused to come with us, sir,' said one. 'He held on to a heavy desk. We had no alternative but to take hold of him and take him out to the carriage.'

'This outrage was witnessed by my colleagues,' said Amity. 'I shall call them as witnesses when I bring a court action against the police.'

Maison regarded him coolly, unmoved by this threat. He asked, 'Where did you get your information from? About the lunatic in the Louvre.'

'I refuse to answer,' said Amity. 'A newspaper man protects his sources. Anyway, the information in my article is already known to the public, so you have no grounds for keeping me here.'

'This particular source seems to know more than is available to the general public. The murder of Monsieur LeMarc, for example. That was not generally known to the public.'

'So?' said Amity.

'So, that suggests to me that your source knows more than the general public about that particular death.'

'So?' repeated Amity, his tone challenging.

'So, this person could, in fact, have been involved in the murder of Paul LeMarc,' said Maison. 'In which case, by concealing his identity you are an accomplice to the murder.'

'That is nonsense!' snorted Amity derisively.

'We will see what the court decides when you are charged as an accessory after the fact to Monsieur LeMarc's murder.'

'Wait!' burst out Amity. 'Are you planning to keep me here?'

'For the moment,' said Maison. 'If you refuse to co-operate I will have you transferred to a prison on remand while you await trial.'

'Excellent!' exclaimed Amity joyfully, a broad grin on his face.

Yes, thought Maison ruefully, *this is what all the radicals and communists want. To be locked up and made a martyr, bringing them notoriety and fame.*

'Take him away and lock him up,' Maison ordered the uniformed officers.

247

'I demand a solicitor!' announced Amity.

Maison pushed a sheet of paper across the desk to him. 'Write down your solicitor's name and address,' he said.

'No,' said Amity, sitting up straight and folding his arms. 'First, I want the editor of *Les Voix* here so I can talk to him. He will arrange a solicitor for me.'

'Very well,' said Maison. 'I will pass on your message to him. What is your editor's name?'

'Anton Loussier,' said Amity.

Maison made a note of the name on a pad, then nodded to the officers. 'Take him away.'

CHAPTER THIRTY

As Daniel and Abigail walked through the main entrance of the Louvre, Daniel looked doubtful.

'I'm not sure if we should be doing this,' he said. 'This will be our fourth visit to the Louvre as tourists, as opposed to calling to continue our investigation.'

'We have spent hardly any time here just looking at the museum's treasures,' countered Abigail. 'These are the wonders of the world, and when will we get back to Paris again?'

'I know,' said Daniel, 'but we have a commission from the Louvre to find out who murdered these people.'

'And we are doing that, and doing it properly,' insisted Abigail. 'But there is one more exhibit here that you just have to see. This is special.'

'You've shown me the special pieces,' said Daniel. 'The Leonardo da Vincis, the statue of that goddess.'

'The *Winged Victory of Samothrace*,' said Abigail. 'But there is one piece you cannot come to Paris and not see: the *Venus de Milo*.'

'We can see it after we've finished with the case,' argued Daniel.

'No, because we don't know what's going to happen. We were both nearly shot dead the other night. I've been arrested and put in a condemned cell, with the threat of the guillotine hanging over me.'

'All of which are unlikely to happen to us again,' said Daniel.

'Any of them are very likely to happen again,' insisted Abigail. 'And if it does, I want to know that we got the chance for me to show you the *Venus de Milo*.'

'It's that important to you?' asked Daniel.

'It is,' she said. 'We're here in Paris with access to the Louvre, but we've barely scratched at what they have to offer. Just this one more, the *Venus de Milo*, in case we don't get the chance to see it again.'

'We will,' said Daniel.

'We may not. So, follow me.'

A short while later they found themselves looking at the famous marble statue, almost seven feet high, of a woman naked from the hips upwards, with a tasteful loose skirt carved in marble covering her lower limbs.

'Venus de Milo,' said Abigail. 'Though that's her Roman name. She's also known as Aphrodite, which was the ancient Greek name for her.'

'So was she Greek or Roman?'

'She was carved by Alexandros of Antioch, a Greek sculptor, some time between 150 and 125 BC.'

'So around the same time as the other one you showed me: the goddess Victory with the wings.'

'Roughly.'

'Where does the "de Milo" part come in?' asked Daniel.

'From Milos, the Greek island where the statue was discovered by a farmer in 1820. A French sailor who was present when he dug it up persuaded him to sell it to the French government.'

'She's lost both her arms,' said Daniel.

'Most of these ancient pieces of sculpture that were buried for a thousand years were damaged in some way. The *Winged Victory of Samothrace*'s head went missing. The Venus's arms. If you go to any museum and look at the ancient relics on display, bits of them will be missing. But, fortunately, there's enough left intact to give a good idea of what she would have looked like originally.'

Daniel nodded. 'I've never really paid much attention to ancient sculptures. Or paintings, come to that.'

'Was it worth it?' asked Abigail.

Daniel smiled. 'If I'm shot dead during the rest of our stay in Paris, I will die happy.'

'Now you're mocking me,' she said, annoyed.

'No,' he said. 'I mean it. You have introduced me to aspects of culture and the arts that I never noticed. Before, they were just background, of no importance. Now, they put history and the arts in a whole new light. When we get back to England I shall insist you take me round more museums, and make me look at what's in them, not just concentrate on who killed who and why.'

Emile Chevignon sat on the bed in the private room in the medical block at the national barracks and raged silently at the injustice of his situation. The humiliation of being rescued from the Prefecture of Police by the intervention of the Minister for Defence was bad enough, but to be stripped of his rank as captain! What was even worse was being given the news by a lieutenant colonel. General DeLaGarde had not even deigned to talk to him since his return to the barracks, leaving all communications to be made through Lieutenant Colonel Bass. It was a snub of the worst kind!

'A temporary measure,' Lieutenant Colonel Bass had told him when informing him of the removal of his rank of captain, 'just until things blow over.' But there had been no indication of when that might be, nor what his present rank was. Did he have a rank? The situation was a nightmare!

He had obeyed orders, carried them out to the letter, despite the general's insistence – passed on to him by the lieutenant colonel – that the general had never ordered Chevignon to shoot the Wilsons. Lieutenant Colonel Bass had stressed this to Chevignon, with further instruction never to say any such thing. If he was asked, he was to say that he acted completely on his own initiative. But it was a lie! General DeLaGarde had given him clear instructions: to eliminate Dreyfus's lawyer, Labori, and the English couple, the Wilsons.

Yes, both had failed. Labori, the man he'd entrusted with the assignment, had botched it, merely wounding him. That was why he'd taken on the task of getting rid of the Wilsons himself, and he would have succeeded if it hadn't been for that clerk from the British Embassy intervening. How had it happened that he had been there? What was his name? Belfont, that was it. Well he'd have his revenge on this Belfont.

The Wilsons, too, he held responsible for his situation. They would also pay. As would that damned policeman, Superintendent Maison, who should have protected him, instead of which he'd betrayed him to General DeLaGarde.

DeLaGarde! Chevignon's sense of cruel injustice rose to dimensions he could barely cope with. To save the general's face, he – Chevignon – had been confined to this private room to be tested for a nervous breakdown, for God's sake! Once word spread, his career in the military would be over. The force to which he'd dedicated his life – the army – had betrayed him and was preparing to turf him out.

Well, he wouldn't go without a fight. He'd go down fighting, and he'd take those who'd landed him in this nightmarish position with him. He had their names. All he needed now was to get out of this place, and arm himself. Once he had a pistol again, those people who'd put him here would feel his wrath and tremble.

Daniel followed Abigail into a large room dominated by four enormous landscapes, one on each of the four walls.

'I thought we'd finished,' he said.

'We have,' said Abigail. 'But just in case we don't get the chance to return for a proper look . . .'

'We've been through this before,' said Daniel.

'Yes, but these paintings are special. *The Four Seasons*, by Nicolas Poussin. They are seen as the pinnacle of French painting.'

'I preferred some of the painting we saw at Lucas's café in Montmartre,' observed Daniel.

'*Classical* French painting,' clarified Abigail. 'Each painting represents a different time of day, a different season of the year, and depicts a subject from the Old Testament.' She pointed at the painting showing a luxuriant and heavily vegetated wood. '*Spring*. Depicting Adam and Eve in the Garden of Eden.'

She pointed to the next one in which some people seemed to be meeting in a cornfield. '*Summer*,' said Abigail. 'Also known as *Ruth and Boaz*.'

'Boaz?' asked Daniel.

'He was a wealthy landowner. Ruth is the one kneeling before him. She was a widow in difficult financial circumstances.'

'And he's taking advantage of her?' asked Daniel.

'You don't know your Bible,' said Abigail. 'He was a good man, and when she asked him to marry her, he did.' She pointed to the third. '*Autumn*. A time of harvest. It's also known as *The Spies with the Grapes of the Promised Land*.'

'Who are they spying on?'

'That's debatable,' said Abigail. 'You need to go back to the Old Testament.' She pointed to the fourth painting, which showed a deluge of water flooding the landscape. '*Winter* or *The Flood*. You can just see Noah's ark in the distance, on calmer waters, while the people in the foreground are doomed to die under the rising waters.'

'And this is the pinnacle of French classical painting?' queried Daniel.

'You're not impressed?' asked Abigail. 'Look at the way he's painted the trees; they look real.'

'Not as real as Constable's landscapes,' said Daniel. 'Now when he paints a tree, it looks like a tree.'

'When did you look at a real Constable landscape?' asked Abigail.

'When we were at the National Gallery,' replied Daniel.

'You didn't mention then about his trees looking so real.'

'Because we were investigating a murder there, and that seemed more important. But, if we're talking about art and you want to know what I like, I like Constable's landscapes. They may not have biblical themes from the Old Testament, and mean something deep, but they make me feel like I'd like to be there.'

Abigail fell quiet and looked again at the four Poussin paintings.

'You think I'm wrong,' said Daniel.

'No,' said Abigail. 'I was just thinking you're right. A painting is different things to different people, and I can see why you would go for a Constable rather than one of the Poussins here. Constable makes you feel the world's a good place to be.' She nodded. 'I like that.'

She took his hand and kissed him.

'Culture interlude over. Let's get back to work.'

CHAPTER THIRTY-ONE

When Daniel and Abigail returned to the Olive House, they found an envelope waiting for them. Abigail opened it.

'It's from Superintendent Maison,' she said.

'May I?' asked Daniel.

Abigail handed it to him and he studied it carefully.

'He wants us to call on him,' he said.

Abigail stared at him in surprise.

'You read it?' she said.

'Just the key words,' he admitted. 'Then I guessed what most of the others in between meant.'

'I'm impressed,' she said.

'Well, I have spent time studying words where I could. Shop signs. The words beneath the illustrations in magazines and newspapers. I've been gradually building up a small vocabulary.'

'You'll be able to join in conversations soon,' said Abigail.

Daniel shook his head. 'Reading words is one thing; understanding them when they're spoken, especially when people talk fast, is something completely different. But I've been able to pick up certain phrases – the ones that people use most of the time.'

* * *

Superintendent Maison was in his office when they arrived at the police prefecture.

'I can report that there will be no further attacks on you by the army,' were his opening words.

'How can you be so sure?' asked Abigail.

'I called on General DeLaGarde at the national barracks and informed him that if there were any more attacks, he and his senior staff would be arrested and executed and the army would cease to be a political force in this country.'

'And you convinced him?'

'I was very firm.'

'You don't think you've put yourself in danger?' asked Abigail, concerned.

Maison shrugged. 'We shall see. Nothing is predictable in this world. Also, I have talked to Monsieur Deschamps. He will be delighted for you to give a talk at the Louvre. He asks if you can make an appointment to see him so you can discuss details.'

'Did you tell him the real reason for it?'

'I hinted at problems with certain forces and this was the only way to ensure you are able to carry out your investigation.'

'Thank you,' said Abigail.

'I have also had the reporter from *Les Voix*, Julian Amity, brought in to question him about the source of his information concerning the alleged lunatic. He refuses to name his informant.' He grimaced. 'I get the impression he is delighted to be kept in custody because it enhances his reputation as a hero of the freedom of the press. To be honest, I'm not sure how long I can keep him locked up. He seems determined not to reveal his source.'

'Would you mind if we talked to him?' asked Abigail.

'To what end?'

'Sometimes people are prepared to tell civilians things they won't tell the police.'

'Why would they do that?'

'Because they think there might be some way out of their situation that non-police people might be able to arrange.'

'A deal of some sort?'

'We've had that kind of thing in England.'

Maison thought this over, then he said, 'It might be worth seeing what he has in mind. It might give us a clue to his informant's identity.' Then he added quickly, 'Of course, if there is the possibility of a deal it can only be done with us, the police.'

'We agree,' said Abigail.

'Very well,' said Maison. 'If you wait here I will arrange for you to be taken to Amity's cell.'

As Maison got up to leave, Abigail said, 'One moment, Superintendent, before you go.'

Maison looked at her quizzically.

'We went to see Madame LeMarc.'

'Oh? How did you get on with her?'

'She wasn't there. She's no longer living at that address. She left the house to live with her lover somewhere else, but the landlords weren't able to supply us with their new address.'

'Her lover?' repeated Maison.

'Yes. His name's Luigi. A young man built like a boxer, we understand. They were having an affair at the time Paul LeMarc was killed.'

'We knew nothing of this!' exclaimed Maison. 'Where did you get this information?'

'From the neighbour who lived next door.'

'Our inspectors asked the people on both sides if they knew of any enemies LeMarc may have had. They said nothing about this. Nor of his wife having an affair.'

'Some people are reluctant to tell the police things,' said Abigail.

Maison scowled. 'A boxer, you say?'

'Built like a boxer. Muscular. Young. Madame LeMarc apparently got some money after her husband's death from an insurance company.'

'You think this boxer type killed Paul LeMarc?'

'It would certainly make life for Madame LeMarc and this Luigi easier with the husband out of the way, not to mention the windfall of the insurance money.'

'I will have this looked into,' grated Maison. 'I will have the inspector who was in charge of the case brought in and questioned.'

'Yes, I think that's a good idea,' said Abigail. 'It may be just rumour and gossip, of course.'

Maison scowled, then left the room. Abigail told Daniel what she'd told the superintendent, and also what she'd said about Amity.

'What have you got in mind?' asked Daniel. 'After all, it's you who's going to be doing the talking to Amity.'

'I was thinking of making him an offer. A large sum of money for the name of his informant, plus an exclusive story for his newspaper when the murder is caught.'

'I can't see the superintendent agreeing to that. Nor Amity, for that matter. And who's going to be paying this large sum of money? Not us, and not the police.'

'I hope the Louvre will cough up,' said Abigail. 'The problem, of course, is that we can't ask them until we've tentatively sounded out Amity. But if, as you suggest, his informant could be connected to the murders, perhaps even the actual murderer, I think we ought to pursue it.'

Daniel nodded. 'It's certainly worth a try.'

Maison returned.

'It's arranged,' he said. 'I shall take you myself to his cell. After you've finished with him. I will see you here in this office.'

'Thank you,' said Abigail.

The superintendent escorted them to the basement where the cells were located. At this time only one of the six cells was occupied. Maison gestured for the turnkey to unlock the cell door, which was then relocked once Abigail and Daniel had been ushered inside.

Julien Amity remained sitting on the bunk, looking at them with suspicion.

'Monsieur Amity, my name is Abigail Wilson. This is my husband, Daniel Wilson. We have been engaged by the Louvre to investigate the murders of Professor Flamand and Elaine Foret at the museum. I shall be doing the talking because my husband does not speak French.'

Amity did not reply, just regarded the couple warily.

'You wrote the piece in *Les Voix* suggesting that there is a lunatic loose at the Louvre who carried out the murders.'

'That is correct,' said Amity.

'In that article you said you had been told this by an insider at the museum.'

'That is also correct,' said Amity.

'We have been advised by Superintendent Maison that you decline to identify your informant.'

Amity nodded. 'Again, correct. A journalist must protect his source in all circumstances. It is only that which guarantees the freedom of the press.'

'Absolutely,' said Abigail. 'And there is also your integrity.'

'That is true,' said Amity, although this time there was a hint of uncertainty in his voice, wondering where Abigail was going with this.

'I do not mean just your integrity as a journalist, but as an artist. Because when I read your piece I was aware that you were writing not as just a reporter, but as an artist. A creative talent.'

'Thank you,' said Amity, but his tone was definitely wary.

'I am guessing that you have aspirations to write more than just reportage. You have a novel inside you. More than one, I expect.'

This time Amity did not reply, just waited and watched Abigail, obviously wondering what she was going to say next.

'In that, you are in the tradition of such people as Zola, or our own Charles Dickens, who began as reporters but developed as the great creative writers they are, respected by the whole world for their talent. I can see that same talent in you. But, for you to achieve that, you need to be recognised as the writer you are by more than the readers of *Les Voix*. You need to be with a major publishing house. People who admire your integrity, and your writing style.'

'Perhaps,' admitted Amity reluctantly. 'But it is a very packed world out there, writing. It is not easy to get one's name to stand out from the crowd.' Sourly, he added, 'For one thing, it takes money, and *Les Voix* do not pay the higher rates.'

'That is usually the way with newspapers on the socialist wing,' said Abigail sympathetically. 'That is why, sooner or later, the celebrated writers I am referring to needed to be attractive to the larger and more commercial markets.'

Amity frowned, puzzled. 'Where is this talk leading?' he asked.

'Before my marriage my name was Abigail Fenton. Before I became a detective, I was an Egyptologist.'

'Abigail Fenton!' exclaimed Amity. 'I read about you in an archaeological magazine. You were at Haware with Flinders Petrie. And, last year, you led a major expedition to a sun temple in Egypt, the first woman to do so.'

'Indeed,' said Abigail.

He looked at her, bewildered. 'But what are you doing here?'

'I told you, we are investigating the murders at the Louvre. We wanted to talk to you because you have information that could help us: the identity of the person who told you about the lunatic.'

262

He shook his head. 'I cannot. As I've already said, it's about the freedom of the press, which is sacrosanct to a journalist.'

'But you are more than just a journalist. You are an artist, as I've already said. I can help you achieve that without losing your integrity.'

'How?'

'I have contacts with the editor of many top-class magazines and some of the major international newspapers, such as *The Times* of London. The French-language magazine *Égyptienne* has published articles by me. I can help promote you as a creative writer.'

He shook his head. 'These are promises that need never be fulfilled. I have had many people promise to promote my work, publish my stories, but all of them have been empty. That is why this particular story is so important for me. It will gain me the fame I need, which I will lose if I give away the name of my informant.'

'Not necessarily,' said Abigail. 'What we can offer you for the name is a large sum of money, plus an exclusive and a book deal for you when the murder is caught. And at the same time you will have anonymity about the identity of your informant, until such time as you want to reveal it when the case is over, and you can claim credit for breaking the case. No one will know you told us the name.'

'Except the police.'

'No,' said Abigail. 'This agreement will be between us. We will not pass it on to the police.'

Amity thought it over, then he announced, 'This proposal is one I would be prepared to consider,' he said. 'Except for one thing. I do not know the name of my informant.'

'But in your piece you said he had close ties to the Louvre.'

'Because that is what he told me. But he did not give me his name. He wanted to remain anonymous.'

Abigail frowned. 'Surely, if you told that to Superintendent Maison, he'd have to free you.'

'But I don't want him to free me,' said Amity. 'When the time comes I will admit I do not know his name and the police will be forced to release me. But, in the meantime, I will be seen as a hero, a defender of the freedom of the press. People will trust me with stories in the future, knowing they are safe with me because I would go to prison rather than reveal my sources.'

Yes, thought Abigail. *I thought that was what this was all about.*

'How did you meet your informant?' she asked.

'He came to the newspaper offices and asked for me. He said he had inside information to sell about the murders.'

'And you paid him?'

'Of course. That's how it works.'

'How could you be sure he was telling you the truth?'

'He gave me his word.'

'That doesn't count for much.'

'It does among the Apaches.'

'The Apaches?' said Abigail, puzzled. 'I know about the tribe of North American Indians, but I didn't know any had come to France.'

Amity shook his head. 'It's what the gangs of youths who hang around the streets call themselves. Apaches. They see themselves as outside society, the abandoned. They can be dangerous to people who they don't know.'

'And they know you?'

Amity pondered this, then he said, 'Just this one. I guess he'd read articles I'd written. Or his friend had.'

'His friend?'

Amity nodded. 'This Apache told me a friend of his knew someone who worked at the Louvre, and they had told him about this lunatic and what he'd been up to. He swore it was true.'

Superintendent Maison looked up expectantly as Daniel and Abigail returned to his office.

'Well?' he asked. 'Did he give you the name of his informant?'

'No,' said Abigail. 'He claims he doesn't know it. However, I believe he's lying.'

'Of course he's lying!' snorted Maison. 'Then we are no further forward.'

'Actually, I believe we are,' said Abigail.

'How?' asked Maison.

'We have to check something. When we return tomorrow, we hope to have the information we need.'

CHAPTER THIRTY-TWO

Abigail and Daniel made their way to the offices of *Les Voix*. The reception area was decorated with posters of a revolutionary nature urging a socialist revolution in France.

'Hardly an unbiased press,' murmured Daniel.

'You'd find it hard to discover a newspaper in Paris that isn't biased one way or another,' said Abigail.

Daniel followed her to a reception desk where a young woman was sorting through some handwritten sheets of paper.

'Excuse me,' aid Abigail. 'I wonder if you can help us? A day or so ago a young man called and asked to speak to Julien Amity.'

The woman nodded. 'Yes, the young Apache. I remember him because we don't get many like him coming in. Usually they're either earnest young intellectuals, or businessmen come to complain about our interpretation of a story.'

'I don't suppose this Apache gave a name?'

'Yes, he did. We're not supposed to allow visitors in until they've given us a name, in case it's someone the reporter doesn't want to talk to.'

'I'd be grateful if you could let me know his name. I'd

quite like to make contact with him.'

'I'll have to check.' She picked up a book marked 'Visitors' and began to leaf through the pages. 'We have strict instructions to keep a record of all callers and who they saw. That's in case there's trouble later.'

She ran her finger down the list of dates and names. 'Here it is. Jean-Luc Dubois to see Monsieur Julien Amity.'

'Did you tell Monsieur Amity his name?'

'Of course.'

'I ask because, as I'm sure you know, Monsieur Amity is currently being kept in prison for refusing to divulge his informant's name.'

The receptionist laughed. 'He's achieved his ambition!'

'His ambition? To be arrested?'

'Arrested for refusing to divulge information to the police. He wants to be the next Émile Zola, in trouble for defying the authorities. He hopes his stance over this will make him famous and the darling of the anti-government movement.'

Inspector Auberge was shown into the office of Superintendent Maison, who gestured for him to take a chair.

'I received your message, Superintendent,' said Auberge. 'I came at once.'

He was a short man, fussily dressed, wearing a long camelhair coat with a dark fur collar over his jacket. His hair was pomaded. He was obviously a man who took great care of his appearance.

'You were in charge of the investigation into the murder of Paul LeMarc, who was killed earlier this year.'

'LeMarc?' Auberge frowned, checking through his memory.

'The head of security at the Louvre,' said Maison.

'Ah yes!' Auberge smiled. Then his smile changed to an unhappy one. 'Sadly, we never found the murderer. He was beaten to death.'

'Yes. Did you have any suspects?'

'No. There were no witnesses to the crime. The local police had a report of a man's body being found lying in the street. He had been beaten about the head with a heavy object. Possibly a piece of metal pipe.'

'There was no sign of robbery?'

'No, sir. His wallet and possessions were intact. We assume it was an intended robbery, but the attacker ran away before he could rob the body. We thought that people arriving had scared him off.'

'But there were no witnesses, you said, so who were these people arriving?'

Auberge thought about it, then said, 'The attacker must have thought he heard noises and believed that people were approaching.'

'Did you consider that robbery may not have been the motive? That he may have been murdered by someone who wanted him dead?'

'That was a possibility,' agreed Auberge. 'But we found no evidence of anyone who wanted him dead.'

'Not his wife and her lover?'

Auberge stared at him, stunned. 'Her lover?'

'Yes. A young man called Luigi. Built like a boxer.'

'I have never heard of this person.'

'Did you talk to Madame LeMarc?'

'Of course.'

'Did you question her about her private life?'

'She was a woman in grief!' protested Auberge. 'It would have been inappropriate to do such a thing.'

'Did you quiz the neighbours and friends of the couple about their private life?'

'No,' said Auberge stoutly. 'There was no need. Madame LeMarc swore to us that she had no idea who might want to harm her husband.'

'And you believed her?'

'There was no reason not to,' protested Auberge.

'You have been incompetent, Inspector,' snapped Maison coldly. 'If you had carried out your investigation properly you would have discovered that she was having a sexual relationship with this young man, and the pair would certainly benefit from Paul LeMarc's death. Not least because of the insurance payout Madame LeMarc received.'

'Insurance payout?' asked Auberge, his mouth now open in bewilderment.

'For her husband's death.'

'I did not know this,' insisted Auberge.

'You did not make enquiries about who benefited financially from his death?'

'We had a lot of other cases to investigate at this time, sir!' blustered Auberge. 'I did not have enough me.'

'None of us have enough men,' snapped Maison. 'But we should do our jobs to the best of our ability. You have not done this. I am considering what action to take against you.

Whether to have you reduced in rank . . .'

'No!' burst out Auberge desperately. 'It was one error, and it was not my fault! It was the men who carried out the questioning!'

'Which was your responsibility.'

'Please, Superintendent, I appeal to you. My wife is ill. She needs medical care. If my salary were to be reduced . . .'

Maison held up his hand.

'There is a way for you to salvage something from this debacle,' he said sternly. 'Find this Luigi and Madame LeMarc.'

'Find them?' asked Auberge, puzzled.

'They are no longer at the address they were when Paul LeMarc was alive. You will find them and question them and see if there is evidence to indicate that they were responsible for the brutal murder of Paul LeMarc.'

'But how will I find them?' bleated Auberge.

'You are a detective inspector. Do your job. Detect their whereabouts and bring them in.'

As Daniel and Abigail made their way back to the police prefecture, they discussed what they'd learnt.

'Louise Perrault mentioned a young man she saw hanging around the corridor in the Louvre around the time Armand Ruffalo was killed,' said Abigail. 'It could have been this Jean-Luc Dubois.'

'He kills Ruffalo and then tells Amity there's a lunatic loose in the Louvre?' Daniel frowned.

'To put up a smokescreen. Divert attention away from himself.'

'You think it could be this Jean-Luc Dubois who killed Flamand and Elaine Foret?'

'It's possible. If he was able to get access to the administration area of the Louvre to kill Ruffalo, there's no reason he couldn't have done the same for those two.'

'But what's his motive?' asked Daniel.

'At the moment, I have no idea,' admitted Abigail. 'We need to check and see if Professor Flamand and his secretary had any dealings with this Jean-Luc Dubois Although it doesn't have to be with him,' she added thoughtfully. 'Remember, Patrice Foret's mother told us her son ran around with a gang of youths. They could be these Apaches Amity has told us about. They sound just like the gangs of youngsters Superintendent Maison mentioned. Maybe this Jean-Luc Dubois was referring to someone else in his gang?'

'But we come back to it, what's their motive?' asked Daniel.

'We need to talk to Julien Amity again,' Abigail told Maison when they got back to the police prefecture.

'Did you find the information you were after?' asked Maison.

'We did. We just need to confirm it with Amity.'

'Who did you see?' asked Maison.

'Again, we'll tell you that after we've talked to Amity.'

The superintendent regarded them suspiciously.

'I believe you are playing games with me,' he said accusingly.

'No, it's just that we need to be sure of our facts,' said Abigail. 'We don't want you to go off on fruitless chase.'

'And after you've talked to Amity you'll tell me?'

'We will,' promised Abigail.

Maison nodded, then called for an officer to take them to the cells to see Julien Amity.

'You lied to us,' said Abigail accusingly when they were in the cell with the journalist.

'What about?'

'About not knowing the name of the young Apache who gave you the story. We've talked to the receptionist at *Les Voix*. She gave you his name, otherwise he wouldn't have been allowed in. Jean-Luc Dubois.'

Amity regarded them, and they could see from the expression on his face that he was taken aback at this. Then he shrugged. 'It was obviously a made-up name. "Dubois" in France is like your "Smith" in England. People use it as an alias.'

'But you still could have given that name to Superintendent Maison. However, you chose not to for the very reasons you said. You wish to be a hero to those who oppose the government and the forces of law and order: the establishment. And, once you've gained the notoriety and fame you're after, you'll secretly hand the name over, while denying it.'

'I will never do that!' said Amity defiantly.

'But you won't object if we do,' said Abigail.

Amity regarded them coolly. 'You are being unfair,' he said.

'We are trying to catch a murderer. You are trying to be famous as an anti-hero. We are very likely both using methods that could be called unfair in order to achieve our aims. We would defend our aim by saying it's for the greater good, to catch a murderer and stop him killing again. Your aim is purely selfish. Fame. So, what can you offer us to stop us giving the

272

name of Jean-Luc Dubois to Superintendent Maison?'

'What do you mean?' demanded Amity.

'You're a reporter with ambitions to be a great writer. We can't believe you saw this vital witness without finding out more about him. You would have needed more so you could talk to him again, if it was necessary to add something to keep your story running.'

Amity fell silent and glowered at them. 'This is blackmail,' he said accusingly.

'Yes, I suppose it is,' said Abigail calmly.

Amity fell silent again, then asked, 'So, what do you want?'

'We'd like to meet your young Apache,' said Abigail.

Amity gave a laugh of derision. 'Do you know what these people are like? These Apaches?'

'You said they were honourable. That an Apache's word means something.'

Amity scowled. 'Well, maybe I was exaggerating. In fact, they are dangerous. *Very* dangerous. I was lucky because this young man had some information he wanted to sell me. If I'd gone into Apache territory looking for it, my life would have been in danger. Do you want to put yourself at that kind of risk?'

'Our work means we are always at risk,' said Abigail. 'We have a suggestion. If you tell us where we could find this Jean-Luc Dubois, we won't tell Superintendent Maison you know his name.'

'I'm not even sure if it is his real name. Like I said, it's quite likely to be false.'

'But you've met him so you'd recognise him.'

'Perhaps, but as I'm in prison that's not a lot of help.'

'Unless we can persuade Superintendent Maison to release you into our care. Then you take us to where you think he'd be.'

'Are you mad? Didn't you hear me say what these people are like? They're dangerous. They're armed with knives. And why on earth would Maison let me out if I haven't told him the name?'

'Because we'll do a deal with him. We'll tell him you don't know the boy's name but you know what he looks like and where he hangs around. You've agreed to take us there. After we've talked to the boy, we'll bring you back to the superintendent, provided he promises to release you.'

'That's nonsense! He'll never agree to that.'

'He might. He trusts us.'

'Even though you've just said you're ready to lie to him?'

Abigail gave a shrug of indifference, 'Very well. If you don't want to do this, we'll go and tell the superintendent about Jean-Luc Dubois.'

'You can't!' protested Amity. 'I gave you his name in confidence.'

'You didn't give us his name at all,' Abigail pointed out. 'We got it from the receptionist at *Les Voix*.'

Amity looked at them, his expression showing he was torn by indecision. Finally, he nodded. 'Very well. See if the superintendent agrees. Although I doubt if he will.'

'So how do we sell this to the superintendent?' asked Daniel as they made their way back up the stairs to the superintendent's office.

'We promise to give him the name of the boy when we come back.'

'We double-cross Amity?'

'Absolutely.'

'Do you think that's morally sound?'

'If Amity was a morally sound person, I'd say definitely not. But he isn't. He lied to us before. He's rigging all this up for his selfish ambition. He's not bothered if the murderer gets caught; all he wants is his time in the spotlight. He's prepared to use us to achieve that; we should be prepared to do the same to him to achieve our aim, which is of far more importance than his egocentric ambitions.'

'Well?' demanded Maison when they walked into his office.

'Amity told us his informant was an Apache boy,' Abigail told him. 'He's agreed to show us where he hangs around so we can find him.'

'And then what?'

'We'll talk to the boy.'

'Are you mad? Do you know what these Apaches are like?'

'That's what Amity said, but we're prepared to chance it, if it leads us to the killer.'

Maison shook his head. 'No, I cannot allow it. There is a good chance that Amity will run off, and you'll both be killed.'

'People have tried to kill us before and failed,' said Abigail. 'Look at Captain Chevignon.'

'You were just lucky that the young man was there to save you.'

'There have been frequent attempts on us in England,' added Abigail.

'That was in England. This is in Paris, a city you don't know.'

'I do know it,' said Abigail. 'I've been here many times.'

'But that was before these gangs began to infest the city. For some reason they've begun to appear this last year, usually in the poorer districts.'

Seeing the expression of interest on Daniel's face, Abigail translated what the superintendent had just said for his benefit.

'Tell him it's the same in England,' said Daniel. 'The poorer areas breed gangs of disaffected youths who go around causing trouble, threatening people.'

'Not just in England,' said Abigail. 'It's the same in every large city.' She then translated Daniel's comment into French for the superintendent.

'That may be,' said Maison. 'But it doesn't change what I've just said. It's too dangerous.'

'There is another option,' said Abigail. 'You could have plainclothes policemen following us. If we run into trouble, they move in and save us.'

Maison fell into a thoughtful silence. Then he asked, 'You really think this is worth putting your lives at risk for?'

'Daniel feels the person who gave the information to Amity is either the killer, or is involved with them,' said Abigail. 'And I've rarely known him be wrong.'

Maison mulled it over, then nodded, albeit with some reluctance. 'Very well. But if there is trouble, my men will move in very fast. They'll also be armed, so there could be shooting.'

'Let's hope they don't shoot at us,' said Abigail, concerned.

'If you get shot it will not be my men. Some of these so-called

276

Apaches are armed with pistols as well as knives. As I've said, they are very dangerous.'

'But you agree? You'll release Amity into our custody?'

'No. I'll release him to accompany you, but he'll be in the custody of the plainclothes policemen who'll be watching. I'll arrange for them to be here tomorrow afternoon. Most of these Apaches stay in bed all morning, so it won't be worth you going until the afternoon.'

CHAPTER THIRTY-THREE

It had been a tortuous task for Inspector Auberge tracking Madame LeMarc down; there had been so many dead ends in his search, until finally he'd discovered she had an aunt working in the vegetable market at Les Halles. A young informer had heard the police were looking for Madame LeMarc and had turned up at his local police station and offered to sell the information about Madame LeMarc's aunt.

'She's a grumpy old woman,' he'd told the police. 'She's always telling me off just because I hang around Les Halles looking for any old vegetables they might be throwing away. If they have, I sell them door to door. She's spread the word among the stall owners to kick me out of there if they see me. So, if there's anything that might get her into trouble, I'd be happy for that. It serves her right.'

'It's not her we're after,' he was told. 'It's her niece, Madame LeMarc.'

'Yeah, but she'll still be upset when the police call on her asking questions.'

This information was passed on to Inspector Auberge, who

called personally on Madame LeMarc's aunt, Iseult Noir, at Les Halles.

'What do you want her address for?' demanded Madame Noir.

'That's for us to know,' said Auberge. 'Have you got an address for her or not?'

'I might have,' said Noir. 'What's it worth?'

'Ten days in jail for obstructing the police in the course of an investigation if you don't let me have it,' said Auberge.

He was still smarting from his interview with Superintendent Maison and set on taking it out on everyone he encountered. The junior members of his squad had already suffered, and now it was this woman's turn to feel his anger. At first she demurred, but when she realised he was serious about arresting her, she gave him the address.

'I had a note from her telling me she'd moved.'

'Did she mention someone called Luigi?' asked Auberge.

'No,' said Noir. 'She told me that her husband, Paul, had died. That was all.'

Inspector Auberge had brought two uniformed officers with him to the address Madame Noir had given him. If it turned out that this Luigi was the murderer, he wanted to make sure he had people who could help him subdue this very fit and active young boxer.

The door was opened by a woman he recognised from his encounter with her shortly after LeMarc's death.

'Madame LeMarc,' he announced. 'I don't know if you remember me? Inspector Auberge.'

'Yes, you came to talk to me after my husband, Paul, was

killed,' she said, watching him suspiciously.

'I need to talk to you again because some new evidence has surfaced that we need to look into.'

'What new evidence?' she demanded. 'Do you think you know who did it?'

'We are following a particular line of enquiry,' said Auberge. 'We'd like to talk to you, and your man-friend, who we understand is called Luigi.'

At the mention of Luigi's name, Madame LeMarc flew into a rage. 'He's no friend of mine! He stole all my money!'

'You had money?'

'The insurance money I got for my husband's death. That bastard Luigi said he'd invest it for me, but instead he stole it.'

'How?'

'He said he'd put the money in some company that would make me rich. I thought he knew what he was doing, but two months ago he came to me and told me the company had gone bust and all my money had gone. And then he left me!' Her voice rose to a shrill shriek at these words, and suddenly she began to cry.

'Did you report this to the police? Him stealing your money?'

'I tried, but when I told them what had happened they said it was nothing to do with them. They said it was a business matter.'

'Did you tell them the name of the firm he invested the money in so they could check on it?'

'I didn't know the name. He never told me. I trusted him! And now he's shacked up with some floozy of twenty or something.' Suddenly, she burst out, impassioned, 'He's got my money! I know it!'

'Do you have an address for him?'

'Yes. I followed them both one day to find out where they were living. Tell him I want my money back or I'll sue him.'

'Why haven't you sued him already?'

'Because he took all my money. I can't afford to pay a lawyer to chase him. And he's hidden it somewhere, so it would be throwing good money after bad.'

'What's Luigi's other name?'

'Domenico. Luigi Domenico.'

Inspector Auberge looked across the narrow road at the terraced house, the address for Luigi Domenico that Madame LeMarc had given him. He'd left the police van parked around the corner, to avoid the risk of Domenico spotting it from his house.

'Your signal will be three long blasts on a police whistle,' he'd told the driver. 'When you hear that, bring the van round immediately.'

He'd then walked with the two uniformed officers who accompanied him round the corner into the street where Domenico lived.

'Right,' Auberge told the two men. 'This is how we're going to do this. Doulet, you go round the back of the house. There's usually an alley that runs between the back yards of these terraced houses. If this Luigi makes a run for it out the back door, you grab him.'

'Say he's armed?' asked Doulet anxiously.

'You've got a truncheon,' said Auberge.

'Yes, but if he's got a knife or a gun, a truncheon isn't going to be much use.'

'Blow your whistle and shout out loudly if he comes out the back door. Gerrard and I will come through the house and join you in overpowering him.'

'Wouldn't it be better if me and Gerrard both went round the back? Then there'd be two of us if he came rushing out the back door.'

Auberge gave the officer an unfriendly look and replied, 'And say he doesn't come out the back door but instead makes a break for it through the front, where I'd be on my own?'

'Then you could shout, Inspector, and we'd come running.'

'And what do you do if the back door is locked?' demanded Auberge.

'Well . . .' began Doulet. Then he dried up. 'It was just a suggestion,' he said defensively.

'You go round the back,' Auberge ordered Doulet firmly. 'Gerrard, you come with me to the front door.'

'Yes, Inspector,' said Doulet unhappily.

'We'll give you a couple of minutes' start to find the back of the house,' said Auberge.

The inspector and Gerrard watched as Doulet trudged unhappily towards the end of the street, then disappeared down an alleyway between two of the houses.

'Right,' said Auberge, and he headed for the target house, Gerrard trailing after him. They arrived outside the front door and banged on it. There was a few minutes' delay, then the door was opened by a young woman pulling a dressing gown around her.

'Yes?' she demanded.

'Police,' said Auberge, showing her his warrant card. 'We'd like to speak to Luigi Domenico.'

She looked at them suspiciously.

'Who?' she asked.

'Luigi Domenico. We've been advised he lives here.'

'Never heard of him,' said the woman, and she began to close the door. Auberge stuck his boot in the gap to stop it closing.

'We're coming in,' he said, and he pushed at the door.

'How do I know you're the police?' shouted the woman loudly.

Auberge scowled and pushed her to one side.

'She's alerting him we're here,' he growled.

Suddenly they heard the frantic sound of a police whistle being blown somewhere at the back of the house. Immediately, Auberge and Gerrard rushed into the house, along a short passage and out through the back door into a small yard. Doulet was standing on the brick wall at the end of the yard, waving his truncheon at a short, stocky man in shirtsleeves. Auberge and Gerrard ran down the yard and jumped on the man, wrestling him to the ground. Suddenly the young woman appeared and began to beat the policemen with a broom.

'Leave him alone, you brutes!' she shouted.

Auberge turned his attention to her, tearing the broom from her hands and pushing at her with the brush.

'Police brutality!' she shouted. 'Help!'

Meanwhile, Doulet and Gerrard had managed to get a pair of handcuffs on Luigi Domenico. They hauled him to his feet. The young woman leapt at Auberge and grabbed hold of the broom handle and tried to take possession of it.

'One of you slap some handcuffs on her!' shouted Auberge.

There was a moment's hesitation as Gerrard and Doulet looked enquiringly at one another, then Doulet produced a pair of handcuffs and put them with difficulty on the struggling young woman, while Gerrard kept a firm grip on the man.

'Got you!' announced Auberge. 'You're both under arrest.'

'What's the charge?' demanded the man.

'Fraud and assaulting the police for starters,' said Auberge. 'Then, possibly, murder.'

'Murder?' exclaimed the young woman, horrified. 'We ain't murdered anyone!'

'That's not what we've heard,' said Auberge. With that, he took out his whistle and blew three long blasts on it.

CHAPTER THIRTY-FOUR

Inspector Auberge went methodically through the house, checking every cupboard, every drawer. He'd sent Doulet and Gerrard to the local police station in the van with Domenico and the young woman, with instructions for them to be locked in separate cells, and then for the two policemen to return to the house in the van and re-join him.

Fifty thousand francs, Madame LeMarc had told him. That was how much she'd received as an insurance payout for her late husband's death. According to her they'd spent five thousand francs – or, according to her, Luigi Domenico had spent them – which left forty-five thousand that he'd invested on her behalf. Or stolen it, according to Madame LeMarc.

Auberge guessed that Domenico didn't trust banks, which meant the money was hidden somewhere in the house. Unless, of course, Domenico had spent it, but Auberge thought it unlikely that he'd spent all of it. A sizeable sum would be here, somewhere, he was sure.

There was a knock at the door and Auberge broke off his search to open it. Doulet and Gerrard were there.

'They're both under lock and key in the cells,' said Doulet.

'Good,' said Auberge.

'There's another thing,' continue Doulet. 'I thought his face looked familiar, so I went through some of the old Wanted posters. Sure enough, he was there. But his name isn't Luigi Domenico. According to this poster, he's Ricardo Pesta, wanted in Rennes, Calais and Paris for robbery and assault.'

'Excellent!' said Auberge. 'Well done, Doulet. There'll be a commendation for you after this.' He gestured at the house around them. 'And there may even be a bonus for us if we find the money he stole from Madame LeMarc.'

Abigail and Daniel returned to Amity and told him they'd got the agreement of the superintendent. 'He said we can accompany you, but he's sending some of his men in plain clothes to shadow us, just in case things turn nasty.'

'The Apaches will spot them.'

'I'm fairly sure the superintendent will select men who look the least like policemen,' said Abigail. 'Where can we find these Apaches?'

'This one told me he could be found in Montmartre.'

'Montmartre?' said Abigail, surprised. 'That's where our hotel is. You mean we're staying in an area populated by dangerous gangsters?'

'Haven't you seen them?' asked Amity. 'Gangs of young men who hang around on street corners.'

'Yes, but I didn't think they were anything special,' said Abigail. 'Every city has gangs who hang about on street corners. They don't wear a uniform of any sort; they look like groups of young men with nothing else to do.'

'You obviously don't look rich enough for them to rob,' said Amity. 'The other thing is, you're English. Robbing and murdering a foreigner, especially the English, will bring a major investigation. The ambassador would be involved. Police would flood into the area and start arresting them. So instead they target the local bourgeoisie.'

'Whereabouts in Montmartre does this particular Apache hang around?' asked Abigail. 'I don't recall seeing any gangs around our hotel, the Olive House.'

'Jean-Luc told me he and his gang hang around near where they're building the Basilica of Sacré-Coeur, at the top of the hill.'

'Yes, we saw it earlier,' said Abigail. 'I must admit it doesn't seem to have progressed much since I was last here about eight years ago, although I noticed the dome has been put on.'

'The dome was finally completed this year,' said Amity.

'It still seems odd for these Apaches to have chosen it as their favoured hangout,' said Abigail. 'A church of such importance seems rather out of character for a bunch of delinquents.'

'Not really,' said Amity. 'The site is right at the very top of the hill, so they get a clear view of everything around and anyone coming up the hill.'

Inspector Auberge faced Ricardo Pesta across the bare wooden table in the interview room at the local police station. The young woman who had been arrested with him was in a cell at the station, loudly making protestations of her innocence. Auberge would deal with her later; right now he was intent on Pesta. Even though Pesta was handcuffed to the chair on which he sat, Constable Doulet stood close guard over the prisoner.

Auberge patted the bag that they'd finally discovered hidden behind a wardrobe, which had been found to contain bundles of banknotes.

'So,' said Auberge. 'Madame LeMarc's money.'

'It's not hers, it's mine,' growled Pesta. 'It's nothing to do with her.'

'Forty thousand francs,' continued Auberge. 'The amount you stole from Madame LeMarc, what was left of the insurance money she received after her husband was killed.' He leant towards Pesta and said pointedly, 'Killed by a very fit young man who beat him to death. Killed by someone who knew his victim's wife would benefit from a sizeable insurance payout when he died.'

'I don't know what you're talking about.' Pesta scowled. 'That's my money.'

'Where did it come from?'

'I got lucky gambling.'

Auberge laughed sarcastically. 'Where?'

'Where what?'

'Where did you win this money?'

'It was a bet with some bloke. I didn't know his name.'

'When did you win it?'

'About a month ago.'

'So the woman you're living with might know.'

'No,' said Pesta firmly. 'She knows nothing about it.'

'We'll see what happens when I ask her about it,' said Auberge.

'No!' said Pesta desperately.

Auberge stood up and turned to Constable Doulet. 'Keep an eye on him, Constable, while I have a word with his female companion.'

Once Daniel and Abigail had reported to Maison what they'd learnt about the Apaches from Amity, they took a carriage back to the Olive House. On the way, Daniel asked, 'When you booked our hotel, did you know it was in an area that was a hotbed of dangerous young gangsters?'

'Of course not. The last time I was here in Paris I knew Montmartre as a centre for artists. Obviously these Apaches, as they call themselves, have just sprung up recently. Anyway, we can take comfort in what Amity said about them not attacking foreigners.'

'That might change when we turn up with a bunch of plainclothes policemen in tow,' observed Daniel with some concern. 'Be prepared for us to get caught up in a street battle.'

There was a letter waiting for them at their hotel from Sir Brian Otway asking if they would call to see him at the embassy.

'We're not going to get much chance to do any proper sightseeing with all this calling on people,' said Daniel. 'And you're supposed to be preparing for your lecture.'

'Don't you prefer to be active?' asked Abigail. 'I've noticed you get irritable when you've nothing to keep you busy.'

'True,' admitted Daniel. 'Let's walk to the embassy. We can do some sightseeing on the way.'

'You want to try out your French on people, don't you?'

Abigail smiled. 'Talking to shopkeepers, that sort of thing.'

'I thought it might be an opportunity for me to experiment. Things like, "*Quelle heure est-il?*"'

'Very good,' said Abigail, 'but will you know what they're saying back to you?'

'I've memorised some times. "*Il est une heure.*" "*Il est deux heures cinq.*" "*Il est quatre heures et demie.*"'

'And what if it isn't one o'clock, or five past two, or half past four?'

'Then I shall nod politely and say "*merci beaucoup*", and look for a clock.'

When they arrived at the British Embassy, they found Sir Brian in ebullient mood.

'I'm glad you got my note,' he said. 'Something wonderful has happened.'

'Oh?'

'I sent a telegram to Sir Anthony Thurrington advising him of the attack on you, and the part that Edgar Belfont played in preventing your deaths. I received a response from him today. He informed the Queen of what happened, and Edgar's part in it, and Her Majesty has graciously authorised the awarding of the Distinguished Conduct Medal to Edgar for his gallantry.'

'That's wonderful!' exclaimed Abigail.

'It will be presented to him at a ceremony at the embassy here in Paris. I am pleased to say I will be doing the presentation as the official representative of the Crown in France. Sir Anthony has arranged for Edgar's parents, Lord and Lady Belfont, to bring the medal to France, so they will also be at the presentation. I would be grateful if you would attend.'

'We will be honoured,' said Abigail enthusiastically.

'Absolutely,' confirmed Daniel. 'Where is Edgar? We must congratulate him.'

'He is in his flat writing a letter to his parents, which he wishes to be sent to them today. He will be delivering it here later to put it in the official diplomatic postbag. I am also planning to invite Superintendent Maison to the occasion, in order to keep Anglo-French relations in good order.'

'An excellent idea,' said Daniel. 'Although Captain Chevignon seems to have got off scot-free, the superintendent did his best to invoke the law in this case, despite the threats to his own safety and his career prospects from the army.'

'I'm not sure if Chevignon will get off completely,' said Otway. 'I have made representations to my counterpart in the French diplomatic corps, and he has taken steps to ensure that Chevignon's career in the army will be at an end. He has been stripped of his rank, and I believe that after a certain amount of time he will be dismissed from the force. And, what is more, it will be a dishonourable discharge. There is a good chance he will take what is known as the honourable way out.'

'Suicide?' asked Abigail, shocked.

'Possibly even assisted,' said Otway. 'The army can be very unforgiving. By the way, how are preparations going for your talk at the Louvre? We're all looking forward to it.'

'I have to admit that I've let our investigations into the

murders of Professor Flamand and his secretary take priority,' said Abigail. 'But I've arranged to see Monsieur Deschamps to see if there's anything in particular he wants me to raise. It will be a wonderful opportunity to take advantage of the treasures the Louvre has to offer.'

Inspector Auberge faced Pesta's (aka Domenico's) female companion across the table. Her name was Emilie Lavalle, age twenty-five years, and she'd remained resolutely silent since arriving at the police station. She hadn't even given the police her name; they'd discovered that from a neighbour, who'd informed them that Emilie Lavelle and Luigi Domenico had moved into the house some time before and were generally orderly and well-behaved, except sometimes when they had been drinking, in which case there were often outbursts of shouted abuse at one another, which sometimes escalated into violence. 'More her against him,' the neighbour had added. 'She packs a powerful punch. I've seen her lay into him.'

It was for this reason that Auberge had decided to keep the handcuffs on Lavalle.

'Tell me about this money we found in your house,' said Auberge.

As before, she gave no answer, just looked sullenly at the inspector.

'It's the proceeds from a murder,' said Auberge. 'Insurance money paid out to Madame LeMarc, the widow of a man who was killed by Luigi Domenico, also known as Ricardo Pesta. We intend to charge you with aiding and abetting in this murder. You can save yourself from the guillotine if you tell us what really happened. Were you with Pesta when he killed Paul LeMarc? Was it you who was his accomplice, or was it the wife of his victim, Madame LeMarc?'

As before, she remained stubbornly mute, just glared at him with sullen and angry eyes.

'He has told us the killing and getting hold of the money was your idea,' lied Auberge. 'He has sold you out. So why protect him? You can be out of here if you tell us the truth. For your own sake, talk!'

Lavalle continued to stare menacingly at the inspector.

'Talk!' repeated Auberge.

Instead, she suddenly let fly with a gob of spit, which splattered on the inspector's face.

Auberge glared at her, then reached in his pocket for his handkerchief and wiped his face.

'I hope he's worth you dying for,' he growled.

CHAPTER THIRTY-FIVE

Emile Chevignon marched along the corridor towards the office of General DeLaGarde, flanked by a uniformed soldier on either side. He felt full of expectation at being summoned this way. It could only mean his reinstatement to his rank of captain. At last! He accepted that the army had to go through the protocol of temporarily removing his rank from him while he was officially undergoing medical treatment for a nervous breakdown. *Nervous breakdown!* He snorted to himself derisively. It was a fiasco. But it was just the army covering themselves until such time as they could rectify the situation. The lack of any direct contact from General DeLaGarde had worried him slightly. But when the soldiers had come for him just now and told him that the general had summoned him, his immediate reaction had been relief. Soon he would be back in his uniform decorated with his captain's insignia, instead of wearing these ridiculous civilian clothes.

The soldiers and Chevignon stopped outside the door of the general's office, and one knocked on it.

'Enter!' called the general.

The soldier opened the door and announced, 'Former

Captain Chevignon as ordered, sir!'

Former *captain*, thought Chevignon. *Not for much longer.*

The general gestured for Chevignon to march forward to his desk, which Chevignon did. The two soldiers saluted and then left the office, shutting the door.

Chevignon stood stiffly to attention in front of the general's desk. The general did not rise.

'There has been a development in your case,' announced DeLaGarde.

Good, thought Chevignon. *I'm being brought back into the fold.*

'The British ambassador to France has made representations to the head of the French Diplomatic Corps. As a result, the President has ordered the Minister for Defence to take action. You will still not stand a civilian trial, because such a trial would impact very negatively indeed on the military. However, you will be dismissed from the service.'

Chevignon stared at the general, shocked. He listened in horror as the general continued, 'I requested, on your behalf, that it be an honourable discharge, with you leaving with the rank of captain and the relevant pension, but the minister – under great pressure, I believe – insists that it must be a dishonourable discharge.'

'But, sir . . .' burbled Chevignon.

DeLaGarde held up his hand to silence him. 'The minister and I have done all we can, but the political forces need to be appeased.'

'The British . . . !' exploded Chevignon angrily.

DeLaGarde jerked to his feet and glared at Chevignon. 'It

is not the British who have landed you in this predicament! It was your own stupidity and incompetence. You allowed a civilian – this clerk at the British Embassy – to overpower you. You failed in your objective of eliminating the British couple, the Wilsons. Before that, despite your assurances, the attempt to neutralise the lawyer for the traitor Dreyfus was a disaster. The case in Rennes still continues. Your recent exploits have been a litany of failure that have put the reputation of the army at risk. Any officer with a grain of honour would consider his position. You will return to the room you currently occupy and await your summons to a tribunal, which will advise you of your fate.'

With that, the general barked out, 'Escort!'

The door sprang open and the two soldiers entered and stood to attention.

'You will escort Monsieur Chevignon back to his quarters. You will lock the door to his room and bring the key back to me.'

Chevignon opened his mouth to say something in his defence, but one look at the general's grim expression and he closed his lips, resigned.

He marched between the two soldiers back to his room. He walked in and the door closed behind him. He heard the key turn in the lock and the boots of the soldiers as they marched away.

He looked at the dressing table. A pistol had been left lying on the top.

He walked over and picked it up. He opened the chamber. There was one bullet in it.

* * *

296

Abigail had elected to go on her own to the Louvre to see Georges Deschamps, mainly because conversation in French alone with the curator was easier than a difficult mixture of French and translated English. Daniel had said he was pleased to wander around on his own, trying out his elementary French on shopkeepers, so Abigail settled down in Deschamps's office, keen to get her mind back on the pyramids of ancient Egypt. They had already decided her talk would centre on her recent expedition, funded by Arthur Conan Doyle, to Abusir and the Sun Temple of Niuserre. Abigail had been pleased to find that the Louvre had relics and artefacts from an expedition to Niuserre's pyramid at Abu Ghurob two years before, which had been led by Professor Flamand.

'It will be good to make the link between the sun temple and Niuserre's pyramid, and to use this talk to highlight the work of Professor Flamand,' said Abigail. 'I'd like to make the evening a tribute to his memory.'

'That will be extremely welcome to his colleagues here at the Louvre, and to the French archaeological establishment as a whole,' said Deschamps enthusiastically. 'But you mustn't downplay your role at Abusir. The first woman to lead an expedition to the area.'

Abigail smiled. 'Not something of which the professor would have approved, considering his opinion of women in archaeology,' she said. 'I will do my best to combine my own experience at Abusir with the professor's work at Abu Ghurob. The two sites are less than a mile away from each other so there is a certain amount of crossover.'

'I'm sure you're aware that tickets for your talk sold out

virtually as soon as they went on sale. You'll be guaranteed a full house.'

'Let's hope they are supportive. There may be some who share the late professor's view of female archaeologists. Archaeology itself is a subject that some people can get very passionate about.'

'Passionate but polite,' said Deschamps.

Abigail gave a wry smile. 'I have attended talks on ancient Egypt at which opposing views on Piazzi Smyth and the Pyramid Inch were so fiercely held that fights actually broke out.'

'Ah, the famous Flinders Petrie.' Deschamps smiled. Then, changing the subject, he asked, 'Have there been any developments into your investigation into the murders?'

'There has been a recent one that may prove promising. You will have read the story alleging a lunatic at large in the Louvre?'

Deschamps's face darkened with anger, and for a moment Abigail thought he was going to thump his fist on his desk to express his rage.

'Absolutely outrageous!' he fumed. 'The board have consulted our solicitors to explore suing that rag for slander.' Suddenly he frowned, concerned. 'You're not seriously considering that as a possibility?'

'No no,' Abigail assured him quickly. 'But some of the information contained in the piece has led to us look into the person who fed the story to the reporter at *Les Voix*. In particular, we feel that the person who mentioned the death of Paul LeMarc is someone we need to talk to. After all, it's not considered common knowledge, unlike the killings of the professor, Elaine Foret and now poor Monsieur Ruffalo.'

'Do you know who this person is?'

'We do,' said Abigail. 'He's a member of a gang of Apaches who hang around the streets of Montmartre. Our next task is to seek him out.'

Deschamps looked concerned.

'I would caution you to be very careful when dealing with these Apaches,' he warned. 'They can be very dangerous indeed.'

'We shall be fine,' said Abigail, with a confidence she did not completely feel. 'Superintendent Maison is providing us with police protection.'

Chevignon was sitting on the bed in his room, reading, when he heard the door to his room being unlocked. He looked up and noticed the looks of surprise and disappointment on the faces of the two soldiers who entered. One looked towards the dressing table.

'Where is the pistol?' he asked.

'I have it,' said Chevignon.' I will do what is required, at a time and place of my choosing.'

The two soldiers exchanged uncomfortable looks.

'I'm not sure if that is permitted,' said one.

'It is,' said Chevignon. 'As an officer and a gentleman, I know the code of conduct in matters of this sort.'

The two soldiers were obviously unhappy at this unexpected turn of events.

'We will need to report this to the general,' said one.

Chevignon gave a sardonic smile.

'Very well,' he said. 'If you wish to incur the general's wrath by disturbing him over this matter, that is your right. But you know the general as well as I. You will regret it.'

CHAPTER THIRTY-SIX

Daniel and Abigail stood alongside Julien Amity in Superintendent Maison's office, where Maison was about to address the six plainclothesmen who'd be accompanying them to Montmartre. The six were dressed in various disguises: one as a labourer, complete with a bag of tools; one had a sketch pad and a box of coloured chalks. 'He's going to pose as an artist doing sketches of the basilica,' Maison informed them.

'Very Montmartre,' said Abigail approvingly.

Three of the others wore rough clothes and looked like hoodlums, while the sixth wore the long black cassock of a priest.

'Is that allowed?' Abigail had enquired of the superintendent.

'His brother is a priest and has given permission to use his outfit if it helps catch a murderer.'

As Maison delivered his instructions to the plainclothes officers, Abigail translated for Daniel's benefit.

'We are in search of a young Apache who goes by the name of Jean-Luc Dubois, although we are not sure if that is his real name or an alias,' Maison announced.

He gestured towards Abigail, Daniel and Amity. 'On the

right are the two English detectives, Monsieur and Madame Wilson, who I have authorised to lead this search. The other man is Julien Amity, a reporter with *Les Voix*, the scurrilous newspaper that never ceases to attack the police.'

'I protest!' exclaimed Amity.

'Shut up,' snapped Maison 'You are here under sufferance. If I had my way you'd still be in a cell.' To the officers, he said, 'Monsieur Amity is the only one who has laid eyes on this boy we are seeking. He is the only one who can recognise him. We understand that this gang of Apaches hang around the Basilica of Sacré-Coeur at the top of the hill in Montmartre. Monsieur and Madame Wilson will walk up the hill towards the basilica, accompanied by Monsieur Amity.

'Janvier and Trossard will be already at the top in their respective roles as a priest and an artist. Lapointe, who is acting the part of a labourer, will keep a discreet distance behind the Wilsons as they walk up the hill. Andoluce, Pettit, and Jacquet, the ones posing as tough hoodlums, will amble along up the hill on the other side of the road, apparently looking for mischief to commit. They will be on the move because we don't know where this gang of Apaches will be. They may be at the top by the basilica; they may be halfway down the hill.

'The plan is that when Monsieur Amity sees this Jean-Luc Dubois, he waves at him and calls out that he needs to talk to him. The hope is that this Jean-Luc will separate from the rest of the gang and go to talk to him. Monsieur Amity will introduce him to Monsieur and Madame Wilson.

'It's possible the boy will run away. If that happens, this is where you come in. Your job is to apprehend this boy. It's likely the other Apaches will come to his aid. You have all been issued with pistols, but they are *only* to be used if your lives are in danger. And I mean *serious* danger, if any of these Apaches produce guns and try to shoot you or the Wilsons or Monsieur Amity.

'I have arranged for two patrol vehicles to be in the area. If there is trouble, sound your whistles and the vehicles will come to you with reinforcements. I must stress the safety of Monsieur and Madame Wilson is your highest priority here.'

Amity looked as if he was about to protest at this, but then decided against it.

'I will see you all back here after what we hope will be a successful mission,' Maison concluded.

Emile Chevignon walked out of the barracks wearing civilian clothes and carrying a bag with his few personal possessions, no longer an officer in the French Army. Cashiered! The indignity, after all his years of faithful service. At least he'd been spared the humiliation of being paraded before the other ranks and ceremoniously stripped of his insignia, and having his sword broken. But he knew that was just General DeLaGarde protecting his own reputation, rather than sparing Chevignon's feelings.

At the thought of the general, a sense of rage rose within him. How could the general treat him like this when he'd only been carrying out the general's orders?

He stopped at a newsvendor's stall and bought a copy of *Le Temps*. He then made for a café he had frequented when he was in the service, curious to see if any of his former fellow officers might join him. He ordered a coffee and then opened the newspaper. His eye caught a headline: 'Bravery award for British Embassy diplomat'. As he read the article, his rage built up even more and he experienced a headache more painful than he'd ever known before.

We understand that Edgar Belfont, a junior diplomat at the British Embassy in Paris, is to be presented with a medal in reward for his courage in foiling a recent assassination attempt in the streets of Paris. We understand the targets of the assassination attempt were an English couple, Mr and Mrs Wilson, who are currently in Paris on vacation. We do not know the identity of the would-be assassin. However, we do know that it was the bravery of Monsieur Belfont in disarming the attacker that prevented a dreadful tragedy from happening. The British ambassador, Sir Brian Otway, told this reporter: 'We are immensely proud of Monsieur Belfont, and it will be my great honour to present him with this gallantry award, the Distinguished Conduct Medal, on the direct orders of Her Majesty, Queen Victoria at a special ceremony to be held at the British Embassy on 23rd August.' We understand that Monsieur Belfont's parents, Lord and Lady Belfont, will be in attendance, as will the people he saved from a deadly fate, Monsieur and Madame Wilson.

Chevignon became aware that he was gripping the newspaper so tightly that his fingertips were tearing the page. *How dare they*, he thought vengefully. This Edgar Belfont was not a hero. He had not challenged Chevignon face to face; he was a lucky fool who had crept up behind Chevignon and attacked him.

He checked the names again. Edgar Belfont. Sir Brian Otway. Monsieur and Madame Wilson. All the people who had brought him down would be at this ceremony. As would Chevignon. He would shave his moustache off and wear a grey wig to avoid being recognised. He would dress as a servant, there to collect glasses from the people present. He had been to such ceremonies before; he knew they needed servants in attendance and how they would dress.

He would also make sure the chamber of his pistol, which he'd taken with him from the barracks in his bag, had a full round of six in it.

Those who had brought him down would pay the price.

Daniel and Abigail could see Amity's nervousness as they climbed the hill towards the Basilica. Despite the presence of the four plainclothesmen trailing behind them, he was shaking and twisting his hands together.

'Calm down,' said Daniel softly. 'You're perfectly safe.'

'You don't know these Apaches,' said Amity unhappily.

'We know their equivalent in London,' said Abigail. 'They're just boys.'

'Vicious boys.' Amity shuddered. 'They have knives.'

They continued up the hill. Ahead of them they saw Trossard, the artist, perched on a small stool and sketching with chalks. Janvier, wearing his brother's priest clothing, stood close to the actual basilica, studying what looked like a copy of the Bible. A gang of about a dozen youths were lounging by a fence that edged where the basilica was still under construction, smoking and talking amongst themselves. Every now and then a tussle would break out between two or three of them and they'd wrestle, each hauling the other about, until one of them fell to the ground.

'There they are,' whispered Amity.

He stopped and looked behind him nervously.

'Don't look around,' hissed Abigail. 'You'll draw attention to the men behind us.'

She took a firm grip on his elbow and propelled him forward, towards the gang of youths.

'You're hurting me!' complained Amity in a whine.

Abigail relaxed her fingers on his arm, but still kept a gentle hold on it.

'Do you see him?' she asked.

Amity gulped. 'Yes.'

'Call him.'

'Say he doesn't come?'

'Then we'll go to him.'

Reluctantly, Amity headed for the gang, his pace slowing the nearer he got to them. The youths had abandoned their wrestling games and were focusing on the three people approaching them.

'Patrice is there,' whispered Daniel to Abigail.

'Who's Patrice?' asked Amity.

'The brother of Flamand's secretary. The one who was killed at the Louvre.'

Patrice had obviously just seen Daniel and Abigail.

Immediately alert, he called out, 'Look out! *Les flics!*'

At this, the youths began to run, separating and scattering.

'Which one's Jean-Luc?' asked Abigail.

'Him,' said Amity, pointing to a short youth with long, lank, greasy hair who looked about fifteen.

'Jean-Luc!' called Abigail. 'We need to talk to you!' Then, as he backed away, she added, 'We have money for you!'

It didn't work. Jean-Luc ran, but then skidded to a stop as he realised the artist had got up from his stall and was running towards him. Jean-Luc turned and ran in the other direction, but when he saw the priest hurrying towards him, he stopped. By that time, Daniel and Abigail were running towards him. Jean-Luc reached into his pocket and pulled out a knife, which he held towards them.

'Stay away from me!' he called.

Suddenly the rest of the watching plainclothesmen were on the scene, the three toughs and the builder rushing at the gang, trying to catch them as they attempted to escape.

Daniel took off his coat as he ran and threw it at Jean-Luc, the cloth going over the blade of the knife. Daniel's speed brought him up close to the boy and he chopped down on the boy's arm, and the knife clattered to the ground. Jean-Luc reached down to scoop it up, but Abigail's foot came down hard on the knife, trapping it. He swore and aimed a punch at her, but she dodged it and let fly with a punch of her own, her fist hitting him in the chest, sending him stumbling backwards and he tumbled to the ground. Before he could get up, Daniel was on him, pulling the boy's hands behind his back.

'What's the French for "handcuffs"?' he asked Abigail.

'*Menottes*,' said Abigail. She shouted to the plainclothes policemen, who were now engaged in battles with the youths who hadn't made their escape, '*Menottes ici!*'

Janvier, the priest, left the youth he was battling with and hurried over to Abigail, producing a pair of handcuffs with which he secured Jean-Luc's wrists.

One of the other policemen produced his whistle and let blow a long blast on it, something he repeated until there was the clatter of horses' hooves on the cobbles and then a police van appeared.

CHAPTER THIRTY-SEVEN

Daniel sat to one side of the superintendent's desk, watching silently as Maison and Abigail questioned Jean-Luc Dubois and doing his best to pick up any words of French he thought he might recognise. Two burly uniformed officers stood directly behind Dubois, ready to move if the boy should start anything violent, but so far the youth seemed cowed.

Daniel reflected how Maison seemed to have accepted them as almost equal partners when it came to the Flamand murder investigation; he couldn't imagine the superintendent offering the same sort of co-operation to any other civilians. It was thanks to Abigail, of course. Not just that she spoke fluent French, but she was an acknowledged internationally famous Egyptologist who had impressed Georges Deschamps and the board of trustees at the Louvre when she'd agreed to give a talk at the museum. Already, just a few days after her talk had been announced in the press and in the Louvre newsletter, all the seats had been sold. For the Louvre, having Abigail talk about her life and work was a major coup.

But now, sitting next to Superintendent Maison and facing

the sullen youth who sat across from them at the superintendent's desk, Abigail was once again a Museum Detective, investigating a series of murders in one of the most famous museums in the world. *We've come a long way since we first met in Cambridge six years ago*, he thought.

'You're the person who told the reporter at *Les Voix* about this lunatic at the Louvre,' said Abigail. It wasn't a question; it was a statement said with such assurance that Dubois didn't even attempt to deny it.

'I was just passing on what someone else had told me,' he defended himself.

'Who?'

Dubois hesitated, looking around him as if desperate to find a way out.

'If you don't tell us, we'll assume no one else told you. That it was you who came up with the story,' said Maison.

'Yes,' said Dubois eagerly. 'That's what it was. A story to make some money.'

'But you were very specific about the names of the victims,' said Abigail. 'Professor Flamand. Elaine Foret. *Paul LeMarc.*' She leant towards him and asked pointedly, 'How did you know about Paul LeMarc?'

The boy gulped nervously.

'I don't know,' he said.

'The only person who'd have put his name on the list of victims was the person who killed him. Did you kill him?'

'No!' exclaimed Dubois desperately.

'Then who gave you his name?'

'Patrice,' burbled Dubois.

'Patrice?'

'Patrice Foret.'

'He was the one who told you there was a lunatic loose in the Louvre?'

'Yes.'

'How did he come up with this story?'

'From his sister. She worked at the Louvre. He told me she worked for Professor Flamand and she knew what was going on there.'

'When did Patrice tell you this?'

'After the steward was killed.'

'Armand Ruffalo?'

'Yes, but he didn't know his name. It was the journalist who knew the steward's name.'

'But it was Patrice who told you that Paul LeMarc had been killed by this alleged lunatic?'

'Yes. Those were the three names he said: Professor Flamand, his sister, Elaine, and Paul LeMarc.'

'And he told you the different ways they'd been killed? Flamand stabbed, his sister poisoned and LeMarc beaten to death?'

'Yes.'

Maison turned to Abigail and asked, 'Do you have any more questions?'

'No,' said Abigail.

Maison gestured for the two uniformed officers to take Dubois to a cell. After the youth had been taken away, he asked her, 'Do you believe him?'

'I do,' said Abigail. 'We need to find Patrice Foret.'

'You think he is the killer we are looking for?'

'I think it's possible,' said Abigail. 'If not, I'm sure he knows who it is.'

Superintendent Maison knocked at the door of the terraced house. From inside came the call of an elderly woman: 'Who is it?'

'It is Superintendent Maison of the police,' Maison called back. 'I need to talk to you, Madame Foret.'

'You'll have to give me time to get to the door and open it,' he heard Madame Foret call back.

He remembered the last time he had called on her after her daughter had been killed. He had noticed that she was blind, but very capable, able to find her way around the room. She was also acutely tuned in to every movement he made, her head turning this way and that as he moved about. A formidable woman indeed.

There was the sound of a chain being pulled back, then the door opened.

'I am sorry to disturb you, *madame*, but I need to talk to your son, Patrice.'

'Why?' she demanded. 'What's he done?'

'May I come in?' he asked. 'We don't need the whole street to hear what we say.'

'I don't mind,' she said. 'At my age, what have I to be ashamed of?' Then she gave a sigh. 'Except my son.'

She opened the door wider. 'Come in. Go through to the kitchen, where we sat last time you came.'

'Thank you,' said Maison, walking in.

'And wipe your feet,' she said sharply. 'There's a mat there by the door. Just because I'm blind it doesn't mean I don't keep my house clean.'

Maison wiped his feet, then walked through to the kitchen. Madame Foret shut and locked the door, then followed him.

'I hope you're not sitting in my chair?' she demanded.

'No, *madame*. I remembered which one was yours from my last visit. I shall take this one on the other side of the stove.'

Madame Foret waited until they were both seated, before repeating her question. 'What's my good-for-nothing son done?'

'We want to talk to him about a friend of his: Jean-Luc Dubois.'

'One of those raggletaggle urchins Patrice hangs around with by the Sacré-Coeur,' scolded Madame Foret. 'My neighbour, Madame Nettle, has told me about them. They are a disgrace to the neighbourhood, and my son is a disgrace to this house.'

'I assume he is out. When will he be back?'

She shrugged. 'Who knows? He wasn't here yesterday and he hasn't been here today. He does this sometimes, stays away for days at a time with those pals of his, getting up to who-knows-what mischief.'

'Is there any particular place he goes?' asked Maison.

'If so, I don't know where it is. He rarely talks to me.'

Maison looked at the old woman with a feeling of deep sympathy. What could he tell her? That they were looking for her son as a possible suspect in a series of murders? No, it would be too cruel to say it aloud to this woman who'd already lost her husband, then her daughter. And at this moment it was just speculation.

'Do you have a recent photograph of Patrice?' he asked.

She looked at him suspiciously. 'You want to get your policemen to show it around?' she asked.

'Yes,' said Maison. It would be unfair to lie to her, and also counterproductive. She was too sharp to be fooled.

The old woman pointed at three photographs in wooden frames on the dresser. 'There's one there. The others are Elaine and my late husband. It may seem silly for a blind woman to keep photographs on display when she can't see them, but I know they're there. I touch them. It helps me.'

'May I borrow the one of Patrice?' asked Maison. 'I shall return it to you as soon as it's been copied. I promise it won't be damaged.'

She sat and thought it over, then said, 'I'm blind. You could have taken it and thought I wouldn't know it was gone.'

'I would never do a thing like that,' Maison assured her. 'I know these photographs are precious to you.' He paused, then added, 'And you'd know it was gone when you went to touch it, and you'd know it was me who took it.'

She chuckled. 'I like you, policeman,' she said. 'Take it. But bring it back.'

'I will,' Maison promised. 'Thank you.'

CHAPTER THIRTY-EIGHT

Emile Chevignon moved around the large function room at the British Embassy, collecting up empty glasses and plates where the remains of the hors d'oeuvres being served to the guests at the ceremony had been left. It was the function of a menial and he seethed with silent rage as he did it, filling a tray and then taking it to the kitchen where the staff washed the glasses and crockery. None of the people here who ignored him as they prattled brainlessly to one another were fit to lick his boots. But this was the best way he could infiltrate this travesty of a ceremony. To celebrate the oaf who had brought him down, who had ruined his mission! It was an outrage.

He knew how these ceremonies were organised; he'd been in charge of enough of them during his military career. Extra staff were hired: waiters and waitresses to serve the drink and canapés. And at the bottom of the heap, the anonymous men in white tunics whose job was to clear up the detritus, the empty and half-empty glasses, the crockery and cutlery, to ensure the function room always looked pristine. They were the class of worker that no one took any notice of, unlike the waiters and stewards on duty.

Chevignon had made contact with an acquaintance who

worked for the catering company that provided the staff for this occasion. Marcel Moreau had provided the same kind of services to Chevignon for some military events such as regimental dinners. Chevignon had approached Moreau and told him that he had made a bet with a fellow officer that he could infiltrate this event. 'A hundred francs!' he told the caterer. 'But it is not the money, it is the satisfaction of showing this idiot that it can be done. So I will give seventy-five francs of the money to you if you can arrange for me to be employed at the event as one of the white-tunic cleaners.'

'You are not planning some sort of prank that could get me in trouble?' Moreau had enquired anxiously.

'Absolutely not!' Chevignon assured him. 'You know me, Marcel, as an officer and a gentleman. This is just to prove to this person, who has challenged me, that it can be done. And so that there is no chance I will be recognised, I shall shave off my moustache for the occasion.'

'It is that important to you?'

'A bet is a bet, and to defeat this particular person is very important to me. To prove that I am right.'

Moreau pondered it, then asked, 'And you'll pay me seventy-five francs?'

'As soon as I receive the hundred francs.'

And so it had been agreed. Chevignon had shaved off his moustache, rendering him, as far as he was concerned, invisible, and arrived at the back door of the embassy and joined Moreau's cleaning crew. He'd hung his outdoor jacket up in the kitchen then slipped on the white uniform tunic. He'd left his pistol in the pocket of his jacket until he was ready to use it. He didn't want to take the chance of the pistol banging against something as he hurried around carrying out his duties and arousing suspicion.

He also needed to wait for the right opportunity to make his move. He needed his targets to be together: this Edgar Belfont, Superintendent Maison and the two interfering English, the Wilson couple. These were the four who'd ruined his life.

He'd identified Edgar Belfont, the young man accompanied by an elderly couple, who he'd discovered were the young man's parents. Marcel Moreau had stressed to Chevignon these were very important people and must be treated as such. Moreau had also pointed out the British ambassador, Sir Brian Otway. 'At no time must there be any sort of interaction with these four,' Moreau had told him firmly. 'They are the guests of honour.'

Chevignon watched the crowd assemble as the various guests arrived. Superintendent Maison arrived, resplendent in his ceremonial uniform, the breast of his tunic adorned with medals and decorations. Chevignon made sure that he kept well away from the superintendent; he was the only one who might conceivably recognise him.

The Wilsons were late arrivals, dressed mundanely in their everyday clothes. Chevignon assumed they'd decided not to purchase or even hire special outfits for the occasion, but just wear what they'd brought with them. *What peasants they are*, he thought scornfully. *Surely the purpose of such an occasion as this is for people to dress as grandly as possible, to show themselves off.* Such dismal, dowdy people, and they had humiliated him! Well, he would have his revenge tonight!

* * *

Patrice Foret sat in the yard at the rear of a butcher's shop next to a pile of offal, hearts, lungs, intestines, stomachs. The stench was overwhelming, which was one reason he'd chosen it as his place to seek safe refuge. It kept most people away, reducing the chance of someone stumbling upon him.

He knew he couldn't go home, nor could he hide out with any of his gang; the police would be watching them, keeping an eye on their houses.

This was all Jean-Luc's fault. Patrice didn't know how or what had gone wrong, but it had been Jean-Luc who'd brought the law to the gang's hangout at the top of Montmartre. That shout of 'Jean-Luc' from that reporter had given things away. Julien Amity.

It had seemed a good plan. Send Jean-Luc to the offices of *Les Voix* to find this socialist anti-government reporter, Julien Amity, and spin him the story about the lunatic at the Louvre. Send the police off on a wild goose chase. Instead, the police had come looking for Jean-Luc, along with those two English detectives who'd called at his mother's house, the Wilsons. How had the Wilsons got involved?

How had they made the connection between Flamand and Jean-Luc?

That didn't matter right now; what mattered was that Patrice had to get away. Escape. But where to? To get anywhere required money, and money was something he hadn't got at this moment, and it would be too dangerous to seek out one of his gang to ask for some.

He felt in his pocket for his knife. His knife was the only thing he could trust. People would cough up money when a knife was being pointed at them. Not the butcher and his assistants, of course – they were far more skilful with knives than Patrice was. No, the best targets would be the tourists who wandered around Montmartre. A man or a woman on their own. With a couple it was possible that the man would resist rather than be seen backing down from a confrontation in front of his woman. Yes, a man would be best, he decided. A man on his own. One who looked as if he was damaged in some way. There were plenty of old soldiers around with legs or arms missing. He would seek out one of them.

Daniel and Abigail stood at the entrance to the function room and took in the gathering assembled.

'This looks like a very high-level event,' murmured Daniel. 'We seem to be the only ones not in evening dress or highly decorated uniforms. I said you should have hired a dress for the occasion.'

'Why?' demanded Abigail. 'We're not the occasion – that's Edgar. The last thing I want to do is turn up wearing something that might overshadow the people this event is about. The dress I'm wearing is perfectly suited to this sort of occasion. And if I had hired an outfit, it would have meant you would have had to dress up as well.'

Daniel shook his head. 'I don't think that would have been expected.'

'You don't know that. Look at Superintendent Maison's outfit. I've seen fewer medals and less gold braid on an army general.'

A waiter appeared bearing a tray and offered them drink

and a small plate of canapés. They took the drinks, but Abigail waved away the snacks.

'We'll just leave crumbs everywhere, all over the carpet,' she said as the waiter moved on.

'I'm sure the embassy have made allowances for that,' said Daniel, disappointed as he saw the tray with food vanish.

'Trust me, it's not easy to stand talking to people with both your hands full, one holding a glass of drink and the other with a plate of food. We'll eat later, once things have settled down.'

Superintendent Maison joined them.

'I am glad you are here,' he said.

'As we were the assassin's targets, we couldn't really stay away,' said Abigail. 'We're both enormously grateful to Edgar Belfont. If it hadn't been for his action we'd be dead.'

'Yes, he's an interesting young man,' said Maison. 'I wanted to tell you that I have distributed a photograph of Patrice Foret to the patrols who police Montmartre in the hope we can apprehend him. I went to see his mother, but she has not heard from him for a couple of days.'

'He may not even be in Montmartre,' said Abigail. 'He could be anywhere in Paris.'

'He could, but street rats like Patrice Foret feel safest in their own areas. It is a world they know well.'

'He's clever,' said Abigail. 'Aggressive, defiant, but clever. That's the impression I got when we met him, however briefly.'

'I agree,' said Maison. 'It is up to us to be cleverer.' A movement near them caught his eye.

'We're about to be joined,' he murmured. 'The guest of

honour and his family are coming to talk to you.'

'Or to you,' pointed out Abigail.

Maison smiled and shook his head. 'I have already had a good conversation with them. They are charming people, but I think their desire now is to talk to you.'

He stepped back and smiled politely at the three members of the Belfont family and spoke rapidly in French, begging their forgiveness, but there was someone he needed to see. He then bowed and moved to another part of the room.

'I believe the superintendent is being courteous and allowing us to talk to you.' Edgar Belfont smiled. 'Abigail, Daniel, I'd like you to meet my parents, Lord and Lady Belfont.'

'This is a great pleasure.' Lady Belfont smiled, shaking hands with both of them. 'Edgar has told us so much about you.'

'And, of course, we're aware of your reputations from the newspapers in England,' added her husband. 'Especially you, Mrs Wilson, and your astounding archaeological experiences in Egypt and Italy.'

'Ah, Mr and Mrs Wilson!' came the genial voice of Sir Brian Otway as he joined them. 'I'm delighted you could make it. But would you mind if I stole young Edgar and his parents from you for a moment? Things we need to talk about over the presentation of the award.'

'Not at all.' Abigail smiled.

As Otway led the Belfonts away, Daniel said, 'Nice people, Edgar's parents.'

'Yes, and it was lucky you weren't holding a plate of food with all that shaking of hands.'

'True,' admitted Daniel.

Suddenly Abagail stiffened at something that had caught her eye.

'What's the matter?' asked Daniel.

'Did you see that waiter?'

'Which one? There are plenty here.'

'Actually, he's not a waiter; he's one of the crew picking up glasses and crockery and taking them to the kitchen for washing. The ones wearing the white tunics.'

'What about him?'

'There's something familiar about him.'

'Show me.'

'He's not here at the moment. He just disappeared into the kitchen.' Then she was alert again. 'No, wait. He's come back.'

'I see him,' said Daniel. He frowned. 'He doesn't look familiar to me.'

'He reminds me of the man who took a shot at us.'

'Chevignon?'

'Yes.'

Daniel shook his head doubtfully. 'We only saw him briefly when he was lying on the ground. The one thing I remember about him was his moustache. That man's cleanshaven.'

'He could have shaved it off.'

Daniel still looked doubtful. 'I don't think it's him. Like I said, we only saw Chevignon for a minute at the most. Then the police arrived and took him away. That man's altogether different.'

'No he isn't. All right, he doesn't have a moustache, but there's something about his cheekbones.'

'His cheekbones?'

'Trust me, Daniel.'

Daniel shrugged. 'I think you're mistaken, but you've often been proved right when I've been wrong. But what would he be doing here working as a waiter?'

'To get close to the people he wants revenge on. In particular, Edgar.'

Daniel nodded. 'I'll go and get Superintendent Maison. You stay here and keep an eye on him.' He studied the man as he collected more glasses. 'He doesn't appear to be armed.'

'A small pistol can be easily hidden.'

'True,' said Daniel. He looked across at where Edgar was standing with his parents and Sir Brian Otway, talking about the presentation. 'Keep an eye on him from a distance. Don't get involved. I won't be long.'

With that, Daniel hurried off. Abigail watched as the man disappeared into the kitchen, carrying a tray laden with dirty glasses. She moved towards the kitchen, then stationed herself beside the exit door. Like most large kitchens, there were two doors, one for incoming traffic, one for exiting.

There was a brief pause, then the man she was convinced was Chevignon appeared, carrying a tray. Her eyes went to the white jacket he wore. She was sure that something in the right-hand pocket was heavier than the left one; it definitely weighed it down and pulled it out of shape. She was also sure whatever it was hadn't been in his pocket before.

She followed the man as he headed in the direction of Otway, Edgar and his parents. The man stopped beside a table on which people had left used glasses, some half-empty, but instead of collecting them he stood and looked around the room.

He's weighing up his next move, realised Abigail.

She moved swiftly and positioned herself close behind him, then poked him hard in the back with the tips of two of her fingers.

'This is a gun in your back, Monsieur Chevignon,' she said quietly. 'If you reach for that pistol in your pocket I shall fire. Put the tray down and raise your hands to your shoulders.'

I will look a compete idiot if I'm wrong, she thought to herself.

The man she thought was Chevignon hesitated, then slowly raised his hands. Abigail dipped her hand into the right-hand pocket of his tunic and pulled out the pistol, which she then slipped into her own coat pocket.

'What's going on?' demanded the voice of Superintendent Maison, appearing beside her.

'In my best French I told him, "*Chevignon est ici*",' said Daniel.

'And he is,' said Abigail. She produced the pistol from her pocket. 'He was carrying this.'

Maison took hold of the man in the white coat and turned him round to face them.

'Chevignon!' he growled.

'It might be better if he put his hands down,' suggested Abigail. 'We don't want to cause a scene on this special occasion.'

'I think it's too late for that,' sighed Daniel.

Abigail was suddenly aware thar Otway and Edgar were

closing in on them, puzzled expressions on their faces.

'What's happening?' asked Otway.

'I believe Abigail has just prevented a mass shooting,' said Daniel quietly.

'I'll deal with him,' grunted Maison.

He took a firm grip on Chevignon's arm and manoeuvred him towards the door, where the uniformed officer on duty had seen what was going on and called a colleague to join him.

'Who was that?' asked Otway, bewildered.

'He looked a bit like the man who took a shot at you,' said Belfont. 'His brother?'

'The same man, but without his moustache,' said Daniel. 'Abigail spotted him. I said it wasn't him and I was wrong.'

'But what was he doing here?'

Abigail tapped her coat pocket. 'He was carrying a pistol. I assume he was going to shoot someone with it. I'd better go and hand it to the superintendent. It is evidence, after all.'

With that, she made for the lobby in search of Maison.

'You mean she disarmed him?' asked Otway, awed. 'On her own?'

'Yes, she does that sort of thing,' said Daniel.

'My God, your wife is some amazing woman. But . . . how did she do it?'

'I'm sure she'll tell you if you ask her.'

One of the embassy officials appeared and whispered something to Otway.

'Of course.' Otway nodded. He turned to the others and said, 'I've been reminded that it is time for the presentation. Are you ready, Edgar?'

'I am, sir.'

'Then I suggest you join your parents.'

With that, the ambassador headed for the low dais that had been put in place in an area adorned with potted plants. To one side sat the four members of a chamber quartet, patiently waiting for their cue to start playing to introduce the ceremony. Otway gave the signal, and they began to play.

'I'll just go and find Abigail,' Daniel whispered to Belfont, who nodded and moved to join his parents.

As Daniel reached the door, Abigail and the superintendent were just walking in.

'We heard the music start,' said Abigail.

'And Chevignon?'

'He's safely in the custody of the police.'

Daniel, Abigail and Maison walked back into the function room. The small crowd had assembled in front of the dais on which Otway now stood. Most were staff from the embassy, along with a few English dignitaries who were already in Paris. There were, too, representatives of the French establishment, resplendent in ceremonial sashes of red, white and blue. Edgar Belfont stood in the front row with his very proud parents.

Otway made a discreet gesture towards the quartet, who brought their rendition to a well-rehearsed conclusion.

'My lords, ladies and gentlemen,' announced Otway. 'We are here this evening to recognise the bravery of a member of the staff of the British Embassy here in Paris, who placed himself in danger to foil an attempt by an armed assassin on the lives of two British citizens, in spite of the fact that he, himself, was unarmed. In recognition of his act of valour,

Her gracious Majesty and Empress of India, Queen Victoria, has personally decreed that he be awarded the Distinguished Conduct Medal for gallantry. It gives me the greatest pleasure to call the Honourable Edgar Percival Arbuthnot Belfont forward to receive this award.'

Edgar Belfont stepped elegantly forward and mounted the dais, then stood to attention as Otway hung the red ribbon bearing the medal around his neck. Otway then bowed to his young assistant, who returned the bow, then turned to face his parents and the audience, who broke into applause. None applauded more enthusiastically than Daniel and Abigail.

'Our hero,' murmured Abigail.

'Our life-saver,' added Daniel in a voice filled with gratitude.

CHAPTER THIRTY-NINE

General DeLaGarde read the letter from Superintendent Maison. It was not really a letter, despite beginning 'Dear General DeLaGarde'; it was actually little more than a curt note. It advised the general that Emile Chevignon had been arrested on a charge of attempted murder. The crime had been committed the previous evening at the British Embassy during a celebratory event attended by the British ambassador and other dignitaries.

> *In view of the highly placed and influential personnel who witnessed this outrage and were present at Chevignon's arrest, there will be no way to avoid a trial. I am sure you will recall the consequences of such a trial to yourself and the army that I outlined to you previously.*

The consequences, thought DeLaGarde bitterly. His own career in ruins. The reputation of the army tarnished. And, what was worse, Chevignon had been involved in the anti-Dreyfus campaign from its early days. He knew all about the machinations behind the scenes that had put Dreyfus on Devil's Island. And he'd been the reason the attempts on Labori and the Wilsons had failed. All of which would be sure to come out at his trial; the prosecution would make sure of that.

DeLaGarde picked up the bell on his desk and rang it. Immediately his door opened and the sergeant on guard duty in the corridor looked in.

'Tell Captain Martin I wish to see him,' said the general.

The sergeant saluted, then disappeared, pulling the door shut. There was a short delay of just a few minutes, then Captain Martin, the general's aide, entered his office. The General passed Maison's letter to him.

'This is a dangerous situation,' he said to his aide. 'Chevignon knows everything about our role in the Dreyfus affair. We cannot afford for him to be questioned in open court by some manipulative lawyer out to destroy the army's reputation.'

Captain Martin nodded. 'You wish this matter be dealt with?' he asked.

'For the sake of the army,' said DeLaGarde. 'There must be no hitches or errors. We are in this situation because Chevignon has blundered too many times. As I understand it, Chevignon is currently incarcerated at the police prefecture, but he will undoubtedly be transferred to a prison on remand to await his trial. That transfer seems to be to offer the best opportunity for . . . settling this matter.'

Again, Martin nodded. 'We will need a good marksman,' he said. 'Someone who's proven his accuracy at distance. I think I know the very man.'

'There must be no more mistakes,' stressed DeLaGarde. 'An error this time could be catastrophic for all of us.'

'There will be no mistakes,' Martin assured him. With that, the aide saluted smartly, then exited the general's office.

Patrice moved along the narrow back alley from the butcher's yard, making for a drinking den called Le Tabard. He knew it was a place where ex-soldiers gathered to drink and swap stories. That was his target, a wounded ex-soldier, his senses befuddled by drink and unable to fight back.

He saw an elderly man appear in the alley from the direction of Le Tabard, struggling along with difficulty on one leg, using a wooden crutch, his other leg cut off below the knee.

Perfect.

Patrice pressed himself into a recess in the wall of the alley and waited, watching the man draw near. As the man drew closer, Patrice could smell the wafts of cheap gin coming off him. The man came level with Patrice and was about to lurch past him, when Patrice barred his way, pointing his knife at the man.

'Give me your money!' he growled.

The man stopped and stared at him, bewildered.

'Give me your money!' repeated Patrice, louder this time.

In response, the man suddenly swung his wooden crutch, smashing it into the side of Patrice's head.

Stunned, Patrice fell to the cobbles, where the man carried on hitting him with his crutch while balanced on one leg and shouting, 'Bastard! Bastard!'

There was the sound of running feet, then four men

appeared, brought by the sounds of the commotion. They all wore ragged clothes and one lacked an arm.

'What happened?' asked one.

'This bastard tried to rob me with a knife!' snorted the one-legged man. 'Me! Who fought a whole army in Egypt!'

With that, he landed another hard blow on Patrice's head, and the youth slumped into unconsciousness.

There was the sound of a police whistle, then two uniformed policemen appeared in the alley.

'Stand back!' called one of the policemen.

'This bastard tried to rob me,' said the one-legged man angrily. 'He threatened me with a knife.' He pointed with his crutch at Patrice's knife lying on the cobbles. 'There it is.'

The policemen approached the unconscious youth, then one pulled a printed handbill from his tunic pocket and showed it to his companion. 'It's him,' he said, stabbing his finger at the printed photograph. 'He's wanted.'

'Is there a reward?' asked one of the other men. 'If so, old Sanditon here should get it. He's the one who caught him.'

'I don't know,' replied the policeman. 'But, if there is, we'll make sure he's rewarded.' He turned to his colleague and said, 'Go and get a carriage so we can take him to the nearest station. I'll stay here and watch him. We don't want to risk him getting up and running off.'

Old Sanditon glared down at the prone body of Patrice and swung his crutch down hard on his head once again. 'Don't worry, he's not going anywhere.'

* * *

The police van pulled up outside the prison. The officer handcuffed to Chevignon led him down the steps at the back of the van and set off towards the prison's iron gates. It was only a few yards to the gates, but to Chevignon it felt an interminable distance. He burnt with the indignity of his situation. Not only to be stripped of his uniform, his rank, his position in the army, but to be treated like a common criminal! It was outrageous. So unfair! He was glad he had no family alive to see his humiliation.

He would have his revenge, of course, he promised himself that. He would expose General DeLaGarde's role in the Dreyfus affair, the plotting and the treachery. It was an injustice that he, Emile Chevignon, a true patriot, should he incarcerated while the men responsible for this whole debacle remained free and in position.

On reflection, the best way to use what he knew was to *threaten* to expose the truth. That would be the deal he'd offer: *give me my freedom and a pardon and let me return to the army in my old rank of captain, otherwise I will tell all and you will all go down.* Their careers would be at an end, and for some of them it would mean prison, and possibly even execution. *Yes*, he thought as they neared the gates, *that will be my way out.*

It was the last thought he would ever have. The bullet struck him in the back of the head and blew his skull apart, his blood spattering the officer beside him, who let out a shriek of alarm and threw himself to the ground next to Chevignon's dead body.

CHAPTER FORTY

Patrice Foret was in a bed in the medical ward of La Santé prison, his skull covered with thick bandages. His nose was broken and the rest of his face was badly bruised. Beneath his pyjama jacket, more thick bandages were wrapped around his upper torso.

'They suspect his skull is fractured,' Superintendent Maison told Abigail and Daniel as they walked towards Foret's bed. 'Certainly, two of his ribs are broken.'

'Who did it?' asked Abigail.

'An elderly one-legged army veteran he tried to rob,' said Maison.

A warder was sitting on a chair beside Foret's bed. He stood up and moved away so that the superintendent and the two visitors could sit down on the chairs that had been provided for them. Another warder stood at the foot of the bed, watching Patrice carefully.

Although Daniel knew that, lacking French as he did, he wouldn't be able to be involved in the questioning of Patrice, he was pleased that the superintendent had included him in the visit.

'How are you?' asked Abigail.

Patrice gave an angry snort. 'How do you think I am? I've been badly beaten up. That brute very nearly killed me. They think I could still die.'

'You had a knife. You were going to kill him,' said Maison.

'No!' spat Patrice. 'I was just going to rob him.'

'Why?'

'Because I needed money.'

'To get away.'

'Of course. I was being hunted. And for nothing.'

'It was you who told Jean-Luc about the lunatic at the Louvre,' said Abigail.

'It was a well-known fact,' said Patrice.

'In that case it's odd that your sister didn't mention it after the professor was killed.'

'She thought you'd done it,' said Patrice.

'She could still have mentioned it after the police cleared me.'

When Patrice didn't respond, but just lay there glaring at her challengingly, she said, 'You made this lunatic up.'

'Why would I do that?' demanded Patrice.

'To hide the fact that it was you who killed them. The professor. Your sister.'

Patrice tried to push himself up, his fists clenched in anger, but then he sank down again. 'Let me go!' he shouted, and once more he tried to struggle up. The warder pushed down.

'If you do that again you will be tied to that bed,' Maison warned him.

Patrice scowled.

'Why did you kill Paul LeMarc?' sked Abigail.

'I don't have to listen to this,' Patrice said sullenly.

'No,' said Abigail. 'You can tell us about it instead.'

'There's nothing to tell!' snapped Patrice defiantly.

'Then I'll tell you,' said Abigail. 'You killed Paul LeMarc because Professor Flamand paid you to. LeMarc was investigating the professor's finances and Flamand needed him to be stopped. He wasn't the kind of person who could do it himself, but he thought you, a young Apache, violent and eager for money, could. So he paid you.'

'He did not pay me!' burst out Patrice, so angry that he spat the words, globs of his saliva splashing on his pyjama jacket.

'He cheated you,' said Abigail.

Patrice fell silent and slumped down in the bed, hiding his eyes from her.

'The professor always had money troubles,' Abigail continued. 'He owed money everywhere. He even borrowed from your sister. But you didn't know that; you thought he had money.'

Patrice looked at her, scowling. Abigail could see that mentally he was in torment, desperate to get out of this but wondering how.

'We have an eyewitness who saw you outside your sister's office on the day she died,' Abigail said.

It was a shot in the dark. Louise Perrault hadn't identified Patrice particularly, but he fitted her description of the youth she'd seen, and the certainty in Abigail's voice as she told him about the eyewitness pulled the rug from under his fragile determination to deny everything. He sagged on the pillows and a tear trickled out of his eye and ran down his cheek.

'The professor lied to me,' said Patrice miserably.

'So you killed him.'

'He cheated me!' shouted Patrice defensively. 'He promised me he'd pay me. He kept promising, but there was never any money for me. He'd taken me for a fool. Because I was an Apache, he thought there was nothing I could do. I couldn't sue him or anything, not after what had happened to LeMarc, because I would get arrested for murder. Flamand said he'd never told me to kill LeMarc, had said he'd just asked for me to warn him off, that's all, and that's what I'd intended to do. Just knock him about a bit. But LeMarc resisted so I had to hit him a bit harder. I thought he was just knocked out when he fell to the ground. It was his fault for fighting back. It was still the Professor's fault that LeMarc died.'

'So you killed the professor.'

'That was his fault. I'd asked him for a long time to pay me the money he owed me, over and over again. In the end he kept avoiding me, so I went to see him in his office at the Louvre. He got angry and told me to get out or he'd call security and have me thrown out. He threatened me. He made me angry. I picked up this knife that was on his desk to try and scare him into giving me the money he owed me. He tried to take it off me and in the struggle he fell on the knife.' He let out a groan. 'That was when my sister walked in. She'd heard the shouting between us. When she saw the professor was dead with his own knife sticking out of his chest, she began to panic. Then she gradually calmed down. She told me that the professor was due to meet someone in his office in a few moments' time. She told me to get out and she'd take care of things. She'd fix it so this woman who was coming would get the blame.'

'Me,' said Abigail.

'I didn't know who it was,' said Patrice. 'I just ran.'

'Why did you kill your sister?' asked Abigail.

'She threatened to tell on me. She was in love with the professor. She told me she'd decided she couldn't let his death go like that. She said she'd tell the police what had happened, but that it had been an accident.' He shook his head. 'I couldn't allow her to do that.'

'So you forced poison down her throat.'

'I did my best to make it look like she'd killed herself.'

'But you knew your sister was a devout Catholic. Devout Catholics do not commit suicide.'

'I didn't think of that. I'm not a practising Catholic. I hate the Catholic faith. I hate all religions. They're rubbish!'

'And the steward at the Louvre? Armand Ruffalo. You killed him to give credence to your story that there was lunatic at large at the Louvre.'

'I felt you were closing in on me. I had to do something.'

Lieutenant Poiret was in the barrack room playing cards with three other junior officers and losing. His mind wasn't on the game; instead his mind was filled with images of Captain Chevignon in a cell at the police prefecture. The indignity!

The unfairness of it all! For one of the bravest people he'd ever known, one of the most loyal to the army, to be treated in this way was intolerable.

It still weighed heavy on Poiret that the captain's fall from grace had started with Poiret's failure to eliminate the lawyer, Labori. *If I had done the job properly, none of this would have happened; the captain would still be here, instead of being cruelly cast out of the life and career he loved.*

The door of the barrack room was kicked open and Lieutenant Schwenk came in, looking angry. The card players paused and looked at him, aware that something was badly wrong. Schwenk hesitated, then came over and joined them and sat down heavily on an empty chair.

'Bastards!' he growled venomously.

'Who?' asked one of the players.

'All of them. The top brass. Bastards!'

'We know that but why particularly today?'

'I've just come back from a mission,' Schwenk told them sourly. 'A *special* mission.'

They looked at him, puzzled.

'But you've been here in Paris.'

'The mission was in Paris.' He spat on the wooden floor as if trying to get a bad taste out of his mouth.

'What was the mission?' asked Poiret.

'An execution,' said Schwenk. 'One of our own.' His face creased in anger. 'I hate them. But I had no choice. The orders came from the very top.'

'What execution?' asked one of the other players.

'It was from a distance. From an attic room in a building.

338

They wanted an expert sniper, and they said my work showed I was the best. It was something I've been proud of, until today.' He lapsed into a brooding silence, before uttering again, 'The bastards!'

'Who was it?' asked Poiret.

Schwenk shook his head. 'I don't want to talk about it any more. I'm going to go out and get drunk.'

With that he pushed himself to his feet and lumbered out of the room. The card players looked at one another with a mixture of puzzlement and concern.

'Who did he shoot?' asked Vian.

'It sounds like his target was a politician, or maybe a businessman,' suggested Thomas.

'No,' said Vian. 'He said it was one of our own.'

'A fellow soldier?' asked Poiret. 'But why?'

'Who knows,' said Thomas. 'Just thank God it wasn't one of us.'

As Abigail, Daniel and Superintendent Maison walked from La Santé Prison towards the waiting police carriage, Abigail said, 'That was a strange feeling, going back to the place where I was imprisoned when we first came here. I still remember looking out of my cell window and seeing the guillotine, and wondering if I'd be its next victim.'

'No,' said Daniel firmly. 'I'd have made sure that didn't happen.'

'You couldn't have stopped it,' said Abigail wryly.

Maison had caught the word 'guillotine' and he said sympathetically, 'La Santé brings back bad memories for you, eh, *madame*?' Then he brightened and added, 'Still, we have the confession from Patrice Foret.'

'I'm sorry we led you down a false trail by suggesting that Paul LeMarc was killed by Madame LeMarc and her lover, Luigi,' apologised Abigail.

'It is no problem,' said Maison. 'As it turns out, that led to us discovering that this Luigi was actually someone called Pesta, wanted for robberies and violence elsewhere in France. We were also able to recover the insurance money he stole from Madame LeMarc. So, your instinct about him being guilty was correct, just not about killing Paul LeMarc.'

They climbed aboard the carriage.

'Where to?' asked Maison. 'Your hotel?'

'The Louvre, if you wouldn't mind,' said Abigail. 'I need to discuss the talk I'm to give there with Monsieur Deschamps.'

'Which is no longer necessary as a ruse to enable you to carry out your investigations,' said Maison. 'The murders of Professor Flamand and Elaine Foret are now solved.'

'Yes, but Monsieur Deschamps only agreed to it to accommodate us. And it is a great honour for me to give such a talk at the Louvre.'

Maison nodded. 'If you will permit, I will be there in the audience.'

'To a talk about Egyptian pyramids?' asked Abigail. 'Are you sure?'

'It will be my pleasure,' said Maison. He called to the driver: 'To the Louvre.'

* * *

Lieutenant Poiret marched along the corridor towards General DeLaGarde's office. It was important, he felt, to appear official and determined and detached if he was to achieve what he intended. Inside, he was far from detached. When he learnt that it had been Captain Chevignon who'd been assassinated by Schwenk as he was being taken to the prison, his rage was barely controllable. Chevignon, his mentor, in fact his military idol. No, not just military, Chevignon had been the best example of a man he'd ever known. If Chevignon had been a woman, Poiret would have said unashamedly that he loved her. The truth was that his feelings for Chevignon were, indeed, those of love. Not that he'd ever admit as such, certainly not to the captain, at least while he'd been alive. But now the captain was dead, cruelly and cynically murdered, he could admit it to himself. But now there was no chance of there ever being any real intimacy to their relationship.

He did not blame Schwenk, the man who'd pulled the fatal trigger. It was obvious from the way Schwenk had spoken to them that he hated what he'd been ordered to do and had only carried out the order under duress. No, there was one man who was responsible for what had happened to the captain, first the humiliations, then his murder.

Poiret arrived outside the general's office where a sergeant stood on guard duty. Poiret snapped smartly to attention and saluted.

'Lieutenant Poiret reporting to the general as ordered,' he said crisply.

The sergeant frowned. 'I've received no instructions that you've been summoned.'

'Those were the orders I received from the general's aide de camp,' said Poiret firmly.

'Very well,' said the sergeant.

He rapped at the door, then opened it and announced, 'Lieutenant Poiret, sir!'

There was no response from the general. Poiret pushed past the sergeant and entered the general's office, stopping and saluting smartly.

The general regarded him, frowning.

'Yes?' he asked. 'What do you want?'

Poiret pushed the door shut, then produced a pistol, which he pointed at DeLaGarde.

'For Captain Chevignon,' he said.

He pulled the trigger and the bullet struck the general in the chest, sending him sliding backwards in his chair. Poiret pulled the trigger a second time, and this bullet took the general full in the face, blowing his head apart.

Behind Poiret, the door was opened and the sergeant rushed in, but before the sergeant could do anything, Poiret had brought the barrel of his pistol to point at his own forehead and pulled the trigger, collapsing in a bloodied heap on the floor.

CHAPTER FORTY-ONE

'Niuserre called the sun temple he built at Abusir, "Delight of Ra",' explained Abigail to the audience packed into the Egyptian Room at the Louvre. Behind her on the temporary stage were two enormous illustrations taken from the Louvre's archives, and usually kept safely in a store room. The first was a map of the area of Abusir, located to the south of Cairo, showing the siting of the pyramids and temples erected close to the north shore of Lake Abusir: the four pyramids of Ranaferef, Khentkawes, Neferirkare and Niuserre, close together, with the pyramid of Sahure nearby, then the Sun Temple of Userkaf a distance away, and the Sun Temple of Niuserre half a mile further on. The other illustration was of Niuserre's sun temple itself, showing buildings of the outer court, including the obelisk in the middle of the court, which towered over everything, then the causeway from the open court to the temple itself.

In his seat at the side of the hall, Daniel watched, as enrapt as everyone else. True, he couldn't understand a word of what she was saying – Abigail was delivering her talk in fluent French – but he remembered her telling him all about her work at the sun temple when she came back to England from Abusir. She'd shown him drawings and maps then, but these two giant illustrations from the Louvre's own archives made everything so much clearer to him. And, even though he couldn't understand her words, he sensed her excitement and delight at her experience in Abusir.

'The solar temple was initially built of mudblocks in the fifth dynasty during the Old Kingdom, but the mudblocks were replaced by stone. Access to the temple from the outer court was difficult at first because the causeway and the temple itself were knee-high deep in water, but we were able to use rafts to transport artefacts and relics from the temple to the outer court.

'The pyramid field of Abusir is a northerly extension of the Saqqara necropolis. Here I wish to give proper praise to Professor Alphonse Flamand, who died so tragically recently, and who was personally responsible for my presence here today at this wonderful museum. It was Professor Flamand who invited me to meet him with a view to our working together, but sadly, due to his sudden demise, that was not to be. However, I know his reputation and the work he did will live on, inspiring future generations of Egyptologists.'

Abigail and Daniel left the Louvre, accompanied by Sr Brian Otway and Edgar Belfont, and made for where the British Embassy's carriage was parked. Her talk had been an overwhelming success. It had taken her almost an hour to get to the exit from the Louvre, so many people had wanted to meet her, shake her hand, congratulate her on her talk, and in particular to thank her for giving it in fluent and flawless French.

'I can't recall a talk at the Louvre as successful as yours,' Otway complimented her. 'The word pictures you created brought the whole area to life. I'm sure that everyone there tonight felt as if they were there at Abusir, surrounded by all those fascinating structures.'

'Thank you, Sir Brian. You're very kind,' said Abigail.

'It was a wonderful way to round off our trip to Paris,' put in Daniel.

'You're definitely leaving?' asked Belfont.

'Yes,' said Abigail. 'We catch the boat train from the Gare du Nord tomorrow morning. We should be back in London by tomorrow evening.'

'We shall miss you,' said Otway. He chuckled. 'I don't think we've had as much excitement involving the embassy in years. Murders! Attempted murders! Thinking about it makes my head spin.'

'Your prophesy over the army dealing with Chevignon turned out to be accurate,' said Daniel.

'Not that that is to be repeated,' cautioned Otway. 'Officially, Chevignon was shot by some unknown assailant for reasons unknown.'

'An unknown assailant capable of surprisingly accurate shooting over some distance,' commented Daniel. 'Sounds like the work of a highly experienced military sniper to me.'

'Or that of a hunter with a personal grudge against Chevignon, which is the suggestion from the army.'

They reached the carriage and climbed aboard.

'Back to the Olive House?' asked Otway. 'Or do you have time for a final celebratory nightcap at my house?'

Daniel looked enquiringly at Abigail, who smiled and nodded. 'That would be a wonderful way to end the evening, Sir Brian, thank you.'

Otway called up to the driver to instruct him to take them to the ambassador's home. As the carriage moved off, he told them, 'By the way, I had a telegram from Rennes. Dreyfus has been found guilty by the military court there and sentenced to ten years' hard labour.'

'Guilty?' said Abigail, shocked. 'But surely the evidence shows he was innocent of the crime.'

'Yes, but this was a *military* court,' Otway reminded her. 'The army were never going to admit they'd jailed an innocent man, and they'd faked the evidence against him.'

'What happens now?' asked Daniel. 'Is it back to Devil's Island for him?'

'No. He had intended to lodge an appeal against the verdict. However, it appears that President Loubet has decided to issue a pardon on his behalf, but only if Dreyfus pleads guilty to the charge originally laid against him.'

'Dreyfus can't do that, surely!' exclaimed Abigail. 'He's innocent!'

'Innocent, but about to spend another ten years in prison, with hard labour, for something he didn't do. He feels, and so do I, another ten years will be the death of him.'

'So he'll plead guilty?'

'That's what I'm led to believe will happen.'

'But how can he trust that the army will stick to that, after what's happened to him? What's to stop them from locking him up for another ten years anyway, once he pleads guilty?'

'The offer is not from the army; it's from the President of France,' said Otway.

'But done to protect the army's reputation!' exploded Abigail angrily.

'The army is very important to the country, and the government. They've been able to get away with an awful lot, as you yourself saw over Captain Chevignon shooting at you.'

'Well, I think it's despicable!'

'It is,' agreed Otway. 'And many French people will agree with you. But just as many will side with the army. The government is caught between two opposing forces. They hope this decision will appease both sides.' He gave a sigh. 'Although, frankly, I doubt it.'

It was just after midnight when Sir Brian's carriage dropped them off at the Olive House.

'A wonderful evening,' said Abigail.

'And I know just the way to make it a little bit more wonderful,' whispered Daniel.

Abigail snuggled into him.

'That is a perfect idea,' she said.

They held hands and walked into the Olive House.

'This has been an amazing experience,' said Abigail.

'It's been traumatic,' said Daniel. 'You under threat of the guillotine, two assassination attempts on us.' He gave a puzzled frown. 'If Professor Flamand didn't send that letter to you, as Elaine Foret claimed, I wonder who did? And why? We now know that it wasn't part of some contrived plot to frame you; Patrice killed Flamand on the spur of the moment.'

'I believe it came from the professor himself,' said Abigail. 'Elaine Foret destroyed my answer to him to maintain the pretence that I'd killed him. Despite all the negative things he said about me, I really feel he was impressed by the work we did at Abusir. He must have heard more about our work when he was at Saqqara; the two places are virtually next door to one another.'

'So it could have led to the two great Egyptologists of the present generation working together,' said Daniel.

Abigail shook her head. 'Both us of were just working archaeologists,' she said. 'Greatness is ascribed by later generations, and often wrongly.'

'You've said that Flinders Petrie is a great, and he's still working,' Daniel pointed out.

'Ah yes, but there's always an exception to every rule,' said Abigail. 'And Flinders is certainly one.' She looked at Daniel and asked, 'Will you be glad to get back to England?'

'In one way,' admitted Daniel, then he added, 'but what memories for us!'

They arrived at the reception desk and took their room key, then she squeezed his hand gently as they made for the stairs to their room.

'Memories indeed!' she said. 'In our hearts, we'll always have Paris.'

ACKNOWLEDGEMENTS

When Susie Dunlop, the publishing director at Allison & Busby who has guided me through my Museum Mysteries series, and also my DCI Coburg World War 2 series, suggested that the 10th Museum Mystery be set in the Louvre, I leapt at it. Like many Brits travelling abroad for the first time in the early 1960s, my first trip 'overseas' was to France, to Paris. There is nothing quite like experiencing an unfamiliar foreign language and customs for the first time. As someone from Camden Town in London who'd left school early, with only the barest exposure to French in the post-war classroom, it was like entering an exotic French variation of the world of Oz, and I loved it. This new book gave me the opportunity to dump my similarly Camden Town-raised detective, Daniel Wilson, in a place where he neither speaks nor understands the language, but it is a matter of life or death for his wife, Abigail, that he must find a way to rescue her from the perilous position she finds herself in. I do hope you, dear reader, will have sympathy for his predicament, and the steps he takes to deal with it.

I must also give a very big and very grateful shout-out to

my editors on this book, Fiona Paterson and Becca Allen. Their knowledge and understanding of French society and history of this time was second to none. Without them I would certainly have struggled much more than I did. It was like having two guardian angels looking over my shoulders as I worked and murmuring 'Avez-vous quelque chose de meillure qualitie?' (or similar). Thank you both, and thanks also to Susie. If you've enjoyed this story set in Paris, it's largely thanks to them. Any factual errors *en Francais* that may have crept in are of my own making.

Jim Eldridge was born in central London towards the end of World War II, and survived attacks by V2 rockets on the Kings Cross area where he lived. In 1971 he sold his first sitcom to the BBC and had his first book commissioned. Since then he has had more than one hundred books published, with sales of over three million copies. He lives in Kent with his wife.

jimeldridge.com